Angel Rising

An Azshael Story

A.D. Landor

Copyright © A. D. Landor 2023

All rights reserved.

All characters in this publication are fictitious and any resemblance to real persons, living or dead, is purely coincidental.

This book is sold subject to the condition that it shall not, by way of trade or otherwise, be hired out, lent or resold, or otherwise circulated without the author's/publisher's prior consent in any form of binding or cover other than that in which it is published and without a similar condition including this condition being imposed on the subsequent publisher.

The moral rights of the author have been asserted.

Dedication

*For my parents who have a front seat with the Angels
- miss you both every day*

*For my sister Roz, nieces Arielle and Sophia
and their fine chaps - Robbie and Bobby*

And a special hug for Colleen the Lurcher!

Acknowledgements

This book would not exist without the support and help of the following:

Johan Bert and family - founder of the feast

Self-publishing guru: Michelle Emerson (michelleemerson.co.uk)

Proofing guru: Carol Sissons

Art guru: K. D. Ritchie of Story Wrappers (storywrappers.com)

Sanity savers: The good folk of the Kingston Games Club at the Willoughby Arms, especially Adrian Joseph, Adrian Lulham, Greg Baker, Jono Tooth, Mikko Lahti (Finland branch), Neil Randerson, Peter Hart, Rob Hrabi, Stu Hollister, Tish Sheridan, Trevor Duguid Farrant

Cheer leaders: Bryan Parke and family, Lorraine Bradley and family, Moreno Airoldi, Paul Mitchell and family, Sean Nelson and all my activation friends at News Broadcasting

Reviewers and influencers: Craig Bookwyrm (Escapist Book Club), Tara D.Morgan (Online Book Club.org), Jamedi, (Jamreads.com), Nathan's Fantasy Reviews, Andrew Mattocks (Andrew's Wizardly Reads), Daniel Lucas (Book 101 Podcast)

Website: www.7th-flight.com created by Jo Hewson

Thanks to everyone who bought a copy of Angel Falling and Azshael for continuing to share his stories with me

Part One

Chapter One

"The only truth that matters is the one that most people want to believe." That old maxim, a popular saying among the Heralds, popped into my mind as a fist sized piece of stone came hurtling towards my face. Thankfully, it was snapped out of the air and crushed into dust just before impact.

"Thanks, Cam," I said as my oldest friend and Throne Angel growled at me.

"Now would be a really good time to focus, Azsh," he said, looking behind us at the Red Roof Inn. It was the place we had come to protect, where Cam's lost Dryad love, Sylvenell, had been forced to take root. Now she and the structure were intimately entwined and any attack on the Inn was an attack on her that Cam took personally.

The Bonded, a collection of former divinities, powers, heroes, and followers that had surrendered to the Seventh Flight of Archangel Anael during the Judgement of their various worlds were angry, although it was not clear exactly what they were angry about. It was fair to say there had always been a level of discontent among them, but in the Lower Landing, where most of the Bonded made their home, the atmosphere had been growing steadily frostier.

I doubted anyone in the sky city above, where the Seventh Flight's Archangel Prince and his Heralds dwelled, had made any move to ask them what their problems were. It was true they were conquered foes who Prince Anael had spared final Judgement in return for their co-operation, but that didn't mean they didn't deserve to be heard, or treated as second class citizens. Of course, that was just my opinion. You'd never hear a Herald say that.

The air above us was suddenly full of beating wings as Angels of the Watch soared in and saw off the small group of Bonded who had chosen to target the Inn. Their Sergeant was Chayliel, a solid block of muscle and grit who, in outward appearance and inward attitude, defined the Citadel garrison known as the Regio.

"Lord Camael," he said, bowing before Cam and ignoring me. "Captain Pesak sent me to request your help. And that of any Angels under your command." I was about to say I wasn't under anyone's command, but this wasn't the time or the place, so I just stared at Chayliel, imaginary daggers cascading off his granite shell.

"I already have my task," Cam said. "Azshael here will go with you." I glared at Camael, but he avoided my look, stood steadfast and said nothing. Emotions were still raw between us, unfairly in my view. They related to the fateful choice his love, Syl, had made in defence of her friends and fellow Inn dwellers. Tensions were still high so I thought it would be better if I left him alone. Chayliel and his wingmen took flight and I followed on.

As soon as we were airborne, I could see why the Regio's Captain had sent for aid. The Lower Landing's central square was packed with protesters, and it wasn't just the Bonded. There were also Succae gathered in the crowd, and they were there in numbers. I was surprised it had not been reported that such an influx had passed through my former command at Vigil Keep. However, things had changed and the renewed peace accord between the Angels of the Flight and the vampiric Succae had delivered new freedoms to our former enemy.

As we drew closer, I could see more detail. The Succae's bare heads bore no marks or tattoos, which meant they were Low-Nin - low caste menial drudges - who were mostly outcasts in their own society. Their animate flesh was occupied by the lesser spirits of the Necrene Well, a vast repository of souls. Low-Nin were doomed to impoverished servitude unless they could find a way to impress someone higher up the food chain in their supposedly meritocratic, honour-bound society.

I landed at the top of Ramp, a steep hill that led up to the Lower Keep and the vital portal that connected the Lower Landing with the Acropolis, the upper part of the White Citadel, which circled slowly in the clouds above. Pesak's Regio were arrayed in lines, shields and shining spears glinting in the morning light. I counted two hundred Angels, but the crowd numbered in the thousands, packed together in the square below. I quickly understood Pesak's concerns and wished Cam hadn't been so quick to dismiss the Captain's call for aid. I thought a Throne power was exactly what this situation called for. Sergeant Chayliel indicated that I should follow him down to where the Regio's commander stood in the front line with his troops. I waited as he made his report, and Pesak beckoned me forward to join him.

"Nice of you to join us, Ambassador," he said with a wry grin.

"Least I could do, Captain," I replied. "Now I see the situation, I believe I have an urgent appointment elsewhere." For just a moment, Pesak's grin faded until I returned it. "I'm an Ambassador, not a Herald," I said, and the look of relief on his face was obvious.

"Right now, I need every experienced Angel I can get," and as he said that, I could see more small units of the Regio returning with other members of the Seventh Flight, who lived down among the Bonded, flying in to add to the defenders on the Ramp. They were welcome additions, but I reckoned that we had nowhere near enough troops if things took a turn for the worse.

"Is Galaeal aware of the situation?" I asked, referring to the Guard Captain of the Legio Alba in the Upper City. Pesak's hesitation in answering told me all I needed to know.

"You must let him know, Captain," I said in earnest entreaty, and I saw a look of resignation on his face. No one liked to admit failure in the Flight. It left you vulnerable to whispering campaigns that you were inadequate and an ineffective leader, yet there was real risk here, and that could result in something far worse.

"You're right of course," Pesak said, and he summoned an adjutant to send word at the double.

It started to snow, and I wondered whether this was an accident or whether word had got to the Citadel above already, and the Powers that controlled the garden's weather had been told to literally cool things down.

"Have they said anything? Made any demands or asked to speak to anyone?"

"Not a word," Pesak said. "It's just been exactly as you see since the coming of dawn a few hours ago."

"They all turned up at once?"

"No – the Succae came first then the others from our side of the Tether. The scouts tell me this is just part of it. The alleyways in the Squeeze are also full to bursting."

I paused to take all this in as the snowfall grew heavier and started to settle on the ground. In the distance, I heard tolling bells coming from the Citadel above and I knew that Galaeal's Legio were aware of the situation and preparing their defences.

"Let me see if I can talk with them," I said, and Pesak looked at me doubtfully.

"Who are you going to talk to, Azshael? No one appears to be leading them. Frankly, that's what scares me the most."

I took flight and headed down to the Ramp's end. My boots crunched into icy fallen snow, and I stood just a few feet away from the first of the massed ranks of protesters. I opened my mouth to speak, but before I could say a word, the strange silence came to a sudden and eerie end. Almost in unison, all the Low-Nin in the crowd suddenly raised their arms and began to sway back and forth. It took me by surprise, and words died in my throat. I had never seen or heard of anything like this before. Then, quietly at first, the Bonded spoke. It started with a handful of voices, but that number quickly grew as did the volume.

"Ex-cel-sis" they said, the common name for the Higher and Ultimate Power whose will we ultimately all served. "Ex-cel-sis," they chanted, and stamped the ground as they did so. Honestly, I was confused. Were they expecting a sudden divine intervention? Or was this a message for our Archangel? If so, exactly what were they asking for – an audience with Excelsis itself? Such an idea was so outlandish as to be laughable. Even if such an audience could be granted, what did they expect the outcome would be? Anael had spared the Bonded once but was probably working to his own sense of mercy. I doubted Excelsis would be quite so generous.

Therein lay the problem. We have judged the living and the dead of countless planets without challenge. That was until the Succae, a race of immortal wraith-like spirits bound in dead flesh, chose to resist. They had fought us in a terrible war of attrition that had left our Prince and his followers in unprecedented territory. Neither side had lost but neither side had won. It was the first known failure of any of the Judgement Flights.

The passage of time, however, was surely on the side of the Succae as more of their spirits were called from the Well and bound in flesh. Their construct forces could also be built anew. For our side, the war had cost many Angels' lives that could not be replaced without a retreat and call for reinforcements. In the Armistice accord it was agreed that neither side would undertake such actions, but words don't always match reality. Time had also had an impact on the relationships between us and them. Vampires and Angels now walked freely in each other's worlds. We shared knowledge, worked alongside each other, learned new crafts and histories. For my own part, I had even found love with Ischae, my Succae liaison, until she had been brutally murdered by a treacherous Cabal. She had died in the process of uncovering their plot to force the hands of both leaders to return to armed conflict.

Our Prince had an invidious choice. Return and admit defeat or maintain the status quo and let things fall as they may. To return would, by implication, mean that Excelsis was wrong. Such a thought would have theologically profound implications for our entire race, especially as Excelsis's arrival had caused a civil war we had viciously fought in its defence. Princes had perished and many had died in what became known as the War of the Tribes. The present ongoing inertia was a thorn in the Flight's side that had yet to be pulled, its poison drawn. Meanwhile, the wound festered like meat left out too long in the sun.

I tried to make myself heard above the chanting as I called for peace and reason, but if anyone heard me it didn't seem to have an effect. Then things began to take a turn for the worse. The first to move were the Low-Nin, who gathered into tight knit groups of three or more and linked arms. They began to advance a single step at a time and as they did, the Bonded's chants grew in volume and intensity, and I saw them fall in behind the Succae advance.

The entire square's gathering was on the move, and I could see more bodies pouring in from the alleyways, lanes, and ginnels that Pesak had mentioned. It was surprisingly orderly and controlled, at least to begin with. A "polite riot", as it was later called. The first line of Succae ascended the Ramp and pushed against me. I heard Pesak shout orders and a moment later, I was flanked by Angels on both sides, great copper shields burnished to parade perfection, pushing back against the advancing mass. As I was without a shield, I slipped back between the Regio guards on either side of me so that they could present more of a solid front. That was when things began to go badly wrong.

The Succae moved swiftly to try and push through the gap I had created but my flankers were faster, and they bounced off Regio shields that held firm. They swiftly changed tactics and broke free of each other. One grabbed the shield in front while the next man climbed on the first's shoulders and wrapped themselves around the Angel blocking them. The third man crawled on the ground and wrapped himself around the guard's legs. This was mirrored up and down the line, and I could see the Regio soldiers did not know how to react or what to do, as one by one, they began to collapse under the weight of Low-Nin bodies. I heard Pesak call for the next ranks to level spears and I knew we were heading for disaster. Sure enough, the Bonded barrelled forward and the mass moved as one. Four Low-Nin wrapped themselves around me and I tried to take to the air, but their combined weight was too much. I was pulled down into their fierce embrace, buried in a growing mound of bodies that would soon be trampled by the thousands that waited their turn to storm up the Ramp.

Chapter Two

In the end, I was one of the fortunate ones. As I tried to pull myself free of those that had me firmly gripped, I felt the ground shake as the Bonded broke through Pesak's lines. In the resulting charge, I heard the bones of the Low-Nin who had me gripped around the body break under the weight of dozens of Bonded feet. We were eventually pushed sideways and fell from the edge of the Ramp to crash to the ground below. That probably saved me from more serious injuries.

I begged the Succae that had me bound to let go and to my surprise they did just that, their task apparently done. Whichever Master they served on the other side of the Tether would reward them with a step up into a better future existence, even if this one was doomed. I shot into the sky to try and gauge what was happening. I could hear screams and shouts and presumed Pesak had ordered the Regio to do whatever was needed to defend the White Gate. I could see a press at the top of the Ramp where it narrowed into an arched passageway and the Bonded appeared to be stalled at the entrance, which had become a chokepoint.

Regio Angels swooped in on both side of the Ramp, trying to pull protestors off and thin the ranks. It was a good plan but there were just too many of them, and they linked arms to make themselves too heavy to be so easily pulled away. There were some successes and I watched as Angels worked together to prise the odd protester free. They would fly them a few feet away from the Ramp edge and then drop them, to crash in heaps on the snowy ground a couple of hundred feet below.

The temperature was dropping dramatically, and the winds had picked up so that snow swirled into a stinging blizzard that whipped its way around the square. I couldn't tell if it was having any effect other than to make flight more difficult. I flew up to the chokepoint on the Ramp – the passage into the tunnel that led to the White Gate. I could see Sergeant Chayliel and a front row of Angels, resolute and stern-faced, being slowly pushed backward under the combined weight of the press. Low-Nin were being crushed against shields, packed so tightly that they couldn't deploy their grabbing tactics. The mob had become grimly intent on their purpose to the point that they didn't seem to mind killing those on their own side and that's when I realised something was off about the entire situation. There had been other clues, but I had been too wrapped up in the moment to think about them. First and most obviously, the Bonded were not using their remaining powers. Secondly, there was a curious quiet about the protest, and the calls for Excelsis had ended after the move up the Ramp had begun. Third, the mob did not fight back, although I had to wonder how long that could last. Finally, there was the presence of the Low-Nin. They followed orders and had very little initiative of their own, which meant they were pawns in someone else's plan—and that someone was presumably of Succae origin. There was something going on that we were not seeing. or more to the point, *I* was not seeing. I knew the Succae in ways others did not.

I circled back over the square that was still full of protesters and started searching for life signs of the Succae using spirit sight. Below me, the small thin wraiths that occupied the Low-Nin bodies were numerous, but I was looking for masters not servants, so I expanded the radius of my search to take in the alleys and lanes of the area that was called the Squeeze. Again, I came up empty, so I returned to normal sight as the bells from the Upper Landing tolled an alarm call urgently in the distance. I guessed Pesak's defence had ended and the White Gate had been breached.

The blizzard had grown in strength and magnitude, and visibility was diminishing with every minute. There was a sudden blaze of white light away to the northwest and I had a pretty good idea who was responsible. It had to be Camael. I flew in the direction of the Red Roof as fast as I could although I doubted he was in any actual danger. Whoever he was scrapping with was more the point. We really didn't need any Bonded dead—or any Succae—and Cam was not renowned for his subtlety.

As I approached the small square that led to the Red Roof Inn, there was a sudden blur of movement below me, and I saw a group of four or five cloaked people heading away from me towards the Squeeze. I thought to go after them, but I heard a roar from the environs of the Inn and decided I would check on Camael first. I found him on his knees cradling an Angel in his large hands as he rocked back and forth, his face a mask of pain.

"My child, my child," he said through gritted teeth, tears streaming down his face. I stood there, utterly stunned. For once in my life, I had no idea what to say.

Chapter Three

Cam carried the body of our fallen Angel into the Inn and laid her down on one of the long tables. Her youthful beauty was still radiant in death, and I wondered where she had come from and what Cam's attachment to her had been. One thing was certain; she was not one of Pesak's Regio troops. She was too young, and the Regio rarely took females into their Legion, although given our reduced numbers post-war, that was becoming a choice that Pesak would soon need to rethink. There was also something about her simple tunic, leggings, boots, and cloak that looked a step down from the level of the Flight's usual craftsmanship. She looked as if she had come from somewhere else entirely.

"She dead?" Papa Famine asked quietly as our friends and the remaining denizens of the Inn gathered around her still body.

"She sure look it," his wife Mama Feast said sadly, shaking her head. "All that life wasted." There was no question she was dead. Her chest was completely wrecked with both hearts destroyed amid a mess of flesh and bone. I had seen the weapon that had inflicted this kind of catastrophic damage before, and it made me even more confused.

"A Shard Blade did this," I said quietly, looking over at Cam for a reaction. "It's a rare Succae warrior weapon used only by full Ashai warriors, who guard them jealously. How this young Angel got on the wrong end of such a thing, I have no idea." Cam said nothing and stared morosely at the body. "Did you see any Succae?" I asked, but he remained silent, head in his hands. I recalled the cloaked group that I had witnessed fleeing from the small market just down the lane from the Inn and considered whether it was worth going after them. However, the more I thought about it, the more I thought it was probably too late. If they were Succae they would have headed for the Tether and even flying, it was unlikely I would get there before they were gone. If they were local, they could be hidden anywhere in the Lower Landing by now.

In the distance, the alarm bells pealed again, giving the full call to arms. It was a call we had to answer. I headed for the door and Cam trailed reluctantly after me. He stopped to look back regretfully at the dead Angel. There would be time for answers later. We headed directly up through the snowstorm for the Upper Landing, and I tried asking again about his connection to the dead girl. He just shook his head and, using his Throne powers, transformed into a fast-flying Gryphon and left me behind. This was getting strange. As far as I knew, Cam had no family or certainly none he had ever mentioned. We rarely breed among our own kind, so Angelic births are rare, but that didn't mean it never happened. I couldn't claim to know all his long history, just that of the considerable time we had served together in the Flight. Could Cam have had a history before his Throne ascension? Perhaps before joining the Flight? I knew one person who would know – Sariel, the Cherub scribe who was probably older than the two of us put together. I resolved to speak with her later.

I passed through dense clouds, feeling the crosswinds that announced the final approach to the city's sheer white marble walls, grand buttresses anchored in dense grey clouds that washed up like white peaked waves against grey stone foundations. I soared over the walls and saw dozens more golden-armoured troops headed for the Acropolis, Galaeal's Legio Alba in full defensive array.

I followed them and saw a terrible sight, Angels locked in combat with the Bonded who were charging forward into the deeper part of Asuriel's Landing. The Bonded were unarmed and I watched in horror as more Low-Nin Succae impaled themselves on Legio spears to help continue the momentum. It was turning into the slaughter I feared it would be. My guess was they were headed for the steps to the Sky Gate, the portal back to Excelsis's Golden Gates. I decided to head that way, only to see the seven hundred and seventy-seven steps leading to the Sky watch tower manned with Throne Angels and Seraphs, the deadliest warriors of our kind.

I saw Cam in the centre of everything, his red halberd already wreathed in flames. Around him Seraphs shimmered behind walls of force, and other Powers churned the air above, deadly invisible masses. It was going to be a total slaughter.

Then something unexpected happened. Horns of the Hosts rang sonorously in the air and aboard a Golden Chariot, the Archangel Anael burst from the clouds flanked by his elite bodyguards, the Alba Seraphim. It was an impressive sight. In full pomp, the leader of the Seventh Flight passed over the citadel, and golden light poured forth from his brightness, illuminating everything and everyone below. I felt warmth suffuse my inner being, and a sense of peace and calm washed over me. It had the desired effect. Everyone stopped what they were doing, and I watched as the protest lost momentum and came to an end. It was over.

Chapter Four

The following day, the Lower Landing was quiet. It was also bitterly cold, as the Powers had imposed a literal freeze to discourage outside gatherings. Everywhere glittered with frost, and icicles sparkled in the wan daylight. Pesak's Regio guards had been augmented by soldiers from Galaeal's Legio, and they maintained vigilant patrols in full battle armour.

The mood felt ugly, as if the Lower Landing was a brooding creature, nursing its wounds. I retreated to my Sphere to rest and consider what I had witnessed. The image of the dead youth and Cam's reaction to her death were ever present in my thoughts. The mystery of the events of the previous day was a worrying puzzle. It was true that the Bonded had been growing increasingly restless, yet it was also a given that those the Flight spared would be eternally grateful and would always conform to their bond of service. That was an optimistic point of view, and in truth, I had some sympathy for them. We had been too long away from the Golden City, where the Bonded would be rewarded with new positions and roles in service to Excelsis. Those long overdue rewards were a source of malcontent for many of the Bonded; another crack in the Flight's foundations.

The presence of the Low-Nin, outcasts even in their own society, was an additional concern and layer to the mystery. I could not readily discern why they would want to get involved unless they were in service to one of their own kind. Their meritocratic culture meant they were doomed to a life of poverty and servitude unless they could find a way to impress a Vod or other High-Nin Master. It was evidence of a hidden hand whose motives were yet unknown.

I resolved to start the search for answers and went looking for

Cam, but he was not at the Red Roof, and no one had seen him since the previous day. The dead girl had been taken from the Inn, apparently on Cam's instructions, so I headed to the Garrison to see if she was there, only to find both Captain Galaeal and Captain Pesak in the guardroom. Pesak smiled warmly whilst Galaeal looked at me impassively, no doubt concerned about my connections with the Succae. I felt a familiar anger burning at my core. I was far from being the only Angel to have ventured down the Tether and made friends among the Succae, but whenever there was trouble, it seemed to be my name that came to everyone's lips. Galaeal was someone that I thought of as a friend, but given his command in the Upper City, I was sure he was a pawn of the Heralds, which made me instinctively reluctant to trust him. For once, though, I opted for a charm offensive and we three soldiers spent a while talking and reminiscing over a manna infused bottle of wine that warmed the flesh and calmed the soul.

"She's gone," Pesak said finally, after I had steered the conversation in the direction of my interests. Pesak looked sideways at Galaeal who had warmed up considerably during our drinking session, indicating he should pick up the story.

"Yes, but not into the Legio's custody," he said.

"Where then?" I asked.

Galaeal took a while to answer and when he finally did so, I understood why.

"My understanding is that her body was surrendered to the Herald Kokael," he said, and a hush descended on the room.

Kokael—Herald of a notoriously secretive sect called the Irin— was a name I had not heard in a while. They were Watchers, apparently responsible only to the Archangel himself. It was originally thought that Kokael did his bidding, but I had long suspected they worked on a more subtle basis, operating on their own initiative to resolve matters they deemed would be in Anael's interest without informing him or asking his permission until it was too late to change the outcome.

It was said among our own kind that there was not much the Irin didn't know about every Angel in the Flight, and I wondered whether Kokael's star had fallen dramatically given recent events. The Watchers had been notably absent in the recent near disruption of the anniversary of the peace accord with the Succae. They had also seemingly failed to spot the ambitions of my former mentor Benazzarr, who had led the conspiracy and sought to restart the war to force the Prince's hand. If they had been derelict in their duties, Kokael and the Irin would need to be on the front foot with any new developments or threats. I had no doubt that the previous day's events would qualify.

"Do you know where Kokael took the girl's body?"

"To the Mausoleum," Galaeal said with a grimace, and I felt a shudder run through my wings. It was the charnel house, and its Keeper was an Angel of Death.

Chapter Five

The Mausoleum of the Seventh Flight was a grey stone building that looked like a grand tomb. It was set aside behind high walls in a memorial garden that stood close to the House of Memory, where all our fallen were marked in memorial Spheres, mostly created after their death. In the war it had been a distressingly busy place, as the dead were brought here for Passover, a final act of ritual service which meant a return to the fire from which we had come. This was the House of Saur'll, one of a select few Angels dedicated to death in all its forms. He was a deliverer, destroyer, and now a ritual processor of the dead of our kind, and I couldn't think of anyone or anywhere I would rather not have had to visit.

As I climbed the steps and passed the great columns of the entrance arch into the Mausoleum itself, I was aware of the grim silence being disturbed by the sound of my boots. It felt wrong, so I took flight and returned the place to its solemn solitude. Lamps lit the way to a central space known as the Hall of Ascendance, where light from outside filtered through grey motes of dust from a glass dome above. I had attended ceremonies for fallen friends in my time, and this was where their pyres had been built and lit, their ashes ascending in bright sparks through the open roof and on up into the firmament of space. I didn't truly understand how their souls made it back to Excelsis, but it was what we believed happened and none of us wanted to consider the alternatives.

In the hushed hall, I saw no sign of life, yet I felt its presence—and as my sight adjusted to the gloom, I saw a Keeper of the Dead, one of the few attendants the Angel of Death had at his command, drift silently from the shadows. Like me, his unfurled wings carried him a foot or so above the ground, preserving the stillness. He was hooded, wearing simple grey robes and he bowed before me.

"Ambassador Azshael?" he said, his voice calm and quiet. I wasn't really sure if that title was still mine. In the aftermath of the Benazzarr crisis, it had not been taken away, but nor had I ever received confirmation it was truly mine to keep.

"Just Azshael for now, Keeper," I said. "I am not here on official business."

The Keeper nodded, and as he did so, a circular stairwell revealed itself, blocks of stone quietly shifting aside.

"You are expected," he said, indicating with a robed arm that I should descend. So, I was expected? I wondered by whom and for what? I doubted this servant would know more than just that basic fact, so I descended the steps into the lower part of the Temple of All Endings.

I arrived in a narrow passage and at its end, I could see the flickering of a flame. As I drew closer, the passageway opened into a large chamber where the Angel dead would lie on great stone slabs awaiting the ministrations of Saur'll and his Keepers. On this occasion there was only the one body occupying a slab in the centre of the Hall, and I could see a small group huddled around the dead girl, her body naked, the terrible wound that had ended her life even more obvious in the bright light that illuminated her pale skin.

I approached the slab and took stock of those in attendance. First was Narinel the Wise, head archivist of the Flight's Hall of Records. He was absorbed in making notes and sketches of the body and barely acknowledged my arrival. Next was a hooded figure who nodded in my direction but said nothing. I could make out the faint glitter of golden eyes within the hood. Finally, another Keeper stood a respectful distance away from the others, garbed in the usual robes of the Mausoleum's attendants. He paid me some notable deference, which I acknowledged with a terse nod and the briefest ghost of a tight smile.

"I understand I was expected?" I said, my voice suddenly breaking the still silence of the chamber. "Given even I wasn't sure I would be coming here until this morning, that's quite some act of prescience. I would like to know who was responsible for it?"

Narinel sighed, the hooded figure folded their arms, and the Keeper looked upwards. I followed his gaze to see Saur'll descending from above. He was wreathed in shadows, but I could make out the glint of a cuirass and a dark tunic and skirt. His wings were mottled grey, and he wore a silver mask that was set in a scream, stylised eyes where holes for the real ones should have been. I had heard tell that this was because just a glance from such a Power could kill, but until this point, I had presumed it was exaggeration. Now, I wasn't so sure.

"It was I, Azshael," Saur'll said in a gravelly voice that sounded as deep as an ocean. He descended to the ground and the shadows around him concealed his wings in a black haze. I did my best not to look intimidated, but I had to admit he was an impressive and imposing figure. I cleared my throat and was about to say something, but he raised a hand.

"The Throne Power Camael said you would be coming, although he did not say exactly when or why. Just that it was in your nature to be…". He paused before going on to say "inquisitive." I suspected Saur'll was being polite, which came as a surprise. I had always assumed that Angels of Death were resolutely blunt, but clearly, I had underestimated this one or life among the Seventh's Heralds had got to him.

"I suppose that's one way of putting it." I replied, trying to sound ironic, but Narinel glared at me, and I guessed it hadn't landed quite as I had hoped. Saur'll said nothing and turned to Narinel. "I saw nothing in my Witness beyond what we already know," the Angel of Death said, referring to the process of entering the eyes and last emotions of a dead person.

"She was excited and frightened at the same time and then someone stabbed her from behind. She was killed instantly. The Succae weapon fulfilled its purpose." Narinel nodded sagely and made notations on the parchment in front of him that also had a full drawing of the girl's body. "Do we know who she was?" I asked, and the hooded figure nodded. Before they could answer, I spotted a strange mark on the girl's body where her wings joined with her back. It was scarified but identifiable as the mark of a branding iron and it bore an identifiable letter 'J' contained in a circle.

"Her name was Cassiel," the hooded figure said in a distinctively feminine tone "and she was one of the Juvenii."

Chapter Six

It had been literally a lifetime since I had thought about the Juvenii. In the language of my kind, the term means 'young', but that can have many different connotations. Young in terms of age or development, yes, but it can also have a less kind interpretation. Young can also mean naïve or stunted as well as mentally or cerebrally challenged.

Not all that serve Excelsis wish to fight. Many find other roles to follow. Crafters or artisans, entertainers, and scribes to name but a few. For those who refuse any path of service, the Juvenii offer a home. Their sect's name came from Juvenil, an Archangel of pity who at some point in our ancient past, had won an exemption from Excelsis's otherwise rigid insistence on our pledge of service to their cause.

The first Juvenii were misfits and outcast Angels who were troubled souls notable by their lack of achievements to their Principalities and Tribes. In later epochs and under Excelsis's guidance, youthful Angels were tested as they neared maturity, and those few that showed little or no aptitude for service were taken to the Juvenii for adoption. Every Prince was responsible for some of Juvenil's lost lambs, but I had always presumed that the Judgment Flights were excused from that obligation. It was clear now, though, with one of them dead on a slab in front of me, that I was wrong. I looked at the hooded female and admitted my ignorance.

"I did not think the Seventh had such persons among us," I said and Narinel tutted at me.

"Something else you don't know, Azshael. Perhaps if you had spent as much time among your own kind as you did with the Succae you wouldn't be quite so lacking in knowledge."

Quite why Narinel was being so prickly I didn't know, and I was about to retort when the hooded one intervened and saved me from my temper.

"There is no way he could have known," she said, pulling her hood back and revealing herself. It was quite a revelation. She was beautiful. Her skin was as pale as milk, her face an appealing oval with golden eyes that glittered in the gloom. A cascade of black hair crowned by a silver diadem with a dark crimson gem at its centre rippled down her back.

As I wondered where she had been hiding all this time, she continued.

"Prince Anael sent them to Cerule when we first arrived here. They have a Sphere of their own that takes up an island landmass in the southern ocean."

"You mean they were exiled?

"In a manner of speaking, yes. Their leader, Jophael, asked to be separated from the judgment process, so the Prince found a place far away from the Succae's places of habitation, and the Thrones built a landmass where they could sit out the conflict to come."

"Are they all young like her?"

"Not all," Narinel said. "They were accompanied by some mature members of the Flight who, for reasons of their own, volunteered to be part of their sect. It is true, though, that many never age further than this. They just cease to develop, and no one knows exactly why."

"So, Cassiel could have been a lot older than she looks?"

"It is possible," Narinel said.

"Not just possible," the hooded one said. "I'd say more than likely."

"How so?"

"I would need Narinel to check the records to be sure, but I believe that the mark on her back is an old one. Possibly very old indeed, which would make her an elder."

"Who are you?" I said when my brain finally restored the power of speech.

"I am Kokael, Herald of the Irin," she said, and I laughed spontaneously, the incongruous sound echoing around the chamber.

The group looked at me, the incomprehension obvious in their faces.

"I mean…that is…you can't be!" I said, trying to recover some sense of decorum. She looked at me quizzically.

"Kokael is male," I said, and she smirked as Narinel tutted again. I had made a fool of myself, but thankfully Saur'Il spoke and saved me from stuffing more of my feet into my mouth.

"So, if Cassiel was one of a group of exiled pacifists, how did she end up on the wrong end of an enemy weapon and dead on the Lower Landing of the White Citadel?"

Kokael shrugged and pulled her hood back up.

"That is the puzzle, Angel of Endings. It is a mystery that needs solving."

After Narinel had finished his cataloguing of Cassiel's body, he departed without bothering to say farewell. It was clear in my mind that the old goat's goat had been well and truly got, but by what or by whom I wasn't sure. Maybe it was just having to come into Saur'Il's spooky tomb that had set him off. It had that effect on me.

"Tell me about this blade that did such terrible harm," Kokael said, moving close enough to me that I could smell a trace of her perfume. It was like the bouquet of roses after a summer storm has passed and was most beguiling. I felt my mouth open, and words fall out.

"The Shard Blade is a rare weapon even among the Succae. It is wielded only by the strongest of their warriors – the Ashai. Or so I understand."

"So, you're saying a Succae Ashai must have killed her?"

"Not necessarily. It is true that the Blades are jealously guarded, but the Succae were at war with us for a long time. I am sure there are Shard Blades that were lost or taken as trophies. Maybe not many, but there are surely some on both sides of the Tether."

"You know their ways don't you Azsh? You could go to them and find out more. You would do this for me, wouldn't you?" She touched me briefly and I felt myself smile as a warmth spread through me. I was lost in a reverie as her presence intoxicated me; her scent, the touch, her breath upon my skin. It was a sensorial overload, a sea of charm that I would happily have drowned in if not for the Angel of Death's timely interruption.

"Leave him be, Kokael," he said, the chill of his aura breaking her spell. "He is wanted elsewhere." I wondered how he knew that, as she stepped away and her grip on me was relinquished. She pulled her hood back up and walked away, headed back up the stairs without a second look. I told myself that now I knew her gift for manipulation, I would be more wary in the future, but who was I kidding?

"Ambassador Azshael?" The voice came out of the shadows and so surprised me that I stepped back into Saur'Il, who moved not an inch. Stepping into the light, I saw one of the Prince's personal retinue, clad in the white and gold tunic of the Trinity Palace Guard.

"Yes?" I said stepping off Saur'Il's foot.

"The Prince requests you attend him immediately You are to come with me."

"Return before you leave, Azshael," Saur'Il said quietly. I wondered why, but before I could ask, he ascended back into the gloom above. As I left with the Archangel's messenger, I saw the lights that had illuminated Cassiel's body slowly wither and die, surrendering the tomb back into the finality of darkness.

Chapter Seven

It was a short flight from the Mausoleum to the gardens that surrounded the great edifice of Trinity Palace, seat of the Archangel Prince Anael. The Prince's retainer directed me to land on the grand dais in front of the White Keep, a marble circle inlaid with gold and marked with Anael's personal sigil of a stylised sun with flames radiating from its core.

Anfial, the Palace's Chief Steward was waiting on the steps above and he was flanked by two others that I immediately recognised. The first was Vasariah, a Dominion angel or Domini, who was head of the Trinity Palace Guard, the Legio Honores. The second was Darophon, the leader of the Heralds, someone I had plenty of history with, some of it good and some bad. Only Anfial looked even vaguely happy to see me, inclining his head in a small but courteous gesture. I climbed the steps only to find Vasariah suddenly in my face.

"I want you to know it was not my choice to call you here, Azshael," he said bluntly. "Against all our counsel, the Prince insisted you were sent for, although for what reason, I do not know." He looked down at me as if I was an unpleasant odour beneath his nose that he couldn't wait to get away from.

Darophon looked at me and then back at the Domini. "Now, Vasariah, that is no way to welcome the Ambassador. He has shown to have his uses, especially where insight into the Succae is required," the Herald said with little warmth. The Domini didn't look impressed, and he looked even less happy when Darophon added, "and he has a reputation for getting things done." I saw a smirk appear on the Herald Prime's face as he turned to walk up the steps, but it disappeared before Vasariah could have noticed. It was an odd display from the Flight's leading politician, and I wondered what I had walked into.

Anfial led us into the great hall of the White Keep and on into the northern gallery that led to the Archangel's private hall known as the Alba Sanctum. Vasariah's Honores snapped to attention as we passed them. I knew they were all hardened Angels who had won the right to join the ranks of an elite troop, but I had the odd feeling that I was walking among peacocks rather than lions.

The great silver gates that marked the entry to the Prince's Sphere drifted open on our approach, and we all took flight to rise to the grand sky palace that Anael called home. It was a beautiful structure, a Cathedral of light and space floating on a bed of white clouds. The grand façade towered into the sky above, alcoves full of sculptures of the other Flights, their Archangels, and notable leaders of the Seventh immortalised in marble. As we walked up the great steps to the entrance doors, one of the Honores stood forward and stopped Vasariah in his tracks.

"What do you think you are doing, Zerach?" The Domini's voice rose as he was stopped by a burly Angel wielding a war halberd.

"The Prince does not want your company, Commander," Zerach said in a less than tactful tone. I felt Anfial wince as Vasariah looked like he had been struck by lightning.

"Not until this matter is resolved," Zerach added, in a poor attempt to placate his dumbstruck leader. It made me like the man even more. Darophon laid a hand on the Domini's shoulder and whispered what I presumed were reassuring words in his ear. I saw Vasariah's puffed up persona deflate somewhat. He gave me a sour look and flew away down into white clouds that swallowed him whole.

The great doors opened before us and Anfial beckoned us on. The Palace was laid out in a cruciform with great high windows on either side. Light from outside streamed through the stained glass, bathing us in a myriad of colours as we walked. Every ten feet on both sides, there were shadowy passages that disappeared into gloom. In the transept, I saw a group of Honores in a circle around a set of steps that led downwards. Anfial led us past them, and I was surprised how grim and humourless they looked. It was clear that something was very definitely wrong. We ascended more steps into the apse and came to another set of gates. These were gold and marked with Anael's sigil. Darophon moved closer to me and Anfial stood away respectfully, the well-practised move of a steward whose diplomatic skills were flawless.

"The Prince is in a troubled state of mind Azshael," he said. "I would suggest you listen, only ask questions that need answers immediately, and proffer neither opinion nor counsel. That last part is vitally important. It is no exaggeration to say lives are at stake here and could hang on what you say."

So, no pressure then...

Chapter Eight

The first indication that Prince Anael was 'troubled' was the weather that greeted us in his Sphere. Black clouds scudded across the sky, heavy driving rain lashed and whipped, and howling winds shrieked and moaned. It was a less than subtle indication of how the Archangel was feeling. The fact that Anael had retreated here in the first place was a surprise. In fact, I had never been to his Sphere in all my time under his command.

I also missed the usual warmth of his greeting, a vibrant power that coursed through one's being. Now that it was absent, almost the reverse was true. I felt like I was being pushed away, repelled. It was disconcerting, as I had never felt anything like it before, and I felt myself looking at Darophon for reassurance. For his part, the leader of the Heralds wore an enigmatic mask that gave away nothing but a sense of hardened resolve. It was enough to calm my nerves.

The Prince's Sphere was laid out as a vast night garden with all manner of plants and trees in glorious bloom. Great lawns dotted with statuary swept up to a majestic summer palace that stood upon a hill. It was an open structure, ornate and lit by an ambient radiance of warm suffusing light. The storm abated at the entrance to the lawn, content to rage on the borders, the winds ruffling the trees but not to a harmful extent.

Anfial took the lead as we walked to the Palace. It was protocol to be grounded in the Prince's presence unless told otherwise, and soon I could see the Archangel in all his glory. I say glory, but he seemed diminished, sitting on his own in the Palace's central chamber. He did not look up at our approach and his head remained bowed.

"Good my Lord," Anfial said, breaking the silence. "The Herald

Prime and Ambassador Azshael attend at your command." Anael raised his head and with a brief wave of his right hand dismissed his chief steward, who bowed and turned smartly to depart without another word. Anael looked different to me. His radiant aura, usually almost blinding in its intensity, was as low as I had ever seen it. He looked ordinary, and I found it alarming. I had never seen any Archangel in this state before. Addressing Darophon directly, he said, "Has Azshael been told of our concerns?" Darophon bowed and said that nothing had been said yet, for reasons of security. "Then for the sake of Excelsis, tell him," Anael said.

Darophon is not known for his brevity, but on this occasion the master orator kept things surprisingly short and to the point.

"Two nights past when the Host went abroad to quell the Bonded uprising, there was a break in at the Trinity. A significant artefact was stolen, and it needs to be found and returned without delay." At first, my mind wrestled with the concept of anyone daring to break into the Trinity Palace, but clearly, someone had done so and pulled off a spectacular heist. No wonder Vasariah was persona non grata. He and his Honores had apparently failed in their sacred duty to protect the Palace.

"Exactly what was stolen?"

"The White Rood."

Now, I'd like to think that I kept my cool in this moment, but the truth is I was genuinely shocked. The White Rood was not just an artefact, it was the Archangel's symbol of command over the Flight. Gifted to the Prince by Excelsis himself upon his appointment as our leader, it was an essential piece of regalia that cemented his authority and confirmed our divine mission and purpose. My mind raced with thoughts of how our enemies might use this against him and the wider Flight. I was so caught up in these deliberations that it took Darophon's prompt to bring me back to the moment.

"Ambassador, your Prince needs your aid," he said. "We believe there were Succae involved in this theft, as a group was seen fleeing the Palace grounds."

I thought back to the group I had seen in the streets during the riot before Cam's roar had diverted me back to the Red Roof Inn and the body of Cassiel.

"Do we know how many?"

"Anfial can tell you that. One of his staff witnessed them running away."

Anael stirred at that point, and lent forward on his silver throne.

"You are to take a message to Vod Karsz and emphasise my displeasure at this situation. He is to bend every sinew and return that which is mine to me with all possible haste."

I nodded and bowed, but I knew I would have to find different language to get the warlord of the Succae to assist us. It had been my experience that they did not respond well to threats. Whilst our accord held for now, it was a cessation of open hostilities rather than a peace treaty. I wondered if this was a subtle manoeuvre by Karsz, but quickly dismissed that as being unlikely. The Succae do not generally deal in subtle politicking. Their way of telling you how they feel has a more 'punch in the face' level of directness.

On the way back down, I asked Darophon who he thought was responsible but got little by way of answer. It was clear the Herald had his suspicions, but he was keeping them to himself for now, although I found our last exchange of words intriguing.

"I understand you were at the Mausoleum before coming here?" he said, and I was initially surprised at the speed his informants worked until I remembered that it was one of the Trinity's messengers who had come to fetch me from the Angel of Death's halls. They obviously knew where I was which means Darophon did, too.

"Yes, that's right," I replied.

"This is about the Juvenii found dead in the streets of the Lower Landing?"

"Yes. I felt I should try and find out what happened to her," I said, omitting Cam's reaction to the discovery of her body.

"Do we know who she was?"

"Her name was Cassiel," I said.

Darophon looked away for a moment as if retrieving an old memory, but he said nothing more and walked away, his staff clacking noisily on the marbled floor.

Chapter Nine

I went looking for Anfial and soon found him on the steps to the Palace. He was standing with the messenger who had come to fetch me from the Mausoleum. His name was Evangelos, and he was young and eager to please, which made me feel uneasy. Whilst I had no doubt that Anfial was probably closer to the Prince, it was Vasariah, leader of the Honores, who had the most influence here, which made me wonder whether I was being fed his prepared version of events.

As it turned out, Evangelos had not seen much at all, other than a group of three or four cloaked individuals running from the grounds of the palace out into the Princelands. He had witnessed this from a distance and thought they had come from the eastern arm of the Trinity, more commonly known as the Day Hall.

I wrestled with my memory. "Isn't that where the Rood is usually displayed?" I asked Anfial when Evangelos had given his account.

"It is, although it is usually stored with the rest of the Archangel's regalia when the Prince is away."

"So he would not have taken it with him when the Host flew to quell the disturbances?"

Anfial shook his head. "No, the White Rood is more ceremonial than practical. He bears Lightbringer for such purposes. Altogether a more powerful weapon." Lightbringer. Anael's sacred lance, imbued with the light of heaven itself. More powerful yes, but a weapon personal to the Archangel and not relevant to the command and control of the Seventh Flight.

"Did you see anyone flying, Evangelos?"

"It was dark, Ambassador," he said. "I just saw them running downhill. I'm pretty sure no-one was in flight, but they did move fast."

"What was the hour of the watch when this happened?"

"It was three tolls after the Prince had left with the Host," Evangelos said with no hesitation.

"Were there no guards at the gates?"

Anfial abruptly interrupted and dismissed Evangelos, much to my irritation. It was true to say that I had not been tasked with investigating the events of that night, but I wanted all the information I could get before explaining things to Vod Karsz.

Anfial could see the annoyance on my face and sighed.

"My apologies, Azshael, but Evangelos is young and impressionable. I also think he has yet to learn the value of considered silence. I happen to like him, and I don't want him to get into any more trouble."

I noted the use of the word 'more' and asked Anfial what trouble Evangelos could possibly be in?

"Kokael of the Irin has said she suspects he could have been a co-conspirator and wants to take him to the House of the Watchers for questioning. So far, I have managed to convince the Prince that this is unnecessary."

Kokael again. I was beginning to like this assignment less and less.

"Do you know why there were no guards left on the gates?"

"Vasariah took them with him. They followed in the wake of the Host."

"He left the Trinity unguarded?"

"They are the Prince's Honour Guard. It is my understanding they felt their place was at Anael's side. It is the first time the Host has flown since the war."

It was a bold decision from Vasariah, which I suspected had more to do with the chance to distinguish himself in the full view of the Archangel than with securing the safety of the Prince. Either way, it had opened the Palace to intruders who, by the sound of things, had literally walked in and run out.

"Can you show me where Evangelos saw them?

Anfial took me into the Trinity's grounds to the golden gates that the thieves, if thieves they were, had fled through unopposed. The perimeter fencing, fashioned of wrought iron, was clearly more ornate and decorative than it was wholly defensive, and looked unlikely to withstand a determined enemy assault. This was true of the palace estate though, built more to impress than defend.

That the Archangel chose to make his home in a more remote part of the Horta Magna told its own story. He was caught in a dilemma of cosmic proportions. The Flight had, so far anyway, failed in its mission of Judgment for the first time in known history. It was also clear that the Succae were not the murderous, rapacious world enslavers and destroyers they had once been. What did that say about Excelsis? That it was fallible? What then? Was everything we had done for Excelsis wrong? Should Anael return and take up arms against it as Duma Fallenstar had once done? Had we therefore doomed our former Prince of Light to exile and disgrace incorrectly? It was a philosophical and practical quandary that was no doubt vexing our Prince beyond measure, and thus far, no decision had been forthcoming. In the meantime, the accord endured, even with a recent test from a cabal of both Angelic and Succae plotters.

I thanked Anfial who flew back to the Palace as I wandered around the area. The terrain leading back to the elevated keep and its eastern wing sloped upwards across gently undulating folds of land, and I guessed that the troughs were deep enough to conceal people from casual onlookers above—at least until you arrived at the well-maintained hedges that marked the immediate palace environs. Again, these were easy to push past and as I emerged between two of them, I found Vasariah waiting for me at in the paved gallery that ran along the side of the halls.

The commander of the Honores looked a deal less haughty than he had been a few hours earlier. It was like someone had stabbed his ego with a pin and it had slowly deflated. Despite our frosty first meeting, I had some sympathy for him as I remembered what it was like to fall out of the Prince's favour, or worse still, earn his disapproval. It was like a warm hearth fire suddenly being extinguished and cold air seeping into your bones. We are conditioned to want the Archangel's attention, and to take it badly when it is denied. It's just the way we're built.

"Greetings again, Ambassador," he said, the look on his face showing he now regretted his earlier rudeness.

"Greetings, Vasariah," I replied, with what I hoped was a conciliatory smile.

"Are you taking over the investigation?"

"Taking over?" I replied, brushing stray foliage from my tunic. "Taking over from whom?"

"The Irin," he said, with a level of reasoned disgust. "I think Anael believes either I or one of my soldiers was involved."

I was so surprised I gasped, and I could see any barriers between myself and Vasariah immediately disappear. The idea that one of the Honores, the most loyal of the Host, would embarrass their Archangel was, to my mind at least, ridiculous. Yet, if Anael suspected it, I suppose I had to as well, but I had no doubt who might have placed that idea in the Prince's mind. The question, though, was why?

"Vasariah – I have not been tasked with establishing what happened here. The Prince bade me speak to the Succae Vod about his people's activities on this side of the Tether and ask for his assistance in finding the White Rood -- if it is on the Succae moon."

"I see," Vasariah said, although from the look on his face, he was puzzled.

"Given there were so many Low-Nin involved in the disturbances, I think the Prince is just being careful."

"Asuriel's Landing and the White Citadel are a good hour's flight from here, Ambassador. I doubt any stray Succae would have managed to get here without being picked up by a patrol."

It was a good point, yet if Evangelos's account was to be believed, intruders had been seen leaving the Palace grounds on foot, and all the patrols had probably been pulled into the Landing once the true numbers of protestors had been understood by Captain Pesak's guards.

"You left after the Prince had called the Host?"

"Yes, we did."

"How long after?"

"About thirty minutes or so."

"So that left the area without guards for how long?"

Vasariah bridled slightly, but I said nothing and kept my gaze neutral.

"Probably half a day or so all told, although I sent most of the watch back after the Prince had calmed the masses, so possibly a couple of hours less than that."

I could tell that Vasariah knew he had made an error of judgment. Whether that was a result of being caught up in the moment, devoted loyalty or naked ambition remained to be seen. Of the three, the last felt least likely, as he was the commander of the most prestigious military post in the Flight, which made this lapse of discipline even more curious. Although I didn't know him well, Vasariah's reputation was formidable, and now he had put it at risk. Something felt wrong, and it was time for the key question.

"So why did you and your troops follow the Prince that day?"

Vasariah didn't respond right away. He looked around him and gathered his thoughts.

"Things have been difficult," he said simply, and then added "since that trouble with Benazzarr." He was referring to my former mentor, who had led a cabal of Angels and Succae intent on restarting the war by committing an atrocity on the anniversary of the armistice. It had been a close-run thing.

"The Prince began to see traitors in the shadows everywhere. The Irin were called in to interrogate everyone here. They have a way of trying to turn the smallest trespass into a suspicious motive. It has been very wearing," he said bitterly. "I think I was so on edge, so alert to any perceived failure to support Prince Anael, that I thought it would be better to be seen to be with him rather than not."

I had been wrong in my assumptions of motive. It was fear that had pushed Vasariah into his decision to leave the Palace unguarded. Anael was not noted for being forgiving of these sorts of errors, and I thought Vasariah's days in command of the Honores were probably numbered, even if the White Rood could swiftly be found.

I said I would do what I could to return the artefact as soon as possible, and I said I felt for him. I may even have suggested that Anael could be reasonable, but we both knew that wasn't the case. I was about to leave when Vasariah asked me if I wanted to see the vault where the Rood had been housed. Whilst I knew I was not tasked with investigating the theft itself, I thought it could be useful to see, and followed him back into the eastern arm of the palace.

The first thing that surprised me was that he took flight once we reached the central nexus of the Day Hall. When Vasariah had said 'vault', I had presumed he was talking about going down, but he ascended upward, flying hundreds of feet above the Archangel's throne to the top of the Hall's tower. Here, hidden in the shadows of its high vaulted roof, I could see an opaque crystal structure that would surely be almost impossible to see from the Hall below. I had to admit, I had never seen it before, even though I had been in Anael's throne chamber many times. It was a compact rectangle with a hatch in its northernmost face that would be a squeeze for an Angel of my height and bulk to get through. Vasariah ran his hand over the entrance hatch, and it popped open with the softest of clicks.

"Wards?" I asked, pretty much asking him to confirm the obvious.

"Yes."

"Known to whom?"

"All the palace guards. Anfial also has access, as do a few of Narinel's Cherubim. They are the sacred keepers of the Flight's regalia and have the ceremonial duty to dress the Prince when such ritual observance is required."

"When is that?"

"There are days in the calendar – Flight anniversaries, Excelsis venerations. That kind of thing."

I will confess that all this was unknown to me. I was never one for ceremonies and days of observance unless there was no option but to attend. Also, it was fair to say that such rituals had been on the wane since the war with the Succae had begun. It made me think that Anael's unquestioning devotion to Excelsis might have wavered in the wake of the unsuccessful attempt to judge the Succae. That, or Anael had found little to celebrate or mark except failure.

I negotiated my way through the hatch with a little difficulty, but then was able to stand upright in a true box of wonders. Here were the Prince's jewels, glittering in multi-hued majesty. The orb and sceptre that confirmed his status as an Archangel Prince were here. Sacred weapons, ritual clothing and other treasures were on display, and I couldn't help but marvel at the achievements of the Prince of the Flight whose will I served.

I noted an empty chest that had fallen to the floor and asked Vasariah if this was where the White Rood has been stored. He nodded in affirmation. The box was around five feet long, about a foot deep, and lined with purple velvet. I could see the impression the Rood had left and judged it to be more of a wand than a staff. That was unless it was like Nimrod, the shape-changing spear that the Fallenstar had surrendered to me so many years before. I made a mental note to try and find out more about it when I had time to visit Narinel and the Flight archives.

In my mind's eye, I imagined Cassiel being able to fly up here where the Succae could not. She was also exactly the right size to easily fit through the hatch, but how she had bypassed the wards and got involved in a plot to embarrass Anael in the first place? I understood the Juvenii to be completely removed from the business of the Flight, so what possible motive she would have had seemed elusive. Maybe I was trying to make connections where there weren't any, but I have never believed much in coincidence, and it seemed odd that Cassiel's death and the theft of the White Rood had taken place within hours of each other just as a massive disturbance had spread chaos and confusion.

Chapter Ten

It was only when the walls of the White Citadel came into view that I remembered that Saur'Il had asked me to return to the Mausoleum before I went to meet with the Succae. I decided that whatever gem of wisdom the Angel of Death had to impart, it could wait. The fact the House of the Angelic Dead gave me the creeps might also have been a factor in my decision.

As the white marbled city walls revealed themselves through dense grey clouds, I felt the usual turbulent winds that came from the grand city in the sky. The arrival landings were packed with troops, and I saw groups of them depart in their squadrons, disappearing into dark clouds as they headed to the Lower Landing below. I had a bad feeling, seeing this many of the Seventh Flight's soldiers being deployed at once. It appeared we were expecting more trouble. I had hoped the Bonded had made their point, but this suggested otherwise.

I landed on the long processional that led to the great gates of the White Acropolis and breathed a sigh of relief that Galaeal's Legio Alba were in their usual guard positions. Vasariah would have been one of their number at some point before joining the Honores. I was hoping to speak to the Legio's leader, as if anyone could speak to Vasariah's reliability, it would be him. He was, however, notable by his absence and none of his troops knew where he was.

Instead, I headed for the Athenaeum, the central nexus of the Acropolis, the inner city. It was a large square surrounded by grand statues that immortalised the five Archangels who had led the Flight before Prince Anael had taken command. A six plinth had already been laid down for him, and I wondered whether his statue had already been carved, waiting, like all of us, for the day things would change.

The Athenaeum was dominated by four great structures. To the north was the Herald's Hall, where the day-to-day administration of the Flight was run. It was here that Anael's council, led by Darophon, sat and ruled in his name. To the east was the Hall of Records and to the south, the Scriptorium, where Narinel and his scribes chronicled our history and learnings with pen and paint. Finally, to the west stood the great temple to Excelsis. Here, the forever flame, a literal part of Excelsis, burned eternally. It was said that as long as the flame was alight, the Seventh Flight would endure. Personally, I thought this was a myth, but it never ceased to surprise me how many of the Flight took it to be a literal truth.

I made my way to the Scriptorium in search of my oldest friend, Sariel. She was one of the Cherubim and to outside appearances, looked like a child, but was actually the oldest of our kind I had ever known. The Scriptorium was usually a place of quiet order, but on this day, it was a hive of activity. Cherubim flitted this way and that, carrying scrolls, books, ledgers, and other items of reference, from the archives to the Registry Hall, where a group of soldiers gathered around a long table. Here, Narinel was busy sorting the incoming material with the help of his archivists.

I spotted Galaeal standing behind the massive bulk of Lamechial, leader of the Legio Alba. I tried to attract his attention, but he was too deep in conversation with his commander to notice. Then I felt a tug at my belt and turned to see Sariel looking up at me. She had a serious look on her face, which was unusual, because the Cherub I knew had a relentlessly sunny disposition. I had relied on it to get me through my darker times. Sariel just had that power to put a smile on your face.

"What are you doing here Azz?"

"Actually, I was looking for you."

"I heard you'd been sent down the Tether. I hope you're not dawdling!"

"No, not exactly. I need some information before I go, and I thought you'd be the best person to talk to."

Sari smiled briefly. "Of course! Who else?"

"What's going on here?"

"Search squadrons on the orders of the Prince. They're looking for mischief makers."

"Mischief makers?"

"Yes. Among the Bonded. You know; tricksters, hucksters, cheats, deceivers, rogues, and the like."

I did. The Flight had a rather large proportion of these characters among the Bonded. They were often tied in a symbiotic relationship with the pantheon leaders whose capture usually ended all resistance. There was something in their nature that made the arrival of Judgment and the fall of the order which they so railed against that made them our natural allies.

"Anyone in particular?" I asked, thinking about the Red Roof Inn and its occupants. Some of them could certainly be classed as tricksters, depending on how wide the definition spread.

"Lamechial has been tasked with rounding them all up for questioning. All those they can find, of course."

I had a bad feeling that things were about to get even worse in the Lower Landing, the sprawling shanty town that the Bonded called home.

"But why them, specifically?"

Sariel gave me a look that pretty much told me she knew but couldn't share the information.

"Look Sari, I have been tasked by Anael to speak to the Succae on this matter, so any and all information of use should be shared with me."

Sari thought about it for a moment and beckoned me away from the Registry.

"Alright, Azz," she said as we made our way back into the archive's passageways.

"But you didn't hear this from me."

We headed out to the steps of the Athenaeum's square, and as we walked around the quad in the shadow of the statues of the Archangels, Sariel told me what was going on.

"You know that after Anael pacified the Bonded, the squadrons detained a number of those who had been involved in the trouble?"

I nodded.

"Well, all the Succae they caught had no idea why they were there. Many couldn't even remember coming up the Tether at all."

That was news and an oddity in itself. I had only seen Low-Nin involved, and I knew their existence was based purely on one thing – advancement. It was hard to see what reward they could have earned from taking part in the Bonded's rebellious protest unless a hidden hand was pushing them on.

"That's not all," Sari said, warming to the topic. "Many of the Bonded also have no real recollection as to why they were so keen on asking for Excelsis. I mean, some of them trotted out familiar complaints about their lot as usual, but there was no specific understanding of what had driven the protest."

"What are the Primogi saying?" I said, referring to the most powerful of the Bonded, former leaders of pantheons, who had benevolently, for the most part, surrendered to the Flight to spare their worshippers unnecessary tribulations, and accepted a life of exile as a result. They had a reputation for aloofness, and I knew that many of the rest of the Bonded held them in varying levels of disdain. However, I was also sure they knew more about our indentured followers and their lives than any of our kind would ever know.

"The word is nothing at all. At least so far. I believe Darophon has summoned Charomos and Aethi to appear before the council later." Charomos, a god of just rule. and Aethi, a goddess of earth and fire, I knew only by their formidable reputations.

"Were they seen during the protest?"

"No, but there are Heralds who believe that they are behind the protests, even with the collective amnesia that seems to have overtaken everyone."

"I take it Darophon isn't convinced?"

"I don't know for sure, but I guess not, given all the research he has asked us to do."

I had to say I was with Darophon, and I doubted the pair would have much to add. It was true that our long-delayed return to Excelsis was overdue. I just didn't think the protest and the strange involvement of the Succae Low-Nin would be their way of making their feelings known. The Primogi were more overt than covert, yet all gods are cunning, and an innate distrust of those we had judged ran deep in the Flight's psyche, and would never be eradicated. We're a suspicious bunch.

"So, what did you come here for?" Sari said, bringing me out of my thoughts.

"Ah, yes. I am after information on the White Rood."

"The Prince's sceptre? Why?"

I paused for a moment as I realised that Sari had no knowledge of what had happened at the Trinity Palace, or at least if she did, then she was unaware of what had been taken. I decided to err on the side of caution and told her I wasn't yet at liberty to say, but that when I could, she would be one of the first to know. Given that knowledge was Sariel's stock in trade, I was surprised when she shrugged and said nothing further on the matter. That was fair enough, I supposed, as ultimately, she would know everything there was to know. Clearly, patience was an archivist trait.

She led me back into the Scriptorium and told me to wait in her cell. It was a place of work and a simple affair. A grand table and lectern dominated the centre of the chamber, and there was a tall, three-legged stool where I was used to seeing her perched as she worked on the copying and illumination of various scrolls and books. These latter were stacked high on the table whilst the scrolls occupied every nook and cranny. Also on the desk were inks and tools of her craft. I had no doubt she would be kept busy for a long time to come.

"Here we are," she said, rounding the corner with a bound tome in her arms that was nearly as tall as she was. She laid it flat out on the table, and I could see the crinkly leaves of parchment bound between cream leather boards worn with age.

"What's this?"

"It's the Prince's codex. Part biography, part philosophy and, of most interest to you, an inventory of the Archangel's most treasured possessions."

She opened the lock on the clasp and started turning the pages. It was a thing of wonder, and I could see the painstaking way it had been illuminated over the ages. It was divided into several sections, and she skimmed past leaves of text to the rear of the book, where there were sketches and illustrations of various weapons, armour, and other regalia, before coming to the entry for the White Rood itself.

Sariel had described it as a sceptre, but to my mind it looked more like a staff. Carved from white wood, it was about five feet long and crowned by an intricate carving of a dove that looked remarkably lifelike, as if a real bird had somehow been petrified and frozen in place. At the other end was a sharpened spike coated in silver. Along the haft, more detailed pictograms of Anael's history had been carved in bas relief. It was elegant and understated for a gift from Excelsis. In addition to the detailed drawing, I saw notations along the side of the page, some actual words, and others just letters.

"What do these mean?" I asked, and she hovered next to me to get a better look.

"Oh, those are archivist references," she said. "The E there indicates it is from Excelsis and the R stands for regalia."

"What about the N there?"

"That's Narinel's shorthand for 'see him for more information'."

"I thought all the details were here?"

"That's usually the case. But in theory, anyone could request access to these volumes. So, where the Prince has requested it, certain details are kept under the direct care of the Archivist Prime."

"In the Black Library you mean?"

"Azsh! It's not called the Black Library at all."

Sariel might have protested, but that's how, in hushed and reverent tones, the rest of the Flight referred to the forbidden archives. It was said that many of the secrets about the Flight, the Prince and even Excelsis itself were deliberately hidden away from the rest of us. I doubted that to be entirely the case, but given what I had seen and done in the Prince's name I wouldn't have been that shocked to discover it was.

"Do you know what it could be?" I was not desperately keen to meet with Narinel, but I did have a need to know all there was to know about the Rood before appearing before Karsz.

"Well, it's only a guess, but I would think something like this would have a power or powers of some sort. You'll need to talk to Narinel to find out more."

It was certainly a fair thought. I had been thinking this staff was a ceremonial item, like a symbol of office, but what if there was more to it? Could it be a weapon? And if so, what damage could it do? As I was dwelling on that, the door to Sariel's cell suddenly opened, and Narinel, Lamechial and Galaeal all walked in. I was pretty sure I heard Sariel swear—but maybe it was me.

"What is going on here?" Narinel said in his most stentorious tone. Initially, he caught me off guard and I may have shuffled a bit and looked at Sari, who gave me a look that was as cool as ice. Before I could gather my wits, she took over. "I am assisting Ambassador Azshael with his research," she said, "as you instructed."

Narinel looked confused. "As I instructed?"

"You did say to assist anyone looking into the recent troubles?"

Narinel suddenly looked a little lost, and took his usual long pause to think about things. Lamechial, who I did not know well, but who had a reputation as a humourless bully, looked less convinced.

"Those are not Ambassador Azshael's orders," he said haughtily. "Are they?"

I do so love it when I am handed the initiative in such situations. I went on to lecture Lamechial on what it was like dealing with the Succae and how he could not possibly know what was or was not relevant and necessary information. I went on to say that the Vod would expect me to have complete knowledge and be able to answer any questions without reference, so it was up to me and no one else to decide when I had all the details I needed. I could see Lamechial's eyes spark with irritation, but I knew I had won this round. He stepped back and said nothing more as Narinel's mind finally fed its thoughts to his mouth.

"Well, do you have everything you need now?"

"Not quite," I replied. Lamechial twitched and Galaeal grinned at me, his face hidden from his commander's sight.

"There is a notation here in the Prince's Codex that Sariel tells me means you have additional information that is not open knowledge?"

Sariel pushed the tome across the table, and Narinel looked at it for a moment before responding. "Yes. What about it?"

"What is it?"

"Nothing important," he replied. It was one of the fastest responses I had ever had from the Archivist Prime. I gave him a look, but he held my gaze, picked up the codex and, without another word, left with Lamechial and the Legio's captain in tow.

Chapter Eleven

I made Sariel promise to speak to Narinel to try to find out the missing information on the Rood. 'Nothing important' was the least likely answer to my question and I was sure Sariel had it right when she said it was more that Narinel was unwilling to reveal sworn secrets in front of those who did not need to know.

I decided to attend the Herald's Hall to hear the Primogi speak in front of Darophon's council. The entire group were in attendance. Twenty former powerful deities who had been forced to swear allegiance to Excelsis and leave their former worlds and worshippers behind. There was a mournful dignity about these gods and goddesses as they trooped into the circular auditorium. The gods were led by Charomos, once mighty ruler of a morally ambiguous world that was rich in inequality. There, the teeming masses suffered from the casual brutality of an elite class that worshipped their lofty divine ruler.

The goddesses were led by Aethi, a slender beauty clad in green robes who had been a fertility and nature deity the Flight had encountered on numerous occasions. Such powers were known as Travellers, with the ability to exist in multiple universes at once until the process of being Bonded forced them to cease and diminish in power.

Darophon and his Heralds questioned the Primogi for a good hour, but as I had expected, they had no new information to add and were as baffled by the events of the uprising as we were. Charomos answered most of the council's questions, and it appeared the others deferred to him. He claimed to be as surprised as anyone else that the unrest had taken place, and denied any prior knowledge or involvement. It seemed he had nothing but disdain for the Bonded and said he would not oppose any serious sanctions on them as a result. He sounded bored and treated his questioners with a pithiness worthy of a sarcastic teacher of indolent children. I did spot Kokael in the audience, but she ignored me and disappeared into the crowd when Darophon called proceedings to a close.

I took flight and descended from the White City down to the Lower Landing, which was still rimed with frost. There was a taste of ice on the wind, and icicles dangled from every roof that lined the town's alleyways, lanes, and thoroughfares. It hadn't, however, stopped many of the residents from going about their business. In the air above and on the land below, I saw Legio Alba troops keeping a watchful eye on proceedings. Given what I had seen of Lamechial, it was clear Narinel had been told to show the commander what he should be looking for. Personally, I highly doubted that the White Rood would be found hidden in the Landing. It seemed to me that this had been a deliberate act, and possibly the unrest among the Bonded had just been a diversion to give the thieves a clear run at the prize. If that was true, though, it implied inside knowledge of the Trinity Palace and its guardian. It meant an Angel had to have been involved. Whilst I pondered that unpleasant thought, I grew increasingly irritated that Narinel had kept the Rood's full story secret from me. However, there was nothing to be done about it. I would just have to wait until Sariel worked her magic and got the answers I needed.

It was growing late in the Horta Magna's artificial day, and in keeping with the curfew, the sky was darkening, with dusk due within the hour. It was bitterly chill when I arrived in the courtyard of the Red Roof Inn. Inside it was quiet, and whilst it was warm inside, the mood of the inhabitants seemed cold, sullen, and withdrawn. No fires burned in the hearths, but heat radiated from the very walls and floors. I felt Sylvenell's welcoming presence manifest itself in smiling simulacra in the wooden walls.

"Hey, Azsh," said the chief bottlewasher, a Hyena-headed former god by the name of Papa Famine.

"Staying for dinner? Mama is workin' on something special!"

His wife, Mama Feast, was now the Red Roof's innkeeper. I'd

like to say it was in partnership with her submissive husband, but that would be a lie. Papa would forever be at her beck and call.

"Who you wastin' time talking to now, eh? These dishes don't wash themselves!" Mama shouted up the stairs from her kitchen. Papa's ears flattened and he shrugged at me, hurrying down to her call.

"Oh, it you," Mama said when she caught sight of me. "I want a word wi't you," she said somewhat ominously, and signalled I should join her in the kitchen.

"There's odd people hangin' round," she said accusingly, as if I had personally invited them in.

"It's the Red Roof Inn, Mama," I said. "There are always odd people hanging around."

Mama blinked and gave a low growl, which I think meant she took the point, but then she grabbed my arm with a meaty paw.

"They're in the Green Bar. You go check 'em out for Mama." She squeezed my arm and I felt claws dig into the flesh. There are some things you just don't say no to when it comes to dealing with former deities.

The Green Bar was at the furthest extent of the long gallery that ran from the Inn's western end, where the main common room and stage were found. On the way, I saw the diminutive form of Ysabeau, the Inn's resident entertainer, pushing her grand harp on its wooden wheels. In another time, that hair had been regularly soaked in the blood of those that strayed from a forest path to better see her beauty and hear her song. Nowadays, her voice was just as beautiful but far less deadly. She was coming in my direction, and I could see her auburn locks looking dishevelled and adorned with dark streaks of mud. The lace eye mask that she usually wore was at an angle, and I saw her right eye sparking with rage. I could also see that the strings of her harp were coated with a viscous red liquid that, on closer inspection, looked like a gravy of some kind.

"You alright Ys?" I asked, and she suddenly looked up and realised I was there. "Tough crowd?"

"What do you think, Azsh? Some people have no respect for art," she said as I stepped out of her way, and she rolled her instrument past me without another word.

The Green Bar was in a state of disarray, and I ducked to avoid the carcass of whatever Mama had cooked for the guests here smashing off the wall nearby. I didn't think it had been aimed at me. I was just in the wrong place at the wrong time. Raucous laughter echoed through the rafters as various outlandishly garbed men and women cavorted, danced, and generally larked about with little care for the furniture or anything else around them. I was about to intervene when the shrill note of a whistle cut through the noise, and everything went quiet. As a group, they all stopped what they were doing and sat down to stare at me. They were an odd bunch, and it didn't take me long to work out who they were. Tricksters.

I didn't recognise all of them, but I knew the more notorious among them by reputation. The whistle blower's name was Malacaz, and he had once been Charomos's court fool. The left side of his head was shaved, whilst an elaborate fringe draped over the right. He was dressed in painted leathers that were tight on his lean, lithe body. Shreds and patches of multicoloured fabric were tied at his elbows, wrists and knees, a remnant of his time as a fool rather than a symbol of the rebel he had become. Malacaz had shown us the secret ways to breach Charomos's great temple in the sky, and once the Archangel had made his presence known, the jaded divine justiciar had swiftly capitulated. It turned out he was bored sick of his worshippers and thought judgment was well overdue.

To Malacaz's left, and fixing me with a provocative side-on stare, was a sinuous dark-skinned woman with amber eyes. Her name was Virdae, and her skin was covered in black feathers that grew denser where modesty demanded. She moved like the carrion queen I knew her to be. She had led many a hunter to their doom with promises of big game, only to vanish when they were deep in the wilderness. She would watch them die of starvation and exposure there, then pick at their bones at leisure. She came from a primitive world where the people worshipped gods of the hunt and everything, including each other, was fair game. Virdae betrayed her own mother, the goddess Xarion, who had turned her only child into a cleaner of corpses after a falling out over the favouring of tribal champions.

Virdae had helped us hunt Xarion down and gloried in the fiery judgment that saw her destroyed and her tribes accept the end of their world.

On Malacaz's right was a big man with an overabundance of hair that sprouted everywhere – bushy eyebrows, nose and ears—in clumps of black and grey. He had a thick, black beard and sideburns, and hairy hands that ended in sharp fingernails. It was the eyes that stood out most though; deep, wide, and rheumy yellow. This was Marok the Wolf, probably the most ancient of the group and a predator of renown who had once protected a great pack that had nearly driven the rest of his tundra world's species to extinction. It was the goddess Aethi who had tamed the wolven heart and prevented total extinction of the planet's life, but not before Excelsis had heard the calls of the last survivors and marked the world for the Flight's attention.

The other two I sensed rather than saw, and one worried me far more than the other. I felt the breeze of the murderous Kaualakoo trying to get behind me. It's a key part of stabbing someone in the back. Kaualakoo and I had met before, and I was wise to his mastery of stealth and invisibility. Once a man whose murderous finesse had elevated him into a demigod of assassins and ruler of a brutal city state, he had been dethroned by his own kin and left for dead.

I flared my wings and sent him and the last of Malacaz's notables sprawling. Her name was Flynx, and she was a former fox goddess, an animistic spirit who had somehow gained physical form and power before we arrived on her world of sentient beasts who ruled over mankind and hunted them for food and sport. Flynx had cared for and been worshipped by the little creatures that scavenged at the bottom of the food chain. Other than the fact that she could not resist taking other people's possessions, she was mostly harmless. Flynx said pointedly "Not very nice. Very nice not." Then she picked herself up and smiled at me sweetly—which was somewhat disconcerting, but then, like all of those gathered in the mossy surroundings of the Green Bar that afternoon, she was genuinely insane.

Kaualakoo, his face hidden by a wooden facemask with

rudimentary slits for eyes and a wide red gash for a mouth, uttered a low guttural growl at me, and his hands were suddenly full of sharp blades. I was rather hoping things wouldn't come to this, but I called Nimrod into existence and my sacred weapon leapt into my hands, black fire licking across the long leaf-shaped spearhead.

"Enough!" Malacaz said sharply. Kaualakoo ignored him until he said it again, this time more softly. The former King of Killers paid attention, and he faded back into the shadows from whence he had come with a nonchalance that was as sudden as it was unexpected.

"Azshael, Ambassador to the Succae?" He said it as if it was a question, but as we had both met before it seemed that he was grandstanding for his gathered followers.

"Malacaz. Thief, liar, troublemaker," I replied. It was more statement than a question, and it earned me a wide grin in return. "What are you doing here?"

"I have come for your help, Angel," he said.

Chapter Twelve

"Why should I help you?" I said, and Malacaz dropped the insane smile and turned away. He pointed at the door, and one by one, the others of his kind departed without a second glance in my direction. Only Marok the Wolf remained, one padded arm resting on the soft greenwood of the bar.

"It's alright," Malacaz said to him, and the old man nodded and took his leave.

"I've got a problem, and I think you can help me. From what I know, you're not like the others are you? I mean, I have heard tell you are one of the more reasonable ones of your kind. Is that right?"

"Even if it were, the question stands. Why would I help you?"

The Trickster reached into his velvet jacket and pulled out something I had hoped never to see again. A black feather.

"I found this in my quarters last eve. It's the calling card of an assassin isn't it? A warning that they are coming for me. Right?"

I turned the item over in my hand. It did indeed look genuine, and it cast my mind back to a life I had long buried in a past I wanted to forget.

"If it is what it looks like, then yes, perhaps you should be concerned. Although the group that used to deliver these to our enemies on the eve of their demise are long gone. Outlawed by Prince Anael many years ago."

"So what? I am supposed to believe this is just a hoax?"

"It could be that way, yes."

"Or it could be that your Prince is looking for a head to put on a spike! A scapegoat to blame for recent events. Word has it the Albas are coming for us all. Someone has got it into their heads that a Trickster is to blame for all that recent bother, and I am top of the list."

I could see Malacaz was growing more agitated, and as he talked, he paced up and down the length of the bar. He looked genuinely frightened, and I could understand why.

The feather was the symbol of a group of assassins known as the Halokim. During the Wars of the Tribes and Duma's subsequent rebellion, the group had become expert at dealing with troublemakers needing to be removed. In my youth, I had been one of them until I became uncertain as to the purity of the mission and the fact that our leader, Kael, was taking matters into his own hands without direction from the Prince. Eventually, the Halokim were outlawed and disbanded, but Kael had recently reappeared as part of the cabal that had nearly destabilised the truce between the Flight and the Succae.

"He's still out there, isn't he?"

Yes, he was. Sariel and I had left him in a pool of his own blood, but we adapt and heal quickly, and after the dust had settled, he had disappeared.

"Kael would be arrested as soon as he showed his face," I said, although I probably didn't sound as convincing as I hoped. The truth was that someone, somewhere, was sheltering him. A useful asset to have up one's sleeve.

"Even if it's not him, it's your Prince that hands these out, isn't it? So maybe he's built a new hit squad just for me and my kind!"

"Who would have said it was you?"

"Charomos of course! Who else?"

I thought that was unlikely. I hadn't spent much time with the current leader of the Primogi, but he didn't strike me as the type who would idly throw someone to the wolves. Then again, Malacaz did have a special reputation for being provocative, and everyone has their limits.

"Are you responsible for the riots?" I asked nonchalantly, and he gave me a dark look before suddenly bursting into laughter that went on for an uncomfortably long time.

"Oh, Angel, you're too much," he said, wiping tears from his eyes as he subsided into chuckles. "If I had that kind of power, do you really think I would be here asking for your help?"

Okay, he had a point there.

"Alright then. What do you want? And why do you think I can help you?"

"I want to get down the Tether. You know, into the vampire lands."

"Why?"

"Because I'll be out of reach there, that's why."

"You'll also be obvious and stand out like a sore thumb. If assassins want to find you, they'll have an easy time of it."

"Nah," he said. "I have friends down there who can keep me out of sight until this nonsense passes. So, can you help me or not?"

"Why can't you just go down the Tether yourself?"

"Ain't you heard? There are new rules. Your Archangel has nailed everything shut. No travel allowed unless you have permission to do so. I don't think it would be advisable for me to just turn up at the guard station and ask for a permit. Do you?"

I was about to say he would have to weather the storm like the rest of his kind. All Tricksters are natural born liars and as such, there was no way he could be trusted. Then again, I couldn't see what his angle was. If anything, being among the Succae was more restrictive than being one of the Bonded. However, I had a nagging feeling that there was something missing. As I was about to turn him down, I heard a commotion and shouting coming from the common rooms, followed by an almighty crash.

I made my way back down the hall with Malacaz close behind me to see the soldiers of the Legio in a pushing and shoving match with Marok and Papa Famine. The Angels had knocked the Inn's main door off its hinges, and it was now the subject of a tug of war between the two sides. I began to voice my protest and appeal for calm when the wolf and the hyena were sent sprawling backward, and Lamechial and a group of his burlier companions pushed their way in. Troopers filed in behind him and I could hear shouts and screams as they made their way into the Inn.

"What the hell do you think you're doing?" I shouted at the Legio's commander, but he barely looked at me.

"Use your lariats!" Lamechial shouted as Captain Galaeal saw me and signalled I should stand down. I heard a wolf's howl as a transformed Marok was swiftly noosed and subdued with white magic bonds around his neck and legs. Energy pulsed across his body, and he collapsed in a convulsive heap. The Legio meant business and even though he was senseless, they set about kicking and punching the old shape-shifter until he lay still. Papa had meekly surrendered and was spared further violence as he was restrained and pushed out the door into the cold of the evening.

The other Tricksters gave Lamechial's troops a brief challenge, but one by one, I watched them submit to arrest. Even Kaualakoo finally surrendered after being cornered in an upstairs chamber by the troops Lamechial had stationed on the roof. As for the Inn's residents, Mama Feast, Ysabeau, and her spider queen mother were sequestered in the common room as Lamechial took stock.

"Well, fancy finding you here, Azshael," he said in his usual pompous tone. "I thought the Prince gave you orders to scuttle off to your vampire friends, yet here you are, right in the thick of a group of plotters. I find that rather interesting, to say the least."

I could have risen to the bait and lost my temper, but I knew how bullies like Lamechial worked. Losing it would do me no favours or help Papa and the others. Instead, I opted for a more reasonable tone.

"I only preceded you by minutes. Did you follow me?"

"Of course not! We were acting on a tip-off that the Trickster Malacaz had been seen entering this property."

"A tip-off from whom?"

"That," the Commander said, "is none of your concern."

"Well, I don't see him about, do you? It looks like your information was faulty."

Lamechial looked sternly at Captain Galaeal, who shrugged apologetically.

"Strange that all these other rogues would be found here without their leader."

"I thought rogues didn't have leaders. Isn't that kind of the point of being one?"

Lamechial took being caught out in a logical paradox relatively well by completely ignoring me. "Search this place again, top to bottom. I want that Trickster found!"

The Commander went outside into the courtyard to question his prisoners while Captain Galaeal and his soldiers went about their business. As they did so, I waited with Mama Feast and Ysabeau in the common room.

A short time later, Galaeal reported there was no sign of Malacaz. I could tell the Commander was angry, and he ordered the other residents of the inn, excluding myself, to be detained. My protests fell on deaf ears as first, Mama Feast, and then Ysabeau and her mother (in human form) were escorted from the building. Then Lamechial went too far.

"Burn it down," he said,

The first thing that happened was that my sacred spear Nimrod appeared in my hands. I don't remember calling it, it just happened, such is our bond. Galaeal and his Legio soldiers took a step back, but Lamechial and the Angels immediately around him stood their ground. Nimrod had once belonged to the Fallenstar and had drunk deep of Angel blood during his rebellion.

"You can't do that," I said. "This is the home of Sylvenell, one of the Bonded powers. She is entwined with the building now and if you burn this Inn down you will be murdering her."

Lamechial gave me a stern glare and looked unmoved.

"Ambassador. I have the Prince's warrant to take whatever steps I deem necessary in Asuriel's Landing to restore order and catch those behind the recent troubles. Unless you are planning to murder those of your own kind, I would suggest you stand aside and get on with the task the Prince gave you."

My mind raced. Was I really willing to kill my own kind to stop Lamechial's soldiers from destroying my home from home and killing Sylvenell? The answer was an unsettling one. Yes, I was. Time seemed to slow down—and then I realised it had actually done so. I could see Angelfire sparking in the hands of the Albas assigned to the destruction of the Red Roof Inn.

"Well? Think of something Angel." It was Malacaz's voice in my head. "I can't keep this up for long."

I racked my brain, searching for an answer, and then it came to me just as whatever power Charomos's Trickster had used came to an end.

"You said your warrant applies to Asuriel's Landing? Right, Commander?"

Lamechial raised a hand and his loyal troops paused in their manipulation of the fire within.

"I did. Upper and Lower parts of the city."

"Well then, you have no business with this Inn except by my permission."

"What are you blathering on about, Azshael?"

"This is an embassy of the Flight. It is not part of the Landing. It is its own domain and subject only to the rules set by the Prince and his ambassador. Of course, if you have a written warrant from Anael specifically mentioning this embassy, I would be happy to review it."

Lamechial sighed. "Do you really think this is going to change anything? Fine, Ambassador, have it your way. I have what I came…". He looked around and saw that half the Tricksters were gone. I surmised that Malacaz had used the time stop to work some of his companions loose. It was not Lamechial's day.

Then I saw Virdae break from her captors and shift into the black feathered Raven-woman that she was. Her two captors followed her, soaring into the night sky in hot pursuit. I willed her to fly as fast as she could. She was small, nimble, and quick, whereas her angel pursuers were slow and comparatively clumsy, weighed down by armour and weapons. Her form in the night sky made her hard to spot, and she vanished and then reappeared behind them. For a short while, she toyed with her pursuers, out flying them, making them look like ponderous fools. As soon as they got close to catching her, she would vanish and materialise away from them. I saw the exhilaration of flight in the shudder of her wings and heard it in the constant mocking caws that sounded like the laughter of carrion. Then things changed, and one of Lamechial's burly soldiers sent a burning spear arcing into the heavens. It went straight through her and at the end of a sad and sudden descent, she hit the ground. I rushed to her side as her body changed back to its feathered, female form. Lamechial looked on with a face of stone. The bastards had killed her, and none of the Legio Alba seemed the least bit concerned.

I might have won an initial skirmish with Lamechial, but it had come at a terrible price. I watched from the Red Roof's balcony as his soldiers set about raiding nearby properties and arresting more of the Bonded. I found it difficult to watch and hard to believe that my golden Prince would allow this to happen.

"Do you believe me now?" Malacaz said from where he was hiding in the shadows. "The world's gone mad and we're the ones that must pay the price. Get me out of here Angel, please! Lest I pay the same price of death for unfounded suspicion."

Did I trust him? No. Was I able to just stand aside and watch those that had aided us in the past be treated like dirt? No. It was an invidious choice, but in the end, I thought it was true that he was probably better off beyond the immediate reach of the Legio. At least until things cooled down and the White Rood was located. Besides, I knew where he was going, and I had faith that he could be swiftly relocated if necessary.

"Alright, Malacaz, I'll help you get down the Tether, but you are going to need a disguise." He brightened suddenly, and that manic grin was back. "Now you're talking! Being someone else is one of my specialities."

Chapter Thirteen

We left the Red Roof Inn in the dead of night, and the deathly chill bit deep in the swirling winds of the courtyard as I took flight into the dark sky. The Inn I had left behind looked as quiet as I had ever known it, and I felt an emotional wrench as I put my hand on the door to say goodbye to Sylvenell. The wood warmed beneath my hand and her face appeared in the panel. Golden sap leaked from her eyes. Tears for herself and tears for those she had given a home.

"Don't worry, Syl. No one will be able to act against the Inn until I return. This madness is temporary. It will pass, I promise you." I pulled the doors closed behind me and marked them with the ambassadorial sigil.

The flight to Vigil Keep, which guarded the Tether that led down to the Succae moon, was an hour's flight away. Malacaz had taken the form of some sort of small lizard with an armoured shell and was riding on my shoulder, hidden in the dark recesses of my hood. He was curiously quiet, but then so was I. The shocking killing of Virdae had plunged us both into quiet introspection. Nothing and no-one got in my way as I raced across the sky, and soon the pale outline of the mountain range known as Vigil's Teeth came into view. This Shaper-made range of unscalable peaks effectively hemmed in the Tether, which lay on a verdant grassy tumulus beyond. Vigil Keep was in the dead centre of the Teeth, its great walls and gates a solid bulwark of defence. It was the first time I had seen it since the recent attempted coup, and it was clear the Shapers had been at work here as well.

Previously, the Tether had been right outside the walls of the Keep, but now the land had been reshaped and the defences enhanced by the creation of a long and narrow pathway flanked by high walls. The path descended about half a mile down to a grassy plain. It was a deadly bottleneck that would favour the Keep's defenders if it ever came to that, or at least I presumed that was the expectation. I had been the Keep's Commander in the last decade of the Succae war and knew its protocols well.

On this night, the white walls and four towers of Vigil Keep blazed with light, and there were substantial numbers of guards maintaining an aerial watch in the sky above the fortress's perimeter. It was an indication they were on high alert but for what reason, I did not know. It gave me pause, and as an escort patrol approached me, I decided I would modify my original plan of heading straight down to the Succae's moon, and instead pay a visit to the Keep's current Commander, Captain Varael, a former member of the Ophanic order.

Before taking over my command, Varael had been an influential member of the main sect of Watchers known colloquially as the Eyes. Convinced I had become an agent for the enemy, Varael had caused no end of problems for me before my Succae love, Ischae, had been murdered. For a long time afterwards, we hadn't got on, but I had supported him in the wake of the attempted coup, where his actions showed he was an unwilling participant rather than an actual collaborator whose position had been exploited. Since then, we had entered a new era of polite civility that I sometimes felt bordered on the painful.

Malacaz stirred and voiced his displeasure at the diversion by digging his claws into my shoulder, but I told him to be quiet and stay hidden as I turned to follow my escorts to the landing zone on the battlements. Here, Varael's adjutant, Sergeant Sabrathan, waited for me. He was either very observant or I was expected.

"Greetings, Ambassador," he said smoothly as I landed next to him.

"Good evening, Sergeant," I said. "Bright night, tonight."

Sabrathan nodded without giving me any clue as to why the Keep was as bright as daylight. It was obviously a hedge versus the Succae, who it was widely believed preferred shadow and darkness. I wasn't certain that it made a difference to their martial abilities but, rightly or wrongly, it was fair to say we had convinced ourselves that it gave us an edge. I followed the adjutant down into the courtyard and on to the wide stone steps that led up into the great square central keep.

"I'd like to see Captain Varael as soon as possible," I said. Sabrathan looked back at me. "Yes, he'd like to see you as well, but there is a visitor waiting here who told me she needs to see you as soon as you arrive, so if it's alright with you, I will take you to meet her first?" I nodded my assent, and he led me up wide stairs and along a narrow gallery that overlooked the Great Hall below.

I wasn't exactly sure who was waiting for me, but I had an uncomfortable feeling that it was the Irin's leader, Kokael. That she would be a regular presence among the other Watchers here in Vigil Keep was a given, and I was sure, even with our new positive relationship, that Varael owed her far more than he owed me. That would be worth remembering when the Commander and I met. In one of the day rooms where I had once spent much of my time, it was therefore a pleasant surprise to see Sariel sitting in an armchair that was so wide, deep, and plush that it looked like it was devouring her. She looked up as Sabrathan showed me in, and with a beat of her wings rose from her seat.

"Well, it's about time," she said, and for once I could tell she wasn't joking.

"Apologies, Sari. There have been some developments, and I confess to having been delayed."

"I know. I heard about the raid on Syl's place. Is she alright?"

"No, not really," I said. "Hopefully, I have bought her some time so that this mess can be resolved." Sariel nodded and looked at Sabrathan, who was still waiting at the threshold.

"That will be all, Sergeant," she said, the authority in her voice belying her apparently youthful frame. Sabrathan bowed and closed the door behind him. Sariel indicated to me to follow her as she retreated deeper into the room, away from the door. In the centre of the command chambers, there was a large round table made of pale marble with enough space to comfortably accommodate ten to twelve attendees. Inscribed in the white stone was a map of the Horta Magna with key strategic locations already engraved. Red veins in the marble illustrated rally points and lines of defence to resist invasion. Sariel reached into her satchel and pulled out a very old looking scroll. It was in a fragile state, and as she rolled it out with expert care, I could see the writing on it was faded with age.

"What's this?" I said, as she placed small ingots on each corner so that the scroll lay flat on the table. As she did so, it became apparent there was an illustration, as well as writing, in the sacred language of Excelsis. The drawing was of the White Rood, and I remembered I had put pressure on Sariel to find out what Narinel was reluctant to reveal. She had come through for me, but from the intent look on her unsmiling face, it didn't look like there was much cause for celebration. My grasp of the noble tongue of the High Heralds was not strong, so I looked at her expectantly until she understood my ignorance.

"You can't read it?"

"I'm afraid not. Well, maybe a word or two. Can you translate, please?"

Sari sighed deeply and leaned in close to whisper.

"This is extremely sensitive stuff. I really shouldn't be telling you any of this, but having read it, I know you need to know. Suffice to say that if Narinel were to find out I had taken this from the Black Vault, I would be in big trouble."

"I thought you said there was no such thing!"

Sari's face flushed for a moment, then she regained her composure. "You know what I mean!" I did, but I liked it when I could catch her out. The opportunity didn't come around that often.

"So, what is it, and what does it say?"

"This is one of the Flight's oldest documents. It dates to our foundation under the Archangel Kemuel."

"I thought this was about the White Rood?"

"It is! It turns out that the sceptre has been part of the Flight's regalia since the very beginning."

That was new information. I had always understood that the Prince's sacred items were original gifts from Excelsis, but it turned out they were hand me downs.

"So every Prince who rules the Flight inherits the gifts of the previous leader?"

Sariel nodded. It made sense, making each Prince that much more powerful than the last.

"All very interesting, but that doesn't tell us anything about what it does."

"I haven't started translating yet! You asked what this document was, so I told you!"

She had a point. I was aware of Malacaz literally breathing down my neck. I was in a bit of a fix, given what Sariel had said about the secret contents of this scroll, but I couldn't very well ask him to wait outside, so I let her continue.

"This scroll is a detailed account of the White Rood as it was when Kemuel held it during the Tribal Wars."

"I thought this was a gift from Excelsis?"

"It was. Can I please continue without you constantly interrupting me with stupid questions?" Sariel looked irritated, so I shut up and let her carry on.

"Archangel Kemuel was the leader of the Tribe of the Seventh Star, remember?"

I did. He was also a great war leader who had gone on to lead the Seraphic Host, a post I presumed he still held.

"Kemuel was the first Prince Excelsis approached in the Great Manifestations. Kemuel challenged him to prove the powers he claimed to wield by forging a great weapon that would bring the Tribal Wars to an end. The White Rood, or what it has become, is exactly that item, or its descendant, at least."

"Descendant?"

"Yes. I think the original item was a lance. It has taken a few knocks over the aeons, so what we see today has been reconstructed and reforged so that the haft is all that remains of the item Kemuel used to subdue his rivals."

"So, it's mainly a ceremonial item, then, if its powers have been eroded?"

"No! That's the point, and is why this must remain a closely guarded secret. One of the reasons it was so carefully locked away is that there is no indication it has lost any of its potency—which brings me neatly to this scroll." Sariel took a feathered quill from within the folds of her robes, placed an un-inked nib on the top line of the parchment's text, and began to read.

"And then Kemuel, Prince of Stars, did call a stay to the battles and trials of combat, an end to the merciless mutilation of Angel on Angel. A great convocation was gathered, a synod of the Princes of the twelve warring Tribes.

There, it came to pass that each one who claimed dominion over the others was heard by all. Some claimed right by conquest, some by historical precedent, whilst others demanded recognition by moral superiority. Through all this, wise Prince Kemuel listened and bided his time until it was his turn, the last turn, to say his peace."

It was a history lesson I had heard about a thousand times before, and I was getting impatient. "This is all very interesting, but does it happen to mention what the damn thing does?" Sariel gave me a withering look. "If you let me finish then yes, sort of."

"Sort of?"

"Look, Azsh, there is nothing official in the archive that specifically details the Rood's powers, which is why I went looking in the restricted histories area of the vaults. That's where I found this. Now, do you want me to finish it or not?"

"I know what happened, Sariel! We all do! Kemuel gave a big, dramatic speech and everyone agreed to stop fighting. Right?"

"That is one version of the story, yes, but in this scroll there's a rather interesting bit of additional detail. That's what I have been trying to explain to you."

Now I was intrigued. "Alright, go on then. What does it say?"

Sariel found her place again and continued.

"Kemuel channelled the power of Excelsis as he spoke, and his words gained new power in the ears of the gathered host. From the highest Prince to the lowliest soldier, it was as if Kemuel was whispering directly to each one of them. New understanding dawned among them, and harmonious thoughts spread across the gathered Host. All previous enmities were forgotten, and grievances put to one side. Kemuel had united the Twelve Tribes in service to a new power and a new purpose. To serve Excelsis in glory!"

I confess that initially, I wasn't sure what point Sariel was making, and she must have seen the puzzled look on my face.

"Don't you think it's strange?"

"What?"

"That the Bonded rebelled, and they don't remember why? I mean, don't you think that sounds exactly like what happened with Kemuel and the Tribes? And it was the Rood that held the power of Excelsis then!"

"I can see the similarities, Sariel, but you're missing a key bit of detail."

"And what's that?

"The Rood was taken *after* the Bonded rebelled so it can't have been…"

I tailed off as I realised I had assumed the White Rood had been taken during the riots. But what if that was not the case? What if it had been taken earlier and used for exactly the purpose of making trouble for Prince Anael? Although who would benefit and what their motive would be, I couldn't immediately fathom. All I did know is that Sariel had—maybe—dug up something profound.

She looked at me expectantly with a sly smile on her face.

"You're finally getting it, aren't you?"

I was, but I was now very concerned for Sariel's safety. If this was a plan to undermine Anael, then who knew who could be involved.

"Does anyone but us know you removed this from the Black Vault, Sari?"

She shook her head emphatically. "No. I was extremely careful."

"What about Narinel? Did you say anything to him?"

"Not a word, I swear."

"Alright, then you'd best get back to the Citadel. Make sure you put it back where you found it and don't say anything to anyone. Right?"

"Right," she said and raised her thumb in acknowledgement.

I had a sinking feeling. Things had suddenly become very complicated.

Chapter Fourteen

I must have seemed pre-occupied in my meeting with Commander Varael, and that's because I was. My mind was churning over the possibility that the Rood had been taken and used to command and control both the Bonded and the Low-Nin. I had to agree with Sari's conclusion that it seemed to be more than a coincidence that the aftermath of the events of the revolt bore a marked resemblance to the events detailed in Kemuel's history, and the one common denominator was the power of Excelsis bound in the Rood.

The power Kemuel had accessed on that fateful day had later become known as 'Sanctity'. All the Archangels knew its secret, but from what I had heard, the results of using it were usually more instant and of less lasting impact. Then there was the issue of the numbers involved. The power required to influence so many was only in the province of the most powerful of the Princes. Did the Rood really have that much power bound within it?

"Is it not to your taste, Azshael?" Varael's polite inquiry brought me back to the moment. He was indicating the warm infusion of rare flowers and manna that had been placed in front of me. It was a powerful pick me up, said to awaken both mind and spirit.

"Oh, no, Commander," I said apologetically, quickly taking a sip from the silver goblet in which it had been served. "It's perfect." This was true, and I could feel a brightness in my core and a sharpening of both physical and mental acuity as the warmth of the draft moved through me.

Varael had been telling me about the changes that the Shapers had made to the Keep and its surrounds. As he droned on, my mind was trying to make sense of the shreds and patches of the implications of Sari's research. If it was the case that the item had been taken before the day of the revolt, then the thief or thieves must have managed to evade the guard whilst it was on full duty. That seemed unlikely and therefore highly suspect, but I was struggling to see any upside in it for Vasariah. Given what had happened in the aftermath, his very position in the Flight was under threat and he had obviously lost the Prince's trust as a result. I knew from my own personal history how difficult that would be to regain. Could it be one of Vasariah's junior officers? Initially that seemed more likely, but such complex planning would need both an element of luck and probably more than one conspirator. I knew the sort of Angels that made it into the Legio Honores, and I knew they would be reluctant to take such risks for each other. The more I thought about it, the more that idea began to fall apart. There would be more benefit in one of them betraying the others than going through with the theft itself, which made it a non-starter.

"That brings us to the situation with the Succae, Ambassador," Varael said, pulling me back to the moment.

"You know they requested the current alert at the Keep? That the Serrate you worked alongside in that recent unpleasantness delivered their formal petition personally?" Varael had a talent for euphemistic speech, wherein an attempted coup had now become 'that unpleasantness'. More unpleasant for some than others, I thought.

"Lytta came here?"

"Is that her name? Yes, she brought a written request from Vod Karsz. I can show it to you if you like?" He sent for Sabrathan, who was surprisingly swift in delivering the black leather scroll case, which was embossed with decorative serpents that writhed in knots along its sides.

I was disappointed that as the supposed Ambassador to the Succae, no one had asked for me or sent word of Karsz's communiqué. It was a technical breach of protocol, but then I knew my position had never been confirmed and was only used when it suited either side. It also wouldn't have surprised me if Varael had passed it straight on to a Herald, who would, no doubt, have thought no-one else but the Prince would need to know. I was not a consideration in any chain of command, especially where the Heralds were involved.

The letter, penned in the Succae language, was mostly pictographic. For a functional people, the Succae could be surprisingly artistic, and I admired the craft and intricate attention to detail in the imagery. In essence, it was an apology that measures had to be taken in response to the Low-Nin's participation in the recent unrest. Karsz indicated that he would take personal responsibility for tracking down any ringleaders. He offered his Lord Ancestral Vachs, as a liaison who could help question any Succae, although it was further suggested this would be best handled on his side of the Tether. He asked that any detainees we were holding should be returned as soon as was practicable. Then there was a strange coda where Karsz himself had written a few short sentences in the Succae's old language. I was sure only a handful of Narinel's archivists would be able to translate this, but I knew Anael himself was fluent, and my former lover Ischae had taught me the basics. It read as a coded warning that 'unknown forces' were creating a disturbance in his lands, too. He referred to the *Yurei* returning to plague his people. That was not a word I knew. He ended with advice to banish shadows, especially around Vigil Keep, with no further explanation.

"I take it the Prince took his advice then?"

Varael nodded. "Indeed so. I had orders within the hour to light the Keep, double the watch and mount aerial patrols. Essentially return to a war footing."

"When did this missive arrive?"

"Yestereve."

"And the Serrate delivered this herself?"

"Yes."

"Did she come on her own?"

"There was a group of Ashai with her, but they stayed round the Tether whilst she came up to the Keep."

I was intrigued. I hadn't seen Lytta for a few months, but last I had heard, she had become part of Karsz's personal bodyguard. Sending her was as good as Karsz having come himself. It was clear to me now that this problem was bigger than just the events of the revolt a few days past. Unknown forces were in action on both sides of the Tether, and light, literally, needed to be shone into the shadows.

Part Two

Chapter One

By the time I reached the Tether's Garden entrance, my mind was still full of questions, and I almost forgot about my stowaway. Almost. That was because Malacaz had been surprisingly silent, even after we had left the Keep and the chance of being discovered had diminished.

"I think it best you come out of hiding now," I said, and within seconds, he appeared beside me. "I need you to say that you will keep everything you heard in there to yourself." The Trickster smiled that insane smile of his and nodded enthusiastically. "No problem, Angel. I didn't understand most of it anyway."

That, I doubted, but it was too late now. I knew the chances of his keeping his mouth shut were remote, but at least he would be talking to the Succae, rather than anyone else closer to home. That gave me time to make some headway on finding the White Rood and lessened the likelihood of any loose talk getting back to the Heralds. Even if it did, I was certain that the words of a liar and a madman could be easily dismissed.

We descended the Tether that connected our world to that of the Succae, and Malacaz dangled beneath me as I held on to his arm in a tight clasp. From the dark of the night Garden, we descended into the dark of Cerule's moon, the Tether's bright white energy a cosseting aura. As we breached the thin atmosphere, it was immediately apparent that we weren't the only ones who had been doing some re-shaping. A great square tower sheathed the last hundred feet of the Tether's length, and I wondered why it had been constructed, given that we would normally just fly down. This suggested they were trying to keep something from coming up the Tether from their side, a thought that was reinforced by the presence of the armed Ashai I could see forming a defensive ring around the structure. They were the Vod's household troops, known as the Ebon Guard, clad in their distinctive black lacquered armour. Fires burned in wide copper dishes that sat atop flesh constructs that were in themselves ambulatory, as if someone had been cut in half at the waist, but their torso, legs, and feet carried on in a new life. The Ashais' breastplates were so highly polished that I could see the light of the flames reflected in them. It was like each one had a fire burning in their chest.

At the bottom of the steps below a wide stone dais, another Ashai awaited our landing. He wore the distinctive red-stained armour of the Loyals, the inner rank of Vod Karsz's personal bodyguard, the Succae equivalent of the Honores.

"*Kai*," he said, and bowed. It was a formal greeting, and I returned the gesture as protocol demanded. I did not recognise him when he removed his helm and gave a short bow. He was a strong-looking man with high cheekbones and a broad forehead. His face was decorated with a red tattoo that matched the demon on his helm's face plate and I could tell from the blood ink that he was a warrior with standing.

"I have come to see Vod Karsz and his Lords," I said once the formalities had been completed. He nodded curtly and bade me follow him as he walked through the tower archway and out into the dark of the blasted plain. Malacaz stayed close behind me, an apparent servant following in my wake. The Succae did not begin to question his presence, but such was their way. To have questioned him would have been an insult to me. The fact that he came in my company was enough. It made me think that Karsz or his predecessors had eliminated Tricksters from their society. Clever people.

In the distance I could see the angular profile of the Succae citadel city of Scarpe, sharp edged towers and brutal masonry. In the sky I could see the luminescent planet of Cerule that the Succae had once settled and called home until we had arrived to deliver Judgment. A long war had forced them to abandon it for this much smaller moon. Here, whilst Cerule was in the slow process of dying, the Succae's necro powers, based in an energy source they called the Necrene Well, sustained new life. Flora and fauna that had once grown and thrived on the planet's surface now had a new home, although with just the Necrene energy to feed them, they were twisted mutations of their former selves. Cerule's planetary luminescence cast a warm glow over the barren landscape and cast long shadows from anything it shone upon.

The Red Ashai took us to a small fortified encampment where torchlight blazed and more of the mobile firepits walked the perimeter in slow plodding steps.

"You will wait for an escort," he said. It was more a statement than a question, but I knew the path to the city, and I didn't want any further delay.

"No, that's alright. I have been here before. We'll find our own way."

I could see consternation tighten across his face. I imagined that given his status, he was probably unused to anyone disagreeing with him.

"You should wait," he said somewhat forcefully. "It is…dangerous out there."

"Dangerous? In what way?"

I could see he was caught in a quandary. I suspected he had been ordered to say nothing of any problems the Succae might be having, yet if he said nothing and something bad happened to us, he would be in all sorts of trouble. I decided to meet him halfway. "Look, why don't I write a note to say I was advised to wait, but due to the urgency of my Prince's command, I had no choice but to respectfully decline? Something like that help you out?"

It looked like it wouldn't, as his face became stony and I could see him manipulating his blood so that his veins stood out, enhancing his muscularity.

"If you will not wait, I must escort you myself," he said, reaching for his helm and a wide-bladed halberd from one of the camp's weapon racks.

"If it's all the same to you, Angel, I might just wait here for a while." Malacaz had a hopeful tone to his voice which made me suspicious. I was beginning to think that a better plan than just leaving him to his own devices might be to ask the Succae to keep him safe whilst things up above calmed down. The more I thought about it, the more stupid that sounded.

"Why don't you come with me to the Citadel, and I'll ask the Vod to place you under his protection. You did get a black feather after all, and Kael's people operated with impunity down here."

The Trickster took off his jaunty feathered hat and scratched the pale mop of unruly hair that sat upon the right side of his head. I was expecting a big argument, but he put his cap back on and nodded.

"Alright then, Angel. Let's do that."

Now, I was suspicious. It all felt too easy.

Chapter Two

On the way to Scarpe, I discovered that the Red Ashai's name was Kho, and he was a sergeant in the Vod's Loyals. As it turned out, that was about all he was willing to discuss, and any mention of the *Yurei* was met with a non-committal shrug. It made me think he knew exactly what I was talking about, but the topic was off-limits, and after several attempts to cajole him into talking, I gave up.

As we drew closer to the city, I could taste smoke and ashes on the wind. Before either Kho or Malacaz could protest, I spread my wings and took flight to take a better look at what was going on. Scarpe sat in a great bowl shaped depression with the Black Citadel at its centre. Wide streets created a complex grid radiating out from the centre into orderly districts dominated by large square buildings that had a hulking presence. These *Zals,* as they were known, were just the tip of an iceberg, for very few of the Succae's large population lived above ground. Below the *Zals* were huge labyrinthine tunnels that spread for miles and well beyond the city's visible boundaries. To the east, I could see a large part of that district was on fire, although the cold stone of the district's *Zals* was yet untouched. I couldn't tell whether any efforts were being made to curtail the blaze, and I wondered whether that was deliberate.

"Kho," I said as I came back down to the ground, "The Eastern district is on fire." I could only see the sergeant's eyes through his face mask, but I was pretty sure they widened in alarm.

"The Sergeant is needed elsewhere," he said with a respectful bow. "Please excuse the Sergeant, who must regretfully request that the Ambassador now make his own way to the Vod's steps."

I let him go, and he sprinted away at supernatural speed.

"What's all that about?" Malacaz asked as we watched him go.

"I don't know, but he obviously thinks he can make a difference.

I think there's much more going on down here than meets the eye. You wouldn't know anything about that, would you?"

Malacaz shook his head in emphatic denial, and swore blind that he was not in any way involved. I couldn't detect anything to make me doubt him, but again, I had a feeling that it was all a well-performed act. That, of course, is the problem when dealing with professional liars. Everything they say is worth distrusting. I had seen enough Heralds in action to know.

We made our way into the shadowy outer ring of Scarpe, on the edge of the city, where streets were strewn with rubble and the buildings either half-finished or derelict. I wasn't sure why no-one had taken up residence here, but the Low-Nin preferred their own company in the vast spaces below ground. It was something the Succae of standing, who called themselves the High-Nin, reinforced. There was no place for the poor masses until they showed themselves worthy of being noticed, but equally, the High-Nin only wanted to live among themselves and had palatial residences both above and below ground. Here was the borderland, and neither High nor Low had any interest in being here.

Here and there, as we traversed the empty streets, I saw Succae Low-Nin whispering and conspiring in small groups on street corners. As soon as they saw me coming, they ran off, disappearing into the vacant structures whose dark empty casements looked like hollowed-out eye sockets in broken skulls. There was a tense atmosphere that was so thick you could almost cut it with a knife. If it was having any effect on Malacaz though, he wasn't showing it, but I had to keep reminding myself that he was at home in chaos.

In the middle ring, the numbers of Low-Nin on the streets grew substantially larger and I could see occasional patrols of black-armoured Ashai maintaining a vigil from the steps of some of the more impressive buildings along the way. As soon as they saw me, one of them ran over and insisted I took shelter with them.

"Something bad is happening," the Ashai said. "Not safe for you on the streets. You should fly to the upper reach." This was on the Citadel's highest level, and how my kind usually arrived. I was about to point out that I was on foot, as I was with a friend, but as I turned to look for him, he was gone.

I took flight immediately, looking for Malacaz, and I caught sight of him a way ahead. How he had managed to slip away and put such a distance between us, I had no idea although I suspected his ability to briefly manipulate time might have something to do with it. I flew overhead, aware of Low-Nin shouting curses, and I had to dodge the occasional rock or other missile that was thrown at me. Malacaz was being pushed forward in a marching wave of Low-Nin, and he looked my way and shrugged, suggesting there was not much he could do about the situation. From my viewpoint, he looked like he was enjoying it a deal too much, and I wondered if he was whispering words of encouragement to his fellow marchers. I cursed myself for being stupid enough to trust a rogue like him. All he wanted was to cause trouble and tear things down. Well, it was my fault he was here, and I would take responsibility for catching him and handing him over to the Vod and his people. That was the plan, anyway, and I put on a burst of speed to try and catch up with him and pull him out of the crowd by the scruff of his neck.

Chapter Three

I was making good progress, until I was suddenly hauled sideways, and searing pain lanced through my left side. I was heading straight for the side of an angular building with a pointed tower, and I smashed into the pitched roof in an ungainly heap. As I came to my senses, I could see a wide curved blade on a thick chain had pierced my left wing. The Succae called it a *Sarigama* but among the Flight, it was known as an Angel catcher and had been one of the Succae's more potent weapons during the war.

I looked around for my assailant as I felt another yank on the chain, and I was pulled upwards, the blade ripping through feathers and flesh to stop at bone. It was agonising, and I knew I had to act quickly to free myself of the blade's bite. I called on Nimrod to change shape to a short-bladed sword and worked on leveraging the catcher free. As I did, I finally saw my attacker silhouetted against the skyline. They were wreathed in black except for a wide-brimmed hat that seemed strangely out of place with the rest of the outfit. They slowly reeled the chain in, raised their hat in mock salute and leapt off the roof and out of sight.

I sat and recovered as y healing powers kicked in. Wounds slowly closed and feathers replaced themselves. In the distance, the great square that surrounded the Citadel was now teeming with people in a scene that was reminiscent of what had happened a few days ago in Asuriel's Landing. Malacaz was somewhere in that crowd, and I had a feeling he was stirring things up and making them worse. Knowing what I did of the Succae, I doubted there would be any attempt to safely control or disperse the masses and I feared what might come next.

The crowd was still swelling when I took flight and headed for the Citadel's upper strand. After that painful encounter, I decided to fly high and stay well clear of any further unpleasant surprises. As I soared over the square, I could see the crowd was mostly made up of Low-Nin, pale undecorated bodies raising their arms in what felt like silent appeals to higher powers. Could the White Rood be down there, I wondered? Was it secretly being used to manipulate these poor and desperate drudges?

I came in to land, only to find the steps of the upper strand, usually occupied by ranks of Ashai, quite deserted. There was a surprise waiting, however, for standing next to the Serrate Lytta was none other than Malacaz who, in a curious gesture, raised his hunter's hat by way of greeting. I thought back to my night-shrouded assailant and wondered if it could have been he who attacked me, but that didn't make sense. It was, however, more than an odd coincidence.

Lytta looked taller, fitter, and stronger than the last time we had met. Long black hair that had a bluish sheen was tightly tied back tied in braids wrapped in velvet ties and interwoven with bleached white bone charms.

She wore a black velvet *Jhat;* a martial robe inlaid with polished black stones and marked with dark swirling patterns. From the waist down, she wore black velvet breeches and soft dark leather boots. At her side, twin blades were secured in lacquered scabbards that had a visible sheen, one short and one long. Behind her left shoulder, I could see the ivory-carved skull of the pommel of the short-bladed sword she carried on her back. It was not entirely just for show, for I had seen what she could do in full blown battle, and physical weapons were just a small part of what made her deadly beyond imagining.

"Are you alright, Ambassador?" she said. She must have seen the blood stains on my armour and wings.

"I'm fine," I said, although I wasn't sure that was entirely true.

"Are you sure?" Lytta looked at me with that unblinking violet stare.

"Yes," I said with added emphasis. The Succae are literalists so I knew Lytta would not push the point. If I said I was fine, I was fine.

"How did *he* get here?" I asked, pointing at Malacaz, who had seemingly lost interest in our reunion and was looking around at the sharp, brutal, angular architecture of the Shadow Citadel.

"He came to the front gates and presented himself. He asked for me by name, said you had sent him ahead and would be following on in due course. Is that not the case?"

I had to admit I was slightly at a loss. I had thought he was gone, swallowed up by a fervent crowd who would no doubt think of him as their king. At least with the right encouragement.

"More or less, yes, I suppose it is."

"More or less? I take it that means there is some level of deceit then?"

"No, not quite. He simply took the initiative when the opportunity presented itself. There was no pre-arranged instruction, but it was my intent to come to see Vod Karsz. He was tagging along."

"I see," Lytta said, which was impressive as even I wasn't entirely sure of what was going on. She turned and addressed Malacaz directly.

"Who are you?"

Charomos's Trickster bowed deeply.

"I am Charomos," he said with a wicked grin on his face. "Lord of Justice."

"No, he's not," I said, earning a reproving glare from the lying rogue.

"His name is Malacaz, and he once served a god by the name of Charomos. He is one of the Bonded who aided the Flight in the Judgment of his people."

"He is one of your prisoners?"

"Yes, milady, I am!" Malacaz exclaimed with an exaggerated level of woe, and now it was my turn to glare.

"No, he isn't! The Bonded are free to do as they will within reason. They serve with us until we return to the Golden City, then Excelsis will weigh their deeds. For their aid, they will be rewarded with a new life and a new purpose."

"You don't really believe that do you, Angel?" Malacaz went to rest an arm on Lytta's shoulder, but she deftly moved to one side, and he nearly fell over.

I was about to argue, when Lytta picked him up by the throat and shoved him up against a wall.

"I don't like liars," she said through sharp, clenched teeth.

"Do I know you?"

"I'm... sure... I'd... remember," Malacaz managed to say, even though Lytta had a firm hold of his windpipe. She dropped him suddenly and turned away. I could see she was thinking, searching her long memory for some forgotten piece of knowledge."

"Is he known by any other names?"

"Malacaz is the only one I know," I said. Just like the Seventh Flight had visited many worlds in our time and encountered similar pantheons and versions of the same gods again and again, so the Succae had once trod a similar path. Ours had been righteous judgment, whilst theirs had been plunder and enslavement. They had changed; we had not.

"Something..." she said, staring back at him. Malacaz had that mad grin on his face and started to laugh. I saw Lytta reach for the blade on her back and I quickly moved between them. It was a stupid move. I felt a boot firmly planted in my back and was sent stumbling into Lytta, who managed to sidestep me so that we weren't entangled However, it bought Malacaz the time he needed to run to the battlements and throw himself over the side.

I reacted as quickly as I could and took flight as Lytta raced to the edge and looked down. I saw Malacaz fall several hundred feet into a group of Low-Nin, who arrested his descent with outstretched arms. Initially he was buoyed by the crowd, but then he disappeared as they let him drop to the ground and closed in around him. I was pretty sure he was still laughing.

Chapter Four

"I'll go after him," I said, but Lytta shook her head. "He's a rogue, you said, and a shape-changer?"

"Well, yes, that's true." This was turning out exactly as I had feared it might.

"In which case, he could look like anybody down there. You'll never find him now. Besides the Low-Nin are restless and hardly friendly to your kind, as I am guessing you found out on your way here?"

It was a fair point. I told her what had happened and about the mysterious assailant with the distinctive headwear. I could see her take a deep breath.

"I would need to check our histories, but I think I know who that is. Your rogue can wait until later, but you will need to tell me everything about him. I have a feeling that wherever one may be found, the other will also be."

That was all she would say on the matter as she bade me follow her into the dark halls and wide stairwells of the Shadow Citadel. As we descended into the building's core, I saw large numbers of Ashai on watch at various points where torches and braziers burned brightly, banishing shadows and illuminating passages and chambers to a level I had never seen before.

"Who are the *Yurei*?" I asked, as Lytta marched ahead of me with strident purpose.

"How do you know about that?"

"I read the note Karsz sent," I replied. "I am versed in the classical tongue."

"I suppose Ischae taught you that, did she?"

"As a matter of fact, she did."

Lytta marched on in silence, and I couldn't tell if it was condemnatory of my former Succae lover's actions or something else. Like whether she was deciding to trust me.

"You may speak of this with the Vod, but do so with care," she said. "I will indicate to him that you wish to talk in private. Talk of the *Yurei* is not for wider discourse. It would cause undue concern among the rest of the guard."

"Is that why everything is lit? Do they hide in shadows?"

She looked over her shoulder and put a finger to her lips. I got the message.

Great obsidian doors that I knew opened to the Succae's Day Court awaited us on the ground floor. I could hear the crowd outside, but I couldn't understand what they were saying. I looked at Lytta, and saw a strange, wistful look on her face. It was like nothing I had ever seen from her before.

"What are they calling for?"

"Not what," she said. "Who."

"Then who are they calling for?"

"They call for *Ina-Koto-Rai*."

"Who is that? It's not a name I have heard."

"Nor I for many, many, years. That is my old name, and to invoke it is to call for death."

I felt a chill run through my wings as Lytta signalled for the great doors to be opened, and ten Ashai combined to push them open. I was walking with another Angel of Death, although until now, I had never thought of her in those terms.

Inside there were plenty of pools of darkness, and I supposed that Karsz was unafraid of whatever or whoever was hiding in the shadows. He sat on a high black marble throne and was his usual hulking presence. Arrayed on obsidian seats beneath him sat the seven Lords Ancestral who made up the Succae Council. Karsz was darker skinned than when I had last seen him, and his hair had grown long and was braided with impressive bindings of silver and gold. He was dressed in a high-collared martial brocade coat that had been dyed a deep purple with the familiar swirling patterns of the Succae woven in. Laid across his lap was a wide-bladed sword with a gold hilt and ivory grip crowned by a large oval piece of jet mounted in the pommel. A great war spear leaned against the throne on his right. It looked as if it had been blackened and tempered in fire and, for someone of his rank, was alarmingly simple and undecorated. I could feel vampiric malice radiating from it, a disdain for the living that told me it was cursed or maybe, from the Succae's perspective, blessed.

"Ambassador Azshael," he said, his deep voice rumbling through the chamber. "To what do we owe this unexpected and unrequested visit?" It was not exactly a welcoming opening.

"Great Vod Karsz, I come with a request for aid from the Archangel Prince Anael, Leader of the Seventh Flight."

Karsz nodded. "Go on then, and state your Prince's request—but know this, the Succae are not in a giving mood."

"This I see, great Vod. I am sure my Prince would be sorry to learn of trouble in Succae lands."

"It is nothing," Karsz said dismissively. "The Low-Nin sometimes need reminding of their place and their need to strive to be better. They will be corrected, reminded, re-educated." I watched thin, predatory smiles break out on the pallid faces of the Lords Ancestral. I had a bad feeling about the fate of the Low-Nin protesters.

"The Vod is a wise leader of his people," I said diplomatically.

"Enough flattery, Ambassador. What message for the Succae does Prince Anael send with you?"

I had been pondering for a while how best to express what my Prince had asked me to say without upsetting the Succae.

"Great Vod, an unfortunate incident took place during the recent unrest in the White Acropolis. You are aware that Succae were among the protestors?"

"I am," Karsz snapped impatiently.

"There was another incident at Trinity Palace which may have taken place at the same time." I went on to detail the theft, and the fact that a witness had seen suspects fleeing from the Palace grounds. I took care to ensure that there was no accusation being levelled against the Succae as a whole. That if the thieves *were* Succae, they were independent opportunists, probably under some malign influence. Karsz seemed to take it all in and said nothing for a while.

"What was stolen?"

I described the staff in as much detail as I could, but left out any information about its reputed powers. I went on to say it was of part of the Prince's regalia and held sentimental value for him, and that the Flight would welcome the Succae's co-operation in retrieving it if it had, indeed, come down the Tether. Karsz stared at me for an uncomfortably long time, and I could tell he was trying to unravel my diplomatic phrasing and get to the truth of what I was not saying.

"The Prince thinks this was a deliberate act?"

I saw the trap he was laying for me and steered well clear of it.

"Not directly ordered by anyone in power," I said, looking at the Lords, who, in turn, looked at each other. Succac power politics was predatory at best, but I saw no knowing looks or accusatory stares.

"Yet it does seem to be a targeted theft. There is also an odd anomaly,"

"Go on."

"One of my kind, from a sect called the Juvenii, was found murdered after the riot. She was the victim of a Shard Blade." This elicited murmurs from the Lords.

"A Shard Blade is a very rare weapon, Ambassador," Lord Vachs said. "Were any pieces of it recovered?"

I suddenly thought about Saur'Il and wondered if that was why he had wanted me to visit him before venturing down the Tether. I silently cursed my own laziness.

"I think there may be, yes. Can the blade's owner be identified from them?"

Vachs stood up to speak, but Karsz got there first.

"Possibly, Ambassador. Bring them to us, and we can see what can be done. On the business of this missing regalia, I do not see why any of my people would have any business with such an artefact. Certainly not a Low-Nin." The Lords Ancestral murmured their agreement. "Unless there is something you are not telling us?"

I kept a neutral face and said there was nothing further as confidently as I could.

"Then assure your Prince that it is likely his own people he must look to, and not mine." Karsz stood up, and I could see he was getting ready to dismiss me when his Serrate came out of the shadows and signalled him. He stepped down and they spoke in hushed tones. I could see disapproval on the faces of several of the Lords Ancestral, but they quickly resumed their po-faced masks when Karsz turned back towards me.

"My Serrate says you wish to speak to me privately. Whilst I do not really have the time to do so, in the interest of maintaining cordial relations with the Angels I will grant a brief private audience. Clear the court!"

Once the great doors were closed, it was just Karsz, Lytta and I left in the Hall. The Lords Ancestral, perhaps with the exception of Lord Vachs, looked far from happy as they filed out. Partly at the fact Karsz would speak with me alone, and partly that the Serrate had been allowed to stay. As far as I was concerned, it made perfect sense. Lytta knew everything we were going to discuss anyway.

Karsz walked slowly in a circuit of the Day Court, and I walked alongside him, Lytta following at a respectful distance.

"You wish to know about the *Yurei*? That was Karsz, straight to the point.

"We have concerns, Vod Karsz. Are these shadow stalkers a threat to us?"

"No, I do not believe so. I doubt they truly know you exist. They are an old enemy of ours that occasionally escape from the Well to cause havoc. I asked your Prince to take precautions as a contingency, in case they sought refuge on your side of the Tether."

"So, they are spirits?"

"Of a type, yes. They are malevolent collations of energy. Cursed remnants of souls who are hungry and rapacious for that which lies within us. That is what I meant when I said they are no threat to you. They prey on our kind only."

I was only vaguely reassured by Karsz's words. Just because they hadn't met our kind didn't mean they wouldn't prey on us, but I had to take the Vod at his word until there was evidence to the contrary.

"My Serrate tells me you brought a rogue into our lands?" Karsz changed the subject quickly.

"I did. I was planning to ask you to keep him in safe custody until it was safe for him to return to our lands. His kind is being persecuted in a reaction to recent events, and he came to me to request sanctuary." Karsz nodded, and in a reasonable tone said, "Yet now he is on the loose among my people, who are already stirred up. It is likely he will have a negative influence, is it not?"

"I don't know. He is a former Trickster god but in the process of becoming Bonded he should have been robbed of most of his powers. His kind also has a propensity to get themselves caught, so hopefully he can be recaptured before long."

Karsz came to a halt and looked me in the eye. "Hope is but a phantom and of little help in such circumstances, Ambassador. Actions are what matter. You will aid my Serrate in her work to recapture this fool."

"Of course, I will do what I can, Vod Karsz, but I have other duties and tasks that my Prince has already set. If you are sure no Succae could have been involved in the theft of our regalia, then I must soon return to my lands to aid in the search."

I felt Karsz stiffen. I doubt he was used to negotiating when he gave an order.

"Very well, Ambassador. Just bear in mind that if this rogue causes damage of any kind to the order of things, I will hold both you and your Prince responsible. You can then explain your error of judgement to him."

Checkmate to Karsz.

Chapter Five

I didn't know what Lytta had in mind, and I didn't immediately get the chance to ask, as both the Vod and his Serrate swept out through the great black doors of the Court. As they went, the Lords Ancestral flanked Karsz, and a troop of his red armoured Loyals fell into formation ahead of them. They marched forward, and commands were shouted as more sets of heavy doors opened ahead of them. I tagged along at the back, not precisely sure if I was meant to be part of the Vod's entourage or not. No one seemed to pay me any mind, though, so I kept Lytta in sight and presumed she would speak to me about her plans when the appropriate time came.

The group came to a halt in the Citadel's entrance hall, and Karsz and his Lords headed for a sweeping staircase that led up to the battlements and observation platform. Lytta and the Loyals waited as a great portcullis slowly raised and the great outer doors began to open under the efforts of several Ashai.

"What's going on?" I asked, and Lytta looked at me.

"You should stay with the Vod," she said. "This is nothing you want to see."

"What do you mean? What are you going to do?"

Lytta looked at me and I thought a look of sadness passed briefly over her face.

"They have called for *Ina-Kota-Rai*. They have asked for death to walk among them. It is the Vod's command that they are given what they want."

"You're going to kill them?" I had feared the Vod's reaction, but had never thought that his punishment would be on such a scale. There were thousands of Low-Nin in Shadow Square. Did Lytta really plan to kill them all?

"That is up to them," she said simply. "If they stay, they will die. If they walk away, then they will be spared. The Well rewards, but the Well also punishes."

A terrible feeling ran through me like a chill on a summer's day. What if the Low-Nin were under the White Rood's influence? What if their deeds were not their own and they were being controlled by a malign force? If Lytta spotted my mental turmoil, she didn't say anything. She turned and headed toward the exit to the square.

Outside, the crowd had quietened, and I followed her as she walked out onto the great steps. I looked up and saw the Vod and his Lords seated on the platform above. I was caught in a mire of my own making. To reveal the Rood's powers would be revealing secrets to those that most of the Flight and my own Prince would consider the enemy. Yet to say nothing was tantamount to being party to an atrocity that would stain my soul forever.

"Low-Nin! Listen to me," Lytta shouted, her voice echoing across the wide expanse of the square. "I am *Ina-Kota-Rai*, the Sixth Succae Spirit of War. I am the Watcher in the Well and High Executioner of the Inglorious Dead. I have slain gods, cleansed fields of battle, and fed upon the spirits of the heroes of our enemies. I have one wyrd, and that is destruction. There is but one certain outcome to your defiance, and that is final death, for I will crush your bones into dust and send your souls back to the Well, where you will dwell in darkness forever." There was no response. Just an unsettling quiet that felt unnatural.

"Your Vod is merciful and gives you this one chance to walk away and return to your homes. There will be no punishment if you do as he commands."

I studied the crowd, looking for Malacaz or the unknown assailant in the hat, but all I saw were pale, wretched faces. Nobody moved or showed any sign of complying with the Vod's ultimatum. It was downright eerie. The idea that such a huge number would meekly go to their deaths was incomprehensible to me.

"I will give you the count of ten before delivering on my promise as *Ina-Kota-Rai*." Lytta slowly drew her main blade, a long, sharp sword that had a soft red glow.

"Ten."

Come on, I silently urged. Go home.

"Nine."

No one moved except for a few of the ones closest to Lytta, who swayed in an invisible wind.

"Eight." The Serrate began to walk down the steps to the edge of the crowd.

"Seven." The Low Nin made way for Lytta as she walked into the crowd, naked blade at her side.

"Six." I could feel the tension growing and my remaining heart was beating anxiously faster. I looked up to see Karsz standing tall and resolute.

"Five." Lytta had reached the centre of the square and the crowd had made a space around her.

"Four." She rested her sword on the ground in front of her, sharp tip biting into the rocky ground so that it stood on its own, blazing fiercely with a darker shade of crimson. It was as if it had its own pulse.

"Three." She lent down and touched the ground, and I saw white strands of power begin to coalesce around her. As they grew in both size and number, I could see blue lights illuminate within the eyes of the Low-Nin. As the strands spread, so each Succae they touched gained this eerie new look. Before long, thousands of tiny blue lights lit up the night.

"Two." I had to act and tell what I knew. I simply couldn't bear the thought of this many souls on my conscience. I took flight and flew up to the platform where Karsz and his Lords were standing.

"Vod Karsz! I must speak to you!" I landed, only to be corralled by red armoured Ashai, who used their halberds to prevent me from getting any nearer. Karsz did not look my way or show any sign he had heard my call.

"One." I heard Lytta's final ultimatum and shouted at Karsz to heed my words once again.

I tried to take flight and get past the guards, but I knew both the Low-Nin and I were out of time.

Chapter Six

It was nothing short of a miracle. As one, and at the last possible moment, the Low-Nin turned and began to disperse. Silently, they filed out of the square and disappeared into the darkness. Lytta watched them go, and called the power she had channelled back into her hands. It was like watching so many snakes slither back to their lair. The energy fed back into the Serrate's blade and from there, back into the ground. The blue lights winked out of existence.

"What do you want now, Ambassador?" Karsz was suddenly standing in front of me. "You said there was something I needed to know?"

"Yes," I said, as his Lords turned to face me. "I will aid your Serrate in her hunt for as long as necessary. I mean, you were right about my misjudgement. It's my mess, and the least I can do is help clear it up."

Karsz stared at me for a moment. "Is that it?"

I nodded and tried to smile, but my skin felt so tight, I probably just bared my teeth.

"Very well, then." Karsz turned and left the platform, his Lords Ancestral following behind.

Having caught my breath, I took flight and headed to rendezvous with Lytta in the centre of Shadow Square. She was kneeling in front of her glowing sword, and I thought she was making some devotion or prayer. In one swift, sudden move, she stood up and sheathed her blade with studied reverence. As soon as it returned to her grip, the glow dimmed, and by the time it clicked home into its scabbard, it had gone completely.

"I am relieved you didn't need to become *Ina-Kota-Rai*," I said, and she looked at me blankly before giving me the slyest and briefest of winks. She could just have been blinking but I like to think it was deliberate.

"So where do we start?"

Lytta looked toward the east, where the sky was red and yellow. It was where we had seen the fire and clearly, it was still blazing. "That way," she said, and set off at a hurried run. I took flight, careful to try and maintain a safe altitude from any Angel- catcher-wielding assailants. I tracked the Serrate's swift progress through empty dark streets from above. Ahead, I could see the eastern quarter spread out before me. It looked as if about a third of the district was ablaze, mostly the buildings that sat in the densely packed narrow streets leading off the main thoroughfares. These looked like residences to me, although there was no sign of anyone trying to escape or fight the fires. It seemed that my original thought that no-one lived in these abandoned structures any longer was correct, and that this fire would be left to burn itself out. Then I spotted a small square with a squat temple structure at its centre. Here, Ashai could be seen forming a defensive circle around it. Other unarmoured Succae were pushing handcarts from another building across the square. and I could tell they were stacked with large slabs of glistening ice. The temple was made of a black stone that did not reflect the light. It had a pitched roof and was surrounded by a moon garden of rocks, sand, and stone. It looked untouched by the fires around it, but motes of sparking cinders were in the air, drifting towards the building.

Lytta arrived slightly after me and began giving orders to the soldiers. She vaulted up on to the roof in a single jump, and the Ashai worked to pass the slabs of ice up to her and the others who had joined her. I descended, and pitched in alongside them, laying out the ice so that it provided some sort of shield that would slowly melt, dampen the roof, and prevent the place from catching fire.

"This is the Hall of Keeping," Lytta said as we dropped down to ground level. "I want to check something that may aid us in our search." She placed her hands on the black metal doors, and I heard a mechanical sound as they slowly swung open. Once inside, I increased my ambient aura so that I could see. Lytta gave me a reproving glare before moving several feet away from me into the dark interior. The Succae all have perfect sight in the dark, and I gathered my illumination was not helping. It was a vast hall that stretched back several hundred yards. Every ten feet or so there were pairs of basalt columns that were twice my width stretching up into the vaulted roof. Each one was decorated with carvings that detailed Succae history. The columns at this end of the hall appeared to relate the deeds of notable Vods from the early history of the Succae race.

Along the walls I could see fading frescos, where more of the struggle to undertake a renaissance was depicted in detail, and beneath my feet, stark mosaics continued the history. The Succae had once worshipped hungry and rapacious gods who demanded conquest and sacrifice. Later, they had turned away from these evil and pernicious deities and embraced a spiritual renaissance and cultural revolution. They had found enlightenment and left their old ways, and older gods, behind. They developed a strict honour-bound society where lives of service won the right of rebirth and a better new existence. It was not perfect, but marked a massive progression from what had come before.

"Angel?" I heard Lytta call me from deeper in the hall. "Over here." I realised I had been lost in a moment of awe and appreciation. I saw the soft red glow of Lytta's drawn blade and headed in that direction. I called Nimrod to spear shape as I approached.

"What are you doing?" Lytta said as I drew closer, finding her at the top of a set of wide stairs that descended deeper underground. It's a Succae habit, digging holes.

"I saw your blade and thought…" I was suddenly not sure what I thought. I realised that she had drawn her blade as a beacon for me to home in on.

"Oh…" I said, and she shook her head. "There is no threat here. It is a library, not a battlefield." I was about to say that I had been in fights in libraries before, but decided that would sound petulant, so I signalled the Serrate to lead the way.

We descended deeper and passed several more floors where statues and other artefacts of the Succae's histories were on display in a sort of cultural museum. As we passed by representations and relics of their pre-renaissance history, I could see why Excelsis had sent us to judge the Succae. Both the gods they worshipped, the weapons they used, and the powers they had wielded looked ferocious. It was worth remembering that Lytta had been part of that world once, a deadly spirit of war and death whose light had never dimmed. I had no desire to meet *Ina-Kota-Rai* in person. I didn't think it likely we'd get on.

About five floors down and deep in Scarpe's underbelly, we came to another set of vast leaden doors. Lytta laid her hands on them, and they started to swing slowly open. I was immediately struck by the smell of leather hanging heavy in the air. Inside the depository, I could see hundreds of decorated hides of various sizes stretched out on racks that were set back-to-back in ordered rows. They filled the hall and extended beyond the frames to cover every available inch of wall space. Between the frames, there were narrow channels, just wide enough for a single individual to navigate the aisles with care. I looked more closely at the frames nearest me. The hides were of a buttery buff colour, and every inch was filled with the pictographic language of the Succae. I could tell they were telling stories of recent history and recognised the winged symbol for Angel. Lytta had gone on ahead of me, and the glow of her red blade bobbed ahead in the darkness. I was so caught up that I didn't notice something from a recurring nightmare creeping up on me.

Chapter Seven

A hooded face loomed suddenly out of the darkness from behind the frame I had been studying. It was male and bald, with intricate dark swirls and markings on its head, neck, and face, the skin stretched so tight that he looked like a walking cadaver. He smiled to reveal rows of sharp white teeth stark against red gums. I had been up close and personal with a similar looking individual just a few months before, and he had cut out one of my two hearts. It had only been Lytta's intervention that had prevented me losing the other one.

Instinctively, I took flight, and Nimrod leapt to my hands, wreathed in fire. The creature, who I thought was a pagan priest of a flesh cult called the Flensers, looked up at me in surprise. Long sinewy arms unfolded from the robe he was wearing to reveal ordinary hands and long bony fingers. In his right hand was a calligraphic brush, in the other, a stylus. This was not what I had seen of the Flenser who had attacked me. His elongated arms had ended in slender black nails that were razor sharp.

"Bibalis," Lytta said, breaking the moment. "There you are." The man turned and bowed deeply. "My Serrate," he said in a barely audible whisper, and stowed the brush before offering her his hand. She held it for a moment, and I saw him jerk slightly as his energy flowed to her. Lytta looked up at me, where I was hovering above.

"This is Keeper Bibalis," she said. "He is a recorder, keeper of the hides of our history. He fulfils the same function for the Succae as your children—like Sariel—do for your Flight."

I had explained to Lytta many times that Cherubs were not children, but it had now got to the point where I didn't bother correcting her. For whatever reason, she found it amusing, and given the Succae are a dour bunch generally, it felt churlish to deny her a moment of internal levity.

"I am seeking our records for the Succession Rebellion. Can you take me to them?"

"Of course, my Serrate," Bibalis said, and he led us deeper into the hall, where the walls were lined with vault doors. The keeper pulled on a solid lead ring to a vault that was marked '16' and had the letter 'D' entwined with snakes engraved on its fascia. I knew enough of Succae history to know that this related to the sixteenth millennium of their history, and the letter referred to Dursc, the Vod who had led his people into a new progressive era of thinking and behaviours that our historians called the Succae Enlightenment.

The door opened to reveal steps that led down to a long chamber where hundreds of hides had been piled in stacks that were as tall as I was. Bibalis obviously had a filing system, but I could not readily see what it was. He knew which stack to approach and, inspecting the corner of each hide, moved a bunch to one side to pull out around ten of them. He took these over to a reference frame and draped them across it. "These are the ones, Serrate," he said and bowed. "I will be in the Hall when you are done."

Lytta began sorting through them. Most had dense writing in the old Succae language and were fragments of eyewitness accounts.

"I knew many Succae didn't agree with Dursc's path. How long did this rebellion go on for?"

"It was about three months in your accounting of time," Lytta said as she pulled out a hide with writing on one side and drawings on the other.

"A challenger to Dursc arose. His name was Scharo, and he led a cult dedicated to the blood goddess, who was very powerful at the time. Her name was Sangaea."

"Blood goddess?"

"Originally, the Succae drank the blood of those we conquered. It was Dursc who believed—and went on to prove—that it was the energy of life that truly sustained us. Drinking the blood of a living creature is limiting when such energy can be drained from anything that holds it. It was a landmark discovery, but it went against the belief of many who refused to embrace or believe it, even though the evidence was plain to see. It also made Sangaea's worship pointless and broke Scharo's hold over his followers."

"So he resisted?"

"Yes. Initially Dursc tried reasoning with him and invited him to open debate, but Scharo knew that if he did that, he would be made to look foolish. He went into hiding and launched a guerrilla campaign against Dursc's rule."

Lytta turned the hide over to reveal extremely well drawn illustrations on its reverse. The first image was that of Scharo, who looked exactly as I expected. A proud and powerful Succae who embodied the essence of a vampire King. The artist had captured a sculptured handsomeness with hooded eyes and a stern demeanour. I could believe he had been uncompromising.

Behind him was the image of Sangaea sitting on a throne surrounded by skulls. She looked voluptuous, beautiful, and deadly, long red hair framing a lovely visage. Her mouth was wide open in a fanged snarl.

Lytta placed another illustrated hide on the rack, and I immediately had a sinking feeling. There, on the leather canvas, were two faces staring back at me. One was female, wearing a featureless face mask and holding a pair of wicked-looking long knives crossed in front of her. She wore a wide-brimmed hat atop a head of long black hair that framed her face with perfect symmetry. The other was a man with a mad smile on his face. Malacaz.

Lytta said nothing. She waited for me to speak, but I was trying to work out how a Trickster who had helped bring down a god of justice and bring his world to Excelsis's judgment had previously been an agitator in the Succae's renaissance wars. This conflict between order on one side and disorder on the other posed an apparent paradoxical question. The only immediate answer I could find was that Malacaz was mad and that trying to make sense of the deeds of a madman was pointless. He did what he did as it made sense to him at the time. It didn't need to add up for the rest of us. I went on to explain what I knew of Malacaz, which, in truth, was not much. She had never heard of the elitist Charomos, deliverer of justice.

She pulled another hide with dense writing on to the frame.

"What about this one?" I pointed to the masked woman in the hat.

"That is Zamalca," she said. "A highly skilled assassin."

"Another one of Scharo's cultists?"

Lytta frowned. "It has never been truly established. I think Scharo called her from the Well. Her powers were formidable. She was certainly no ordinary Succae."

"You fought with her?"

"Yes, towards the end of the Rebellion. She eventually fell from a great height, and I thought she was dead. The body was never found, but she did fall into fire, so no-one went looking for it."

"If she was a Traveller, she might have found a new life elsewhere."

Lytta said nothing and returned her attention to the hide.

"The person who attacked me on the way to the citadel wore a hat just like the one shown here. Maybe she and Malacaz are connected in some way?"

"If that is the case, why were you not aware of her before? Why was she not with your rogue on your side of the Tether?"

It was a fair point, but I had a nagging feeling that there was a connection between the two. We just hadn't found it yet.

"Zamalca is known in our histories," she said. "She nearly destroyed a Spirit of War, and that is quite a feat."

"That Spirit was you, I take it?"

"Yes, it was. Like I said, she was no ordinary rebel."

I stood a while, pondering what I had learned as Lytta pored over the writing on the skin until she seemed to find what she was looking for. She folded the hide under her arm and headed back up to the Hall to speak in hushed tones to Bibalis. "Where are we going?" I asked as she strode up the Hall's steps and out into the moon garden. Here, Ashai still formed a defensive circle whilst the fires still blazed in the streets nearby. Bibalis had been less than happy with his Serrate removing one of his treasured hides but hadn't put up much of a fight when she had quietly but firmly insisted that it was coming with her.

"We are going to find Rukoi, one of Scharo's former supporters. His name is listed in the records here. Bibalis just confirmed he is still resident in the city"

"Dursc spared him then?"

"He surrendered and pledged his loyalty to the Vods," she said simply as if that was perfectly acceptable. I happened to know that was an exceptionally generous move on Dursc's part. Ischae had once told me how disloyalty to the Vod was the highest of crimes and usually resulted in 'soul death', where both the offender's spirit and physical body were destroyed.

I followed Lytta as she headed out of the eastern district and back towards Scarpe's central square. Before we got in sight of the citadel, she cut west and into a part of the town where large mansions I had once thought were empty shells or ruins that only the poorest would use as shelter sat on wide boulevards. These days I knew different. "So he was High-Nin?" I said, immediately recognizing whose district we had come into. This explained why Dursc had spared him. He had obviously earned enough blood ink to deserve a second chance.

Lytta nodded briefly but said nothing, concentrating instead on the houses, which still looked deserted to me. They were all built in a uniform manner, huge black hulks of angular masonry. Lytta paused as we came to a crossroads and pointed down a lane ending in a mansion plot. It was notably isolated, hundreds of yards away from any neighbour and surrounded by skeletal trees whose branches looked like bony hands reaching out to touch the stonework.

"Did Dursc spare Scharo as well?"

"No, of course not. He chose to fight. There would have been no alternative in his mind."

"How did he die?"

"Karsz killed him."

"Karsz?" I was surprised that Dursc had allowed anyone else to deal with the leader of a rebellion.

"It was his first step to becoming Vod. The first of many such deeds that Karsz did in service to Dursc."

All this had happened long before the Flight had arrived. By my reckoning, over four millennia had passed since these events had taken place, which meant they had transpired on Cerule, presumably around the former Succae capital city of Khrov on the Khast plains. There was nothing there now but blackened ruins and blasted heathland. I realised I had never discovered how or why Lytta's former host had died, and I was about to ask when I saw a strange flash of light from the upper floor of the manse. It was the briefest of flares, and it came and went in the blink of an eye. I could tell from the way Lytta had shifted into a predatory stance that she had seen it too. We were both trained hunters, and old habits die hard.

Chapter Eight

Lytta advanced slowly and quietly in a stalker's gait, steady footstep after steady footstep. Each move was meticulous and soundless. As we drew within a hundred yards of the building, she pointed up at the sky, signalling that I should take flight, but I shook my head and refused for two reasons. Firstly, if these were the *Yurei,* I had no idea what these 'ghost warriors' were capable of and, second, my punctured wing was still in the process of healing. Seeing my response, she pointed to the right-hand side of the path as she moved to the left side, and we advanced quietly to the front doors. I called Nimrod into spear shape, and as we passed beneath the clawing tips of skeletal branches, I could see the heavy double doors were slightly ajar.

We crossed the threshold, and the doors swung open with surprising ease. Lytta darted left whilst I moved slowly and stealthily to the right. We were in a hallway with barren and empty rooms off to each side. If Rukoi spent much time here at all, it didn't look like he was much for creature comforts. We swept through vacant chambers before meeting back in the hall. Ahead, a wide double staircase led up to a landing. I was about to ascend, but Lytta indicated I should wait and disappeared deeper into the lobby behind the staircase. A moment later, she reappeared and waved me over. In an alcove beneath the stairwell, a heavy wooden door was set into the wall. It was open, and as I drew closer, I could smell the distinctive tang of Succae blood. I could tell Lytta had also picked up on the scent as her demeanour had turned feral, skin stretched tight against bone, sharp fangs visible as open mouthed, she tasted the air. It was not the first time I had seen this transformation, but I still found it unsettling.

She took the lead as we went down thick stone steps into Rukoi's underground habitat. The stairs ended in a long passage with chambers off to each side. It looked as if Rukoi had spent more time here than he had in the manse above. In addition to chests and boxes of belongings, there was a bedchamber, a dining room and at the end of the passageway, a library and study, the door to which was wide open.

Inside, light flickered from a lamp sitting on a circular table, and its dwindling flame cast shadows around the room, which was stacked with books and scrolls. Bookcases were packed to the point there was no room for anything more, and their shelves sagged under the weight. A large armchair with its back to us faced into the room, and I saw black blood had pooled around its feet. Here we found Rukoi, dressed in blood-soaked High-Nin finery. He had been bound to the chair with thick brocade that I guessed had been taken from his bedchamber. His chest cavity had been sliced open, and his ribs had been removed. They were piled on the floor by his feet. The Succae are strong and able to endure plenty of injury, and I doubted whether this torture had been enough to kill him.

"Look," Lytta said, pointing at strange holes that riddled his chest and neck. They were round and narrow, smaller than the width of a finger.

"Drain marks," she said, and I wondered what could have done this. I knew of no Succae weapon or power that left such marks.

"Drained by whom?" I asked as she looked around warily.

"Not who," she said ominously, "what. This is Necrene sorcery, the work of hungry ghosts."

"*Yurei,* you mean?

"Perhaps," she said, turning her attention to the table upon which was scattered open books and maps. It looked as if Rukoi had been doing some research before his killer or killers had come calling. The books were stolen from other worlds and appeared to be related to my kind and the myth and legends of the Archangels. I have a natural understanding of many languages, and I was able to recognise various names and places, but there was no sign of anything about Anael or the Seventh Flight. Then, I heard a crunch from below and saw that I had stepped on a scroll that had fallen from the table. I picked it up, and my single heart skipped a beat. It was a drawing of Anael's regalia, including the White Rood. Was this the secret that Rukoi had died protecting? If so, from whom, and why?

"What is it?" Lytta asked as she sorted through various writings and scrolls on the table.

"It's a scroll about Prince Anael and his regalia," I said, passing it to her. She paused as she picked up a token emblazoned with a pair of boxing hares. I had seen something like it before. It was a coin of indenture, and by the lack of wear and tear, I thought it was probably recently minted.

"Rukoi's mark, I presume?" I said, thinking that as a High-Nin, he would issue his own tokens.

"No, I don't think so," Lytta said. "It's a Low-Tsar's coin, although I do not know to whom it belongs."

"A High-Nin owing a Low-Tsar? That's odd, isn't it?"

"It is unusual, but not unheard of. The Low-Tsars are purveyors of all sorts of things, and can be relied on to be discreet."

"Anything else of interest?"

"Rukoi was visiting his past," she said, passing me a sheaf of scrolls. I looked through them and saw his memories of the rebellion as well as devotions to Scharo and the blood goddess Sangaea. Rukoi may have been many things, but a poet was not one of them.

Lytta raised an eyebrow as she read from an open book. "This, however, is treasonous," she said, and pushed across a ledger that had been sitting open on the table in front of where Rukoi had been seated. In fresh ink, he had written a long polemic about Karsz's inadequacies as Vod when compared with Scharo. I felt there was something more than hero worship in Rukoi's flowery language, but perhaps I was reading too much into it. He also implied that he was involved in something big, and that his fortunes were soon to change. There was cryptic language about Sangaea's cult returning to lead the Succae into a new 'blood dawn'.

Lytta turned her attention to a writing desk whilst I looked around the bookcases. As I approached the furthest shelves, I heard a crashing sound. Turning swiftly around, I saw my Serrate had given up on subtlety and had smashed the desk in two. Various gems and other valuables spilled from within, but my focus was on a bound bunch of black feathers that had fallen gracefully to the floor. They were an assassin's marker I was all too familiar with; the mark of the Halokim. Malacaz had been the last person to show me one of these, and now that I paid attention, I could tell they were not the real thing but a good imitation. Had I not had a recent encounter with the group's former leader and seen a real one for myself, I would also have been fooled. I remembered now how Malacaz had been quick to flash it in my face and equally quick to stow it away.

"Your friend Kael?" Lytta said, referring to the Halokim's former leader who had nearly killed both Sariel and me, but found out the hard way that Cherubs are not as harmless as they look.

"No, I think not."

"He is still around though?" It was true; he had been badly hurt but had somehow evaded capture as the cabal's plans to reignite the war between races had nearly come to fruition.

"Yes, that's true, but these are just good imitations of the Halokim feather. If it was Kael, he would send the real thing."

"Interesting that they should be found hidden here," she said, and I could only agree. Rukoi had obviously been deeply involved in some dark plot that had gone wrong and cost him his life. A plan that I was now certain had support and involvement from one or more of my kind.

It was all very odd. If the plan was to unseat Karsz and restore a pagan goddess, why had this High-Nin been tortured and killed? I thought about the Rood and how powerful a weapon it could be in the hands of someone who wanted to control large groups of people at once. Is that what had got Rukoi into trouble? Was he somehow involved in its theft? The scroll I had found proved he was aware of its existence but not what it did or where it was held. He would have needed an Angel to help with that information, but what was in it for them?

"Maybe he was more loyal than it seems," I said, but Lytta held up the ledger. "Doesn't look like it," she said, and she had a point. Yet, Rukoi surely had more to offer living than he did dead. Unless, of course, he had been tricked himself. Led to believe that his glorious vision of a new 'blood dawn' was on its way to becoming real. Had someone used him as a pawn in a bigger game and sacrificed him when he no longer had any real further use? It was the sort of move my people made, and the more I thought about it, the more it made sense.

"I think he was used," I said.

"I was just thinking the same thing," Lytta said. "Maybe he found that out and overplayed his hand?"

"Or he didn't trust his partners. That would explain the torture. He thought he had leverage he could use but underestimated how ruthless they were willing to be."

"Typical High-Nin," Lytta said, with a withering glare at Rukoi's dead body. "They always think they are so important and powerful. Until they find they are not." I was about to agree when I realised the temperature in the chamber had dropped substantially. Lytta muttered something and drew her blade as suddenly, and without warning, the lamp's light went out and plunged us into darkness.

Chapter Nine

Between the glow of Lytta's blade, Nimrod's flames, and my own aura, we were able to see our enemies coming. Two faceless wraith-like figures drifted slowly down the hallway towards us. Their shapes were hard to define as they were constantly shifting and changing, but the overall impression was of tall, thin spectres with long arms ending in dagger like talons. They were pale, transparent, and surrounded by a bluish haze.

Lytta advanced out of the study to meet them. I tried moving to hover above her, but my damaged wing complained too much, so I settled for getting behind her and commanded Nimrod to shape as a halberd to give me better reach. As they drew closer, Lytta attacked, and I moved with her, thrusting at one with the halberd blade. The results were not good. Both of our blades, blessed in one way or another, passed through the wraiths with no obvious effect. It was like waving your hand through fog. The pair manifested facial features on what had previously been blank canvasses, long faces with black pits for eyes and distended maws opened wide in silent screams. Ice rimed both of our weapons, dousing Nimrod's flames, and encasing the glow on the Serrate's blade so that it looked like a hearth fire that had ebbed to embers. They separated out, one swirling around Lytta and the other passing over my head to float on into the study.

"Now what?" I said, turning to face my opponent but staying back-to-back with the Serrate.

"I know not," she said, slamming her sword blade against the wall, the icy sheath falling away. "Try harder." Yeah, thanks Lytta, my ever-helpful companion.

I felt her move away, and I focussed on my own assailant,

returning Nimrod to its state as a long sabre with an extended hilt that I gripped with both hands. It was close quarters down here.

In a sudden flash, the wraith sped forward and shifted from its spectral form to something opaque and much more solid. Claws raked at me and squealed off my armour, leaving dents and scratches behind. I sliced at it, but not before it had taken ethereal form again. It shot past me and passed its partner, which suddenly came at me. I saw Lytta roll away as it clawed at her, but I was too slow. It picked me up and threw me across the study. I smashed into a bookcase and fell to the floor. It collapsed and I was showered in tomes and scrolls.

My pride was hurt more than anything else, but I was lying there, prone. The wraith's corporeal weight descended on me and had me pinned. I felt ice cold, chills numbing my flesh and freezing my senses. I saw my aura diminish as the blue halo that surrounded the creature swallowed the light. Its face transformed, and where once there had been dark eyes and a black maw, there was now a mass of feelers. They were strange, tubular appendages that bulged and then drooled a thick pale liquid all over me. The feelers opened, sheaths for bright red tendrils whose spiked barbs glistened with saliva. I thought about the strange holes that we had seen on Rukoi's body and decided his hideous fate would not be mine.

Maybe it was an instinctive reaction on seeing the wraith's corona, or perhaps my repulsed mind dredged up some forgotten knowledge. I cannot be certain but somehow, I knew that light was the answer. As the creature's face lowered towards mine and tendrils moved in expectation of their next feast like a mass of writhing maggots, I channelled everything into enhancing my own radiance. I blazed with the intensity of a hundred torches, and the monster recoiled with a horrendous screech that made my ears ring. It became spectral again, desperate to escape and sped away from me, seeking refuge in the shadows. I could see a spreading darkness that blighted its luminous form, and it shrank in size as I pursued it, giving the creature no quarter from my bright, bright light. It screamed and howled as an inky blackness devoured its essence, infection spreading like a cancer across its form. It could not evade me, and soon it was all shade and no light, a dying sound like a kettle whistling on the hearth, its terrible death rattle. Then there was just shadow, and it was gone.

I turned to see Lytta's martial dance down the hallway. She was literally bouncing off walls, tumbling and rolling to evade the monster's claws. I ran out of the study and into the hall, and as soon as I drew nearer to it, it turned and fled. If I had been able to fly, I think I would have outpaced it, but as it was, it had enough pace to flee into the manse and out into the air where it vanished from sight.

"*Yurei?*" I said as Lytta joined me on the manse's threshold.

"*Yurei,*" she said in return. "We won't have seen the last of them. Ghosts like that are hungry forever."

Chapter Ten

We spent an undisturbed hour going through Rukoi's study, but it was a cursory search, and the sheer volume of printed matter was beyond our capability to swiftly evaluate. On the face of it, the deceased High-Nin had conveniently left the most relevant of information within easy reach, which made me wonder if there was misdirection at play and if we were being fed a story that, at face value, was credible but which came too easily. Lytta was not in agreement, however. "Highers all think themselves so clever that no-one will ever catch them." I had to admit that sounded like many of the Flight's Heralds, our very own schemers and plotters who often thought they were a deal smarter than they were. That there was such symmetry between our two societies had always been a source of amusement for me. "If you say so," I said, but I wasn't entirely convinced.

"I will get Bibalis to come and do a thorough inventory. Now Rukoi has no use for it, he may as well donate his collection of knowledge to the Hall."

We left the manse and I was expecting us to return to the Citadel, but Lytta surprised me by turning to head further west.

"Where are we going?" I asked.

"There is something I need to do. For my host," she said, and I could tell she wasn't that happy talking about it.

"It won't take long. You can wait outside." Now I was intrigued.

We journeyed to the edge of the western district where High-Nin mansions grew in grandeur and sat on ever larger plots. In some places, armoured Ashai stood watch, and I gathered we were among the homes of the Succae elites. Beyond, and in a basin a few hundred feet below, lay a wide expanse of dark, still water that was as smooth as black-mirrored marble. We headed along the edge, and I could see steep banks of black shale leading down to the water's edge.

Before long, we approached an ornate residence surrounded by a walled moon garden that was neatly laid out and clearly well taken care of. Lytta led me to a tall gate carved from black lacquered wood and marked with elegant scenes of flora and fauna. I saw her pause for a moment and gather herself. It was nothing I had seen her do before, and she must have seen the look on my face.

"You must wait here, Ambassador," she said, but the forceful Succae Serrate didn't sound like her usual self. Instead, I could sense mild irritation and embarrassment in her tone, so I decided it would be fun to add to her discomfort.

"Here? Outside in the cold darkness? Not what I am used to, Serrate. Can I not come in and sit in the garden? I promise I will keep quiet and be no bother."

Lytta was about to argue, but stopped at the sound of the gate being unbolted. It opened to reveal a tall and beautiful woman carrying a lantern that emitted a soft, warm glow. She wore a pale red velvet dress that pooled at her feet and hugged her figure. She had a perfect oval face painted white in the manner of a Siren consort, except that she had blood ink snaking around her neck and jaw. Long, lustrous black hair cascaded down her shoulders, stark against her pale skin. This was no ordinary Succae female. She clearly had status.

"Honoured Serrate, loyal spirit, welcome home," she said with a short bow. Lytta responded with a similar move, and I nodded deferentially, seeing her smile in response.

"Who is this you have brought with you?"

Lytta looked at me awkwardly.

"This is the Ambassador Azshael. He is from the Seventh Flight."

"I am Zolorel" she said simply. "Please come into our home."

Lytta looked surprised. "Zolorel, no. The Ambassador was just leaving." She gave me a look that was part glare and part plea. I was about to cave when the lady of the house intervened. "I am sure none of us want to have *obayaz* owed to each other?"

Obayaz was Succae speak for a social debt. I had laughed when Ischae had first explained it to me, but for the Succae, unpaid *obayaz* was a serious matter. It could mount up over time and stain the vampire soul. In ancient Succae history, entire households had gone to war over something as small and inconsequential as a greeting improperly returned.

"No," I said. "None of us want that but Lytta is right, I can't stay for long."

"How about I make some tea?"

"That would be fine," I said, feeling Lytta stiffen by my side.

Zolorel led us through her moon garden, where everything was ordered and tranquil. Paved paths were swept clean, and small ornate trees were planted in pots at regular intervals. Here and there, small pools were sunk into the ground, and I fancied I could see colourful fish kissing the surface, leaving wide, round ripples in their wake. As we made our way to the ornate house that glowed with the same soft warmth as her lantern, Zolorel asked us to wait while she headed off through an arch flanked with perfectly round boulders that were stark against the grey stone tiles. The pathway led around the building, and she turned the corner and went out of sight.

"Wait here," Lytta said, and she followed her, leaving me alone.

I have always been too curious for my own good, and as my wounded wing was feeling better, I decided to take a look from above and ascended into the dark sky. I looked down on an orchard of thin-looking trees, and saw Lytta and Zolorel standing together in its centre, holding hands. Zolorel reached up and pulled down a branch which Lytta touched briefly, and the tree suddenly burst into radiant bloom with delicate blossoms of bright red and white petals. Even from my elevated vantage point, I could smell a warm fragrance on the air that was enchanting and intoxicating. Zolorel plucked a flower from the branch and pushed back Lytta's braids to place it behind her ear. Lytta did the same in return, and the two came together in the longest of delicate but passionate kisses. I decided to leave them to their tryst, as my smile faded at the memory of similar times with Ischae. Times that were as dead as she was, and the memories burned a sad hole in my soul.

Chapter Eleven

Even though Zolorel was the most perfect hostess, initially I was a poor guest. Tea turned out to be a ritual of hospitality that was long and drawn out. Lytta had changed out of her armour and insisted I did the same. I watched the looks, gentle smiles, and occasional touches between the pair, and I knew love when I saw it. It accentuated the melancholy that had fallen on me before they had returned from the orchard to invite me across the threshold. I suddenly wished I was elsewhere. There is nothing worse than mourning for a lost love in front of those who have their connection so clearly secured.

We sat around a square table in the centre of a wide-open room as Zolorel went through the stages of ceremony, which had to be observed as closely as the steps to an intricate dance. First, the table was cleansed with soap and water. Then, small ceramic cups and an ornate iron pot were laid out, and a black iron frame placed in the centre of the table. On its top, a wide copper bowl was positioned and in the frame's base, a candle in a round copper holder. Zolorel lit the candle and poured a pale coloured liquid from the pot into the bowl. As we waited for it to heat, she lit sticks of incense and placed them in ceramic holders at the table's corners. As the liquid churned in the bowl, she fetched a small ornate tree that looked skeletal and barren. Lytta lent forward and touched it, and green leaves sprouted all over its branches. Zolorel pulled the small leaves from the tree, and they became brittle in her hands. She crushed them over the bowl and as they swirled in, there was a release of a delicate fragrance that reminded me of being in woodland on a summer's day after rain had passed. I inhaled the green essence and started to feel tension swiftly fading away.

Before long, we were drinking and talking together, although how much I drank and what I said, I could not tell you. The haze of incense and the warmth of the infusion wrapped me in a snug haze. My eyelids grew heavy, and I could feel them closing. I woke suddenly to see a tigress with immense jagged teeth sitting across from me. Next to her was a great eagle that spread its golden wings and fixed me with a yellow eye, sharp beak turned in profile. I felt my spirit rising and looked down at my body below. I was slumped, my wings wrapped around me, but I looked safe and happy, so I let myself drift up through the roof and into the midnight sky.

I was drawn to the black water of the lake, and I soared across its expanse, my reflection a perfect ghostly image in the surface's dark mirror. In the sky above, Cerule's colours were electric and more vivid than ever. The planet's blue oceans, green forests, white mountains, and red deserts were visible in incredible clarity. I smiled, but felt any pleasure ebb away as I saw the black shadow eating away at the planet's edges, a slow spreading cancer that was irreversibly killing its host.

I blinked and found myself standing on the lake's surface as if I was on solid ground. I looked up, but there was no sign of Cerule. Instead, I could see four moons reveal themselves one by one, turning from their dark to light sides. I was disoriented, as Cerule only had one moon, and I was certain I could see it as the last of the four. As I watched, I saw black dots growing larger and larger on the second and third moons' surfaces. I realised they were *Yurei*, thousands and thousands of hungry ghosts relentlessly massing and growing in number until they began to fall like so many flakes of deadly snow. I turned to run, but hands from below the surface grabbed me and dragged me down into the deep dark water. I looked down to see Malacaz holding my left leg and the assassin Zamalca holding my right. Together, they pulled me deeper below. My aura dimmed as we descended into the dark fathoms of a lightless abyss.

Then, another dislocation of time and space found me standing alone in the purple surf of an alien shore. A great, black temple of polished stone lying half-buried in the sand loomed large before me like the skeletal remains of a great leviathan. It listed to the right at an odd angle, where the structure had been undermined and had duly subsided.

On the steps, the two tricksters who had dragged me under sat, tossing a colourful conch back and forth to each other. They seemed oblivious to my presence, and now I had time to study them I realised how alike they looked. They had to be twins at the very least, but there was something more. It was like they were mirrors of each other, not just in looks, but demeanour and behaviour. It was unnerving.

"Azshael," said a voice behind me, and I turned to see Cassiel standing in the still surf, her white chemise torn and bloody, her chest cavity open and broken. She looked just as I had seen her lying dead on Saur'Il's mausoleum slab. Behind her stood Camael, tears rolling down red-whiskered cheeks. He pointed past me, and I turned to see Malacaz and Zamalca lying lifeless on the steps as the great, dark doors of the temple started to open. It looked like their bodies had been bound with rope, and I watched as they were hauled up the steps in a series of jerky pulls, to be devoured in the darkness of the temple's interior. I could see two shadows and one of them had Angel wings. I ran for the steps, but before I could see who they were, the great temple doors slammed shut and I woke up.

Lytta looked down at me as I awakened. She was back in armour and the decorative blossom was gone. "It is nearly first phase," she said. "We must go." As we walked back towards the city, I began to tell Lytta of my dreaming vision, but she stopped me dead. "What you saw was for you alone," she said. "It was Zolorel's gift to you for bringing me to her on our anniversary."

"Me, bring you to her? You took me there!"

"Only if you believe in chance," she said. "I do not. As you did not stop or divert me, you share my choice of action and are responsible for allowing me to go to her. Do you understand?"

I didn't entirely, but the Succae are weird about wyrd and the strange provenance of the inexorable power of fate, so I let it go.

She continued, "It was Well magic, vision magic. It is a glimpse of truths unseen, destiny, and possible things to come."

I thought about thousands of *Yurei* falling like so many

snowflakes from a dark moon, and shivered. If that was a 'possible thing to come', I hoped I wouldn't be around to see it.

We parted company at the Hall of Keeping, as Lytta indicated it might be a while before she could identify the Low-Tsar's mark we had found on Rukoi's table. I guessed the Tsars didn't actively register their identities, but perhaps with Keeper Bibalis's help, the hides would reveal references that would guide Lytta to identify the one we were after. In the meantime, I had my own tasks to take care of on the Flight-side of the Tether, the first of which would be a long overdue meeting with a certain Angel of Death.

Scarpe looked quiet as I flew to the Tether tower. On the way, I mulled over the vision I had received thanks to Zolorel's magic, and tried to work out what parts belonged in each category of 'truths unseen, destiny, and possible things to come'. The twin rogues were uppermost in my thoughts. Malacaz had tricked me, but I couldn't accuse him of being a liar, given the feathers we had found in Rukoi's home. I also didn't think he had lied about seeking refuge among the Succae. He'd just neglected to mention he'd be hanging out with his murderous twin. The way they had been helplessly drawn into the temple was a mystery though, and I guessed it would stay that way until I could work out who was worshipped within and what their relationship to the tricksters could be. It did look like whoever the deity was, they had the upper hand. Did that make them its puppets? Willing or unwilling?

Next my thoughts moved to Cassiel and Cam. The fact they had been together seemed to confirm that Cam's grief on seeing her body had been real, although how they had come to know each other and establish such a bond was still a mystery.

Finally, I thought about the Angel in shadow. Who were they? What did they have to do with all this, and were they servants or masters? Architects of hidden things set in motion that I could not yet see or fathom? I did not know the answers, but I was determined to seek them out.

Chapter Twelve

On my return to Vigil Keep, I considered telling Varael about the *Yurei* but thought better of it. Karsz's instructions hopefully meant they wouldn't trouble the Keep and if they did, I felt certain they could be dealt with. I was surprised that Sergeant Sabrathan didn't come to meet me, but neither he nor his Commander put in an appearance.

Once over the Teeth, turbulent winds buffeted me, their cold bite harsh and unrelenting. It made flight a strenuous exercise, and by the time I had got within sight of the outskirts of the Lower Landing, I was feeling tired. I wondered why the Powers were making life so difficult in the air when as far as I knew, the only threat was on the ground. Then I remembered my vision of thousands of hungry ghosts falling to earth and thought perhaps a bit of caution was warranted after all.

My first task was to visit the Red Roof Inn and check in on Sylvenell. It had only been a day in real terms since I had left, but I was hoping that Lamechial had released the inhabitants and that they were all back together. However, as soon as I saw the tavern, shuttered and dark, I knew that those hopes were in vain.

I landed and placed my hand on the solid wooden doors at the entrance, but there was no response. I could tell my ambassadorial sigil had been removed and other wards put in its place. I felt anger coursing through me and burning bright, which is never a good thing. Anger makes me reckless and has its own way of often making matters worse. I wanted to seek out Lamechial and break his stone face, or he could break mine. At that moment, I really didn't care which.

"Azshael," said a voice from up above, and I looked up to see

Captain Galaeal standing on the Inn's ice-rimed balcony. The look on my face must have been murderous, as he took a step away from me as we faced each other.

"Calm yourself, Ambassador," he commanded, but ordering me about wasn't the wisest choice. I flew forward and slammed him against the balcony door.

"What have you done, Galaeal? You and your bastard Commander!"

To his credit, Galaeal did not try to fight me.

"Azsh! Please let me explain. It's not what you think!"

Perhaps it was weariness or the look of sincerity on the Captain's face, but as I felt the hot, red anger of the moment pass, I slowly released my grip on him and stood back. Galaeal took a scroll case from his belt and handed it to me. It bore Prince Anael's mark and the seal was unbroken.

I opened it and read a short note signed by the Prince. It gently admonished me for abusing my powers without reference but said that the Inn and the current protected status of its inhabitants would be respected. Not just respected but enhanced with the Prince's own ward, which would replace my own. To say I was shocked would be putting it mildly.

"Where is Sylvenell? Why can't I contact her?"

"You need to key yourself to the ward," Galaeal said. "Just trace its design, speak the words of keying and it will unlock." I followed his instructions, and sure enough, Sylvenell's face appeared in wooden simulacra. I breathed a sigh of relief as the doors to the Inn's upper gallery opened.

A while later, I sat with Galaeal as we both shared a bottle of warming red wine. I could tell the good Captain was keen to mollify and placate me. That was fine to a certain extent, but I hadn't forgotten his lack of intervention in the death of Virdae, so my tolerance would only stretch so far. To be fair to Galaeal, he would have been immediately dismissed by Lamechial for challenging orders, but that was far from an exoneration. 'Just following orders' had long ceased to be an acceptable excuse in my book, even if it was our way of life. After the small talk had dwindled into a reflective silence, Galaeal said, "Any news on our missing sceptre?"

"Who's asking?" I replied with more of an edge to my tone than I had perhaps intended.

"I am, Azshael," he replied evenly before adding, "but you know to whom I report."

"No news yet. Vod Karsz was emphatic in his belief that no Succae would have taken such a thing."

"You believe him?"

"For the most part, yes."

"How do you mean?"

"I mean that I think he believes what he says to be true. Yet, much as we knew nothing about the Angels in the cabal that sought to unseat our Prince, I suspect he cannot know the intentions of every single one of his people. Low-Nin, High-Nin, the Succae have a complex society and not all walk in step."

"I see," he said, although I don't think he really did, and I could tell he needed something to take back to his Commander.

"Let's just say I am pursuing enquiries to confirm the Vod's belief."

Galaeal looked happy with that. It was a classic progress report that said something was being done without going into messy detail. I imagined that was exactly the kind of thing that Lamechial would appreciate. It spared him from inconvenient detailed questions, too, and even better from his perspective, made it look like he had pushed me into doing what I had been commanded to do. The fact that it was pure fiction wouldn't bother anyone.

"Where are the others from this place?" I asked as Galaeal drained his glass and got up to leave. He looked wary and then shrugged. "It's no secret, I suppose. They have been taken to the cells beneath the temple of Excelsis at the Athenaeum. They are safe there, Azshael, and have nothing to fear." I thought about Virdae spiralling to the ground and was less than convinced.

Galaeal headed for the door and was about to leave when he suddenly turned round. "Oh, I nearly forgot. The Commander of the Honores, Vasariah, asked me to pass on news of your return when I knew of it. Any objection?"

"None at all, Captain. Did he say why?"

"Hoping for good news, I expect. He's been in a bit of hot water with the Prince for a while."

"After the theft you mean?"

Galaeal thought for a moment. "Well, I don't think that has helped his position."

"You mean he was in trouble before that?"

"Yes, indeed. After the events you were caught up in. You know - that recent unpleasantness?"

Here we go again with the 'unpleasantness' I thought. That had to have come from a Herald, given its ubiquity. It certainly sounded a lot better than a coup attempt.

Galaeal smiled and left, a blast of cold air marking his departure.

I sat on my own in the dark and thought about Vasariah's situation. It seemed less and less likely to me that he could be complicit in any theft. It just didn't make sense. What could he possibly have to gain? Even if he could access and wield the sceptre's powers, what would he use them for? Arguably, he could be part of a plot to seek to oust the Prince, but I had seen his face at the news of Anael's displeasure, and it was clear that he was sad and disappointed, not angry. It was the demeanour of someone who had failed and lost, not one that was scheming for revenge. Or at least that was what it looked like to me. However, I had been fooled before.

Chapter Thirteen

I spent a few hours resting at the Red Roof before resetting the ward and bidding Sylvenell farewell as best I could. Now the Archangel had given his support, I thought the Inn would be safe and no-one would dare touch it. My concerns now lay with the imprisoned Hyenae, Ysabeau and her spider queen 'mother', but for now, they would have to wait. I had the business of the dead to attend to.

The wintry sky was lightening as I took flight for the Mausoleum of Saur'Il, and I flew into the first blush of a roseate dawn. It was still freezing cold, but the turbulent winds had abated, and my body seemed to have acclimatised so that it ceased to bother me as much. Within the hour, I could see the towers of Trinity Palace on the horizon and the Mausoleum away to its east. I circled above the great palace of the dead before coming into land. Saur'Il's funereal garden twinkled in the early morning light as ice-rimed plants sparkled like so many diamond facets. I made my way past the great pale stone columns at the top of the wide steps and on into the silent black marbled halls beyond. The flames from the lamps lining the walls of the Hall of Ascendance waned thin, and looked as if they would sputter out at any moment. The crystal dome was shuttered, deepening the oppressive darkness so that the hall felt more and more like a tomb rather than a temple. It was claustrophobic, and I willed the flames of the lamps to stay alight. I wanted to brighten my own aura, but it would have been a breach of protocol, so I exhorted myself to tough it out. As I grew accustomed to the gloom, I became aware of the cenotaph monument, a great block of stone that commemorated those of our kind who had fallen in battle. At its summit, I could make out the distinctive white flecks of the wings and the silvery metallic sheen of the face mask of the Angel of Death.

Saur'Il stood stock still, his face looking down at me. To all intents and purposes, it looked as if he was asleep. Or dead.

"Did you forget my request to visit me before venturing to the Land of the Animated Dead? Or was there another reason for your delay?" His gravelly tone sounded neutral, but I still felt the sting of implied admonishment.

"My apologies," I said. "I got caught up in other events and didn't think it would be good to delay acting on the Archangel's orders any longer than I already had."

Saur'Il spread his great grey wings and dropped slowly and gently to the ground.

"Had you not considered that these things might coincide? That one thing must surely feed into the other? Given you have returned, I warrant you have finally worked that out?"

He had a point, but I didn't much like being chided. Being methodical is a Death Angel trait and I knew there was no point arguing. It would only delay the time I had to spend in the funereal atmosphere of his Hall.

I sighed and tried to look contrite. "Yes, correct," I admitted. "Please accept my apologies."

"No apology is necessary. I was merely trying to understand your actions. You do not seem all that comfortable in my house."

Was I that obvious? Apparently, yes, I was.

"I came in the hope you have recovered fragments of the Lacerate. The Shard Blade that killed our Juvenii, Cassiel? The Succae believe the weapon's maker may be identifiable from the quality of the workmanship."

Saur'Il was quiet for an uncomfortably long moment as we just looked at each other.

"Yes," he said finally. "Yes? Yes what?" I enquired.

"Yes, I have been able to recover some shards of the murder weapon."

"Oh gre-"

"Yes, I believe that a maker's mark can be seen on one of the shards."

"Oka-"

"And yes, there is more you need to know that we should discuss."

I waited for Saur'Il to say 'yes' again but he said nothing more, so I ventured a guess that he'd finished.

The Angel of Death signalled for me to follow him as he led me deeper into the Hall and to a set of winding stairs that led upwards. Here, Keepers went about their silent tasks amid dimly lit braziers. As we drew near, they bowed and retreated quietly into the shadows. Laid out on slabs of white marble were the bodies of three more Angels. These looked like soldiers, and I guessed they had been killed during the disturbances. They looked as if they were asleep, wings folded around them like a shroud, and I could not tell how they had died. The Keepers had dressed them in simple white tunics and cleaned and washed the bodies so that whatever fatal wounds they had received were rendered invisible. Soon, memorial Spheres would be made for them, and in our own way, we would remember them on sacred days. I felt a terrible sadness come over me. The Seventh Flight could ill afford any further losses.

Saur'Il led me to a chamber where Cassiel lay on another white slab. She was clad in a long white shift and wore a crown of white roses interlaced with wildflowers and vines. She looked peaceful and more alive than dead. He went to another slab and showed me what he had recovered from the body. There were five large shards of jagged black crystal and several smaller sharp slivers that I had no doubt would still cut to the bone if carelessly handled. The Lacerate was a terrible weapon.

"What happens next?" I asked.

"A messenger has been sent to the Juvenii sect, who will send a group to escort her body back to her kind. What happens then is a matter for them. The Heralds have told me that no memorial Sphere will be fashioned in her memory, so my work is done."

I had an overwhelming sense of sadness at that moment. I was struggling to understand how such an innocent had got herself on the wrong end of a murderer's blade, and a rare one at that. The Angel of Death must have seen the look on my face as he seemed to read my thoughts.

"It is sad to see a young soul like this gone so soon. If, of course, she was as she looks." His words reminded me of what Narinel had said about the strange arrested development of the Juvenii. It was true that she could be a lot older than she appeared. "I have suspicions," Saur'Il said, his voice but a whisper.

"What kind of suspicions?"

"I examined her hands. She bears the marks of weapons training."

"What kind of weapons?"

"Blades and spears, I would say. She has the same calluses as a regularly trained soldier of the Flight. I did not think that the Juvenii wielded weapons or, if so, then hardly at all. These marks seem to speak otherwise, at least for this one."

I took Saur'Il's point, but I had never visited the Juvenii's enclave and had no idea what they did or didn't do. Their reputation was one of a rejection of a martial life, but that didn't mean they didn't hunt or prepare to defend themselves should hostile forces or dangerous wildlife threaten them. I was, however, beginning to think that I would need to see the Juvenii ways for myself sometime soon. The Angel of Death took a long round case made of sturdy waxed leather from the table, and carefully placed the shards inside it. He sealed the open end with wax and handed it to me.

"May I offer you some counsel, Ambassador?"

"By all means," I said.

"I would be careful of the Irin and their leader." I thought of Kokael, of her stunning beauty and the ease with which she had drawn information from me. I thought this was good advice.

"I have been feeling the same way, but what makes you advise such caution?"

"I have seen many bodies and the reactions of our kind to them. Reading mourners is my gift. Most show anger or sorrow, some show regret, and a few sometimes show guilt as they blame themselves for the demise of another. Occasionally I see satisfaction and then, vary rarely, I see no emotion at all. Over time I have learned that such individuals are ones to be wary of. On the morning you came to the Mausoleum, I saw such a look on the Irin leader's face."

"How was she when she first arrived with Cassiel's body?"

"The Herald Kokael did not bring her here."

"That's not what I was told."

"Kokael came with Narinel, Azshael, but neither of them was sent for or invited by me."

"Who brought the body here then?"

"Camael did." Cam. I hadn't thought about him for a while, but I suspected I knew exactly where he had gone.

"I'll track him down," I said. "He has some questions to answer."

"On his face I saw deep sorrow and deep anger. I thought it strange."

I remembered Cam's uncharacteristic response when Cassiel's body had been found. I did not know him to be overly emotional, and it had shocked me. It was becoming clear that the two had known each other and had a history that I knew nothing of. It would be something for Cam and I to discuss in detail when next we met.

"Do you know when the message to the Juvenii was sent?"

"Word was sent when you left here to go to the Trinity."

That would now be two days, which, by my estimate, meant that only now would a messenger have arrived on their island retreat. I guessed it would be a day more before a bearer party would leave, and then two more to arrive at the Mausoleum.

"I would make a request from you, Saur'Il. I would like to escort Cassiel's body back to her people, but I have much to do in the next few days. Please do not let the Juvenii bearers leave until I return. Can you do that?"

The Angel of Death nodded slightly. "I will do what I can." Good enough for me.

"Is there anything else you wanted to tell me?"

"Has Darophon spoken to you about the Irin?"

"No. I saw him at the Trinity, but I have had no contact since then. Why?"

"It is said in some circles that Darophon was concerned that the deceit of the leader of the planned rebellion you disrupted was not detected earlier. That, after all, is the Irin's purpose. To watch for such plots and intercede before things go too far."

That was new news and explained why the Irin's leader was taking such a personal interest. Benazzarr, the now deceased Herald in question, was a highly devious schemer who had fooled me along with many other senior members of the Flight. The question I expected Darophon and, by extension, Prince Anael was asking was how those whose role was entirely not to be fooled had been taken in by his lies. Had the Irin been quietly complicit or turned a blind eye?

"The coup attempt was some time ago now and the investigations are long over. I am sure Kokael, and her sect have been exonerated."

"Yes, that is true, Ambassador. I am sure you think you know best in such matters."

As I left the Mausoleum, those last words rang hollowly in my ears. 'Think you know best?' That was a subtle way of implying I didn't know the full story, but he wasn't going to be the one to tell me what it was.

Part Three

Chapter One

My journey back down the Tether was, thankfully, uneventful. Vigil Keep still blazed like a beacon, and the Tether tower on the Succae's moon was still under heavy guard. I landed between the tower's ring of guards and the encampment, which was now becoming a fort with wooden walls being hastily erected by an army of Low-Nin.

"Ambassador!" I heard a shout come from the gates and saw my Red Ashai, Sergeant Kho, stride down toward me. "*Kai* Kho," I said, the words suddenly feeling clumsy in my mouth, but the Sergeant didn't seem bothered.

"Come," he said. "The Serrate awaits you." Kho escorted me through the gates, and I could see permanent structures were being erected by Low-Nin workers. I knew they needed no rest or sleep. They would work until their tasks were complete.

Lytta was waiting in a square command lodge that was one of the few structures already finished. She was poring over a hand-drawn map as I entered, not looking up or returning my greeting. She had made her disdain for idle chatter known long ago, and I should have known better.

"Did you recover the Lacerate shards?"

"Yes," I said, hefting the round case from my shoulder.

"Good. The bladesmith is expecting us."

As it turned out, the bladesmith was nearby, overseeing the creation of a small forge in a corner of the fort. As I looked at the industry around me where watch towers and weapon racks were being created, I began to realise that the Succae's peace was being secured by preparation for another war. It made me feel ill at ease, but then I remembered the vision of the hungry ghosts falling from space like a deadly snowfall. It wasn't just Angels that Karsz had to worry about.

"This is Zhik, the blade master," Lytta said as we entered the forge. He was small for a Succae and the ink on his skin so faded that it was hard to read. It meant he was an ancient among immortals, which made sense if what Ischae had told me about the creation of a Lacerate was true. Each one was a labour that took a mortal lifespan to create. It also required the donation of a heritage blade, a Succae sword of war that had earned a reputation for killing. It was said that the blade, at that point, had become a spirit that sought final release in a glorious explosion of deadly force.

Zhik looked at me expectantly and cleared a space on his workbench. I unsealed the carrying case and carefully shook the shards of the blade that had killed Cassiel free from it so that they lay on Zhik's table. The black fragments glistened in the light of the forge and had a malevolent cast about them. The blade master had a look on his face that I can only call rapturous. It was the look of a proud parent or someone who had struck gold.

"So beautiful," he said in a whisper. I didn't think so at all, but I wasn't much of a craftsman, so I kept my mouth shut.

"Did you make this, Master Zhik?" Lytta said, cutting straight to the chase. Zhik waved his hand at her dismissively. "Too soon, too soon," he said, and I presumed he was saying he hadn't had enough inspection time to know. Lytta folded her arms, and I knew that meant she was in no mood for indulging any nostalgia or appreciation of craft. Coming to think of it, mood had nothing to do with it. That was just her. It didn't seem to bother Zhik, though, and he took his time examining each piece of recovered shard in intimate detail. As he went about his evaluation, he whispered a litany that invited the blade to reveal itself to him. It was a process called Blade Song, and I had seen it before. All Succae weapons are believed to be living things, even when in a deconstructed state like this one. The process continued for a good hour. If nothing else, Zhik was meticulous. Finally, he turned to Lytta and said, "No good, no good." I could tell Lytta was surprised as she raised an eyebrow. I was a little less calm.

"What are you talking about?" I said as the master smith returned the pieces back to my carrying case and returned it to me.

"Is not Lacerate!" he said emphatically. I was lost. How could he say something was not what it clearly was. I looked to Lytta for help.

"You mean it was not made by a blade master?" she said.

Zhik nodded. "No song. No life. *Minai* piece."

Lytta nodded. "He says it is the work of an apprentice. Not a true Lacerate."

"Does he know which apprentice?"

Lytta looked at Zhik expectantly, and the little smith sighed and said "Rasnich." This time, Lytta was really surprised. Enough to raise both eyebrows.

As we returned to the command lodge, I could tell Lytta was energised with purpose. "Who's this Rasnich?" I said, my long strides just about keeping pace with hers. She said nothing until we were back in the lodge and the door was firmly closed.

"He is a Low-Tsar, but no ordinary one. It was his mark that I found in the house of Rukoi." I was going to say 'we' found, but decided that this was no time to be a pedant.

"What do you know about him?"

"He was once a High-Nin, but he chose to join the Lowers after Dursc's new laws came into being."

That was the first I had ever heard of any Succae opting to become downwardly mobile. In a society based on meritocratic ideals, choosing to be a part of the underclass was a bold decision to take. Unless your drug was power. In that case, perhaps it made sense. The Low-Tsars were the de facto leaders of the Low-Nin, who kept the seething masses of the lower castes occupied, meaning no-one else needed to worry about them. They gave the Lowers purpose and made a difficult life more tolerable, even if they were wolves among sheep. As I understood it, they were able to get away with all sorts of things that would otherwise be regarded as criminal if it wasn't for the fact that many of those things were at the behest and in the interest of those above them.

"Do we know where this Rasnich can be found?"

"Yes. The records say he is to be found at an arena in the undercity. It's right in the middle of a Low-Nin roost, so given recent events, we will have to tread carefully. I do not want another riot on my hands." Having witnessed the Serrate face down a crowd of thousands in Shadow Square, I understood what she was really saying was that she didn't want to have the souls of thousands of Low-Nin on her conscience. I couldn't have agreed more.

Chapter Two

Descending into Scarpe's undercity was a bit like submerging in deep water. It was an alien feeling, and even though I had lived for a few years in that gloom, it was still dislocating. In those days, I had lived in one of the undertown's top tiers with the moon's surface a short walk away. Where we were going couldn't have been further away from that life I had known and the 'safer' end of Succae society.

Lytta and I paused at the head of one of the hewn pathways on the rim overlooking the vastness of the nine deep round tiers where most of the Low-Nin made their homes. We hid our faces behind hoods and masks and set off down a steep path that zig-zagged its way down the side of a gigantic round hollow. Each tier had its own personality, with the various strata of High-Nin society grouped in the first five tiers in varying levels of splendid isolation. Beyond lay the sixth tier, bereft of homes and permanent structures except for temporary shelters where covered market stalls and tents housed traders, crafters, and anyone else who had something to sell, including themselves. They were not hidden from the elements, but rather from prying eyes.

The Succae emporia and bazaars were the most alive of anywhere on the moon and more than just somewhere to trade; they were meeting places, drinking holes, places of drama, intrigue, love, and hate. It would take several hours to walk around the sixth tier's circumference, with almost every foot of space taken and occupied. I was expecting Rasnich's arena to be located here, but Lytta led me through the crowds before locating a rusty looking cage that was housed on a promontory overlooking the deeper depths with a pulley wheel attached to thick rope.

The seventh to ninth tiers were called roosts and were home to the Low-Nin. Here the Low-Tsars ruled their empires of the hopeless and the hopeful. The Low-Nin were rats in the walls, living in vast warrens hewn from the rockface and dimly lit by hundreds of torches that waned and flickered in invisible currents. Lytta opened the door to the cage and indicated I should get in.

"I'd rather fly," I said, giving the rickety-looking thing a dubious look.

"I'd rather you didn't," she said pointedly. "I think it would be less than wise to reveal ourselves or make too grand an entrance. I am not entirely sure what we are walking into, Ambassador. I advise caution until such time as it is no longer needed, or events dictate a different path." She had a point I couldn't really argue with, so I carefully boarded and wedged myself into a corner. Lytta joined me inside and pulled down the bar that locked us in. She reached up and pulled on the heavy rope, and I felt the cage lurch. Then she let go, and we were freefalling into the abyss. I am used to dizzying descents, so I was happy to see a disappointed look on Lytta's face. She had clearly expected a different reaction.

We shot past the seventh tier and on a few hundred feet more before Lytta pulled on the flapping rope, and we jerked to a sudden stop on another promontory. It was mostly dark when we emerged from the cage, although I could see torches guttering at the entrances to tunnels that spiralled away into unknown depths. Here and there, Low-Nin showed their pale, vampiric faces, but Lytta put one hand on the hilt of her sword, and they scuttled away out of sight. We walked for about half an hour in a dim, smoky gloom, following the eighth tier's jagged lip before arriving at a wide tunnel entrance marked with motifs of boxing hares. These were identical to the ones we had seen on the coin of indenture we had found by Rukoi's body. In the distance, I could hear a rumble, and it took me a moment to realise it was the sound of voices joined in rough unison.

"Sounds like we came on a fight night," I said.

"Every night is a fight night here," Lytta said with disdain. For a spirit of war, she could be strangely detached from any interest in martial displays and the art of violence. Of course, those of us who have had to truly fight for our lives see little appeal in such displays that traduce reality. Once you have witnessed the truth of wars and battlefields, only a fool would wish to return there. Lytta was an immortal spirit bound in a Succae host. I had no idea what a wyrd for war and death spread across eons would do to someone. I guess that explained it – she had seen all there was to see.

The Serrate told me to stay three blade lengths behind her and to be ready as we ventured down the tunnel to Rasnich's arena. The path twisted downward, and we hugged the wall as we went. I found it strange that there were torches blazing in brackets that had been hammered into the wall. I understood the Low-Nin were not as powerful as the Highers, whose powers developed as years went by, but I thought they could all see in the dark. Then I realised that these illuminations weren't for them but were probably for my kind and for those who had come from the other side of the Tether. Rasnich, like all his brother Low-Tsars, was no doubt happy to take donations from all that were willing to give them.

Lytta raised her hand, and I stopped dead in my tracks. We had come to a twisting turn in the tunnel. The voices were louder now, and I could hear a crowd baying, barking, and shouting up ahead. There was bloodlust in their tones, a wildness that was disturbing, as though they wanted to witness the terrible end of some poor soul's life. She dropped back and said, "There are Ashai ahead, but I do not know who they serve."

"I guess Rasnich?"

"Yes, I suppose so," she said, sounding weary. "Stay back. I will take care of this."

"Are you going to kill them?"

"I will try and educate them," she said. "All men make mistakes, but a good man yields when he knows his course is wrong."

I wasn't going to argue with Lytta, but I did wonder how much Rasnich and his soldiers could be considered 'good men'. His part in all that we had uncovered so far looked suspicious at best, yet he was a facilitator of the wishes of the High-Nin. Did the fact he had once ranked among their number make a difference? I somewhat doubted it. He had taken a downward step, and Succae culture would keep him there. I wondered if that could have been a motive for him to have got involved with the apparently rebellious Rukoi, or whether it was just business. I guessed we would soon find out.

Lytta rounded the corner with her sheathed blade in both hands like it was an offering. I could not resist watching her as she approached a group of six armed and armoured Ashai who were clearly acting as perimeter guards.

"Ashai," she said as they looked at her curiously. "I have come for Rasnich." It was a provocative choice of words. Not 'I have come to see Rasnich, or 'I want to talk to Rasnich'. She made it sound like an arrest, and that is how they took it.

In any fight, there are opening moves that are either effective or damn stupid. The former gives you an edge, the latter a sure way to a negative outcome. On this occasion, it was the latter, as one of the Ashai to Lytta's right tried to grab her arm. She casually shrank away from his grip and, standing on one foot, punched him so hard with the hilt of her sword that he literally took flight and slammed into the tunnel wall to slump in a heap. Then she vaulted over the remaining five as they tried to pull their swords from their scabbards. The two warriors in the middle were immediately struck in the side of the head as the Serrate's scabbard flashed back and forth. Their helms shattered under the snap of her venomous strike and they both went straight down to lie senseless on the ground.

The three remaining guards should have surrendered at this point, but whether out of honour, fear, or sheer bloody mindedness, they readied their blades and spread out around her. I have seen Lytta fight many times, and I am always impressed with the sheer fluidity and liquid flow of her motion in combat. The first to attack swept in with a frenzied series of cuts that sliced through the air. Lytta ducked into a low, wide stance and swept his legs from under him so that he fell and landed on his back. Then she was straight on him and slammed the end of the scabbard right in the middle of his forehead. The soldier jerked once and laid still. The two remaining guards attacked at once in what they no doubt thought was a co-ordinated assault. That would have been a strong tactic with any normal Succae, but Lytta's exceptional balletic athleticism meant she was able to spin away from them with inches to spare. They moved swiftly after her, blades cutting and slashing at empty space, until one of them sliced through one of her braids which went flying to the ground. I think it was then they realised who she was, and they paused in shock. Lytta picked up her braid and I could feel the sudden static in the air. The Ashai stepped back, instinctively feeling the change in the Serrate. I realised then that up to that point, she had been toying with them, allowing them to test their skills in a kind of game. It was, however, a rigged game that they could never win. Lytta stowed her blade at her side and suddenly shifted forward. It was a blur of movement, and I saw both their bodies lurch as sharp fingernails pierced leather breastplates and on into the flesh beneath. Their bodies were lifted off the ground as the Sixth Spirit of War, the Succae Serrate, pulled their souls from them. Their bodies jerked like a pair of grotesque puppets as black vampire spirits, entwined in white strands of power, struggled in her grip as all semblance of life left their host bodies to fall to the floor, pale and lifeless. Then, something remarkable happened; she channelled the spirits she had taken back into their bodies. This was something I had never seen before, and it surprised me. The two men twitched slightly as the lights inside them were relit and they regained control over their dead flesh. As soon as they could properly move, they both fell on their knees before their Serrate.

"I have come for Rasnich," she repeated, and the pair whimpered and cried. It took a while for Lytta to get them to stop apologising and answer her questions. Rasnich, it turned out, was not here, but someone by the name of Kjatz was in charge whilst he was away. Rasnich had been gone for over a week, and they did not know when he would return. Furthermore, they did not know why he had left or where he had gone to. On the subject of Kjatz, he was a Low-Nin but had risen to be trusted with the running of the arena, which was just one of Rasnich's ventures as a Low-Tsar. All Ashai are High-Nin, which made me wonder about how they felt about taking a Low's orders, but then, being a soldier requires an ability to do such a thing without question. Maybe they hadn't really given it much thought or perhaps whatever Rasnich gave the men was such valuable compensation that it was worth not doing so. Armed with a description of Kjatz and his likely location, Lytta dismissed the men and told them to return home. They gathered their dazed colleagues and scuttled away from the arena entrance and back down the tunnel.

Chapter Three

We emerged into a round amphitheatre that was packed to the gills with people shouting and screaming. Around twenty feet below us was a pair of square pits separated by a thick heavy gate that was barbed and spiked. It looked unclimbable to me. Presently the gate was closed, dividing the two spaces occupied by naked pale figures armed with rudimentary looking weapons. On the right were two female Low-Nin, who looked emaciated and desperate. They clutched rough-hewn wooden spears with sharp points at both ends. In the pit to the left were two male Low-Nin who looked fitter and healthier, although not by much. These men held long blunt staves, and their hands were wrapped in the manner of fist fighters. A discordant band suddenly piped up, and the spectators fell silent as their cacophony replaced the harsh din of the crowd.

"Come on," Lytta said, and we made our way around the edge of the highest tier through the tightly packed crowd, who seemed unbothered by Lytta's sinuous shouldering and my less agile barging. They were mostly Low-Nin, although I fancied I saw faces from the streets of the Upper and Lower levels of the Landing. There were Angelic faces there, too, but as soon as we made eye contact, they turned their faces away. I can't say what they were doing was wrong, but it wasn't something you'd brag about either.

We arrived at a set of narrow steps that took us down the side of the amphitheatre and away from the crowds of spectators. Here, there were more Lowers drinking blood stimulants that were so strong they could make your eyes water if you got too close to their intoxicating scent. As they drank, they also smoked narcotics from short stemmed clay pipes and chattered away in the high-pitched tones of their special language. For some, the night's activities were already too much, and they lay on the ground, insensible and prostrate. As they saw Lytta coming, the conscious ones fell silent in awe of the Serrate before them. I had seen her allow the Low-Nin to touch her and seek her blessing, but on this occasion, she just ignored them and strode forward towards a gate that led back into the lower level of the theatre. An Ashai stood on watch on the other side, but he quickly opened the door and stood back to let us through.

"Kjatz?" Lytta said, and the Ashai pointed to a set of steps that led down, presumably, to the level of the pits themselves. I looked through the slats and saw that the fight between the naked spear women and the male pugilists had ended somewhat predictably, with the boxers' bodies lying on the rocky floor. One had been impaled straight through the chest, and the other had a spear tip protruding from the back of his skull. It looked like the Low-Nin women had known what they were doing after all. It seemed the hopes of the crowd had been with the men, as they were sullen and quiet. "You may leave now," Lytta said, and at the speed the Ashai departed, he had to be one of the smarter ones.

Below, we arrived in a circular passage that wound round the amphitheatre's circumference. Lowers of varying height, weight, and fitness waited in holding pens for their turn in the pits. It was a pitiful sight, but I presumed that whatever reward Rasnich offered for their participation in this most base and basic level of deadly entertainment had to be worth it.

We found Kjatz in the approximate centre of the Via passage, surrounded by a group of armed Ashai. He was one of the bigger Low-Nin I had ever seen, not quite as wide as he was tall, but there wasn't a great deal in it. He was arguing with one of the spear women, presumably about whatever reward they had earned for risking their lives. One of the Ashai pushed the woman, whose face looked thin and stretched, and she stumbled backwards into her fight partner. There was a lot of shouting, and I could sense things were getting heated. This, however, was Lytta's world, so I didn't want to intervene unless things got out of hand. The arena master suddenly noticed our presence and gave up arguing. He pulled some sort of plant matter from a satchel he carried around his waist and shoved it into the women's hands. They fell upon their knees in thanks and scuttled past us into one of the pens, where they quickly dressed and headed back the way we had come.

"Well, isn't this something! The Serrate, here, among us," Kjatz said in a surprisingly deep and resonant tone of voice that could no doubt have been heard in the lower rows of the amphitheatre. I could immediately tell something was off. Maybe it was that tone, a false front that projected confidence, but beneath ran tense surprise. The body language of the four Ashai around him was also telling. They were staring at Lytta with predatory anticipation. That told me they had already lost. If any of them really thought they stood a chance against the Serrate they would have attacked already. Kjatz had blood ink on his scalp, which told me he was indebted to a High-Nin and I guessed it was probably Rukoi.

"I came for Rasnich," Lytta said, steadily. I noticed she had shifted her stance slightly so that she was at an angle to the group of Ashai whose hands had strayed close to the hilts of the blades at their sides. I could feel the tension of confrontation growing, enhanced by the arrival of three more guards who had come in from the pit gate and were slowly circling around behind us. Their attitude and behaviour spoke volumes about Karsz's grip on power. This kind of open dissent in front of one of the Vod's most trusted servants was highly unusual.

"Where is your master?" Lytta said, and Kjatz laughed.

"Not here, Serrate! He's been gone for a few days now, and no-one knows when he'll be back"

"He should be more careful," Lytta said, showing Kjatz the mark that had been found by Rukoi's dead body.

Kjatz took a moment to look at the coin, then sniffed dismissively.

"It is our mark, but Rasnich has many of these and trades them freely. As is his right."

Lytta nodded sagely. "True. Yet this was found next to a dead High-Nin who was plotting rebellion. Is your master a rebel? Are you?"

Lytta's direct accusation made Kjatz's good-natured mask slip for just a moment, but that was enough to see a frightened feral creature caught in an unexpected trap.

"Come now, Serrate. Why don't you take a seat and watch the action as my guest? We'll make space for you in the champion's seat – best in the arena."

"Kjatz. You didn't answer my question," Lytta said as the arena master retreated into the protective circle of his guards.

"Your blood is running faster, Kjatz. I am the Serrate, and I can see through you. You will tell me where Rasnich is, or I will rip your spirit from you and take it to hell."

Kjatz blanched as Lytta moved closer, and then the dam broke, and the fighting began.

Kjatz moved first. He reached into a pocket of his satchel, and threw something in Lytta's face. She recoiled and, gasping, fell to her knees. The Ashai surged past Kjatz, drawing their blades as they came. I blazed, and it was their turn to fall back as bright white light filled the passage. Nimrod leapt into my hands, and I moved to stand over her as the dismayed Ashai regrouped.

Three of them moved forward in a combined attack on Lytta. I extended Nimrod to halberd length and blocked their blades, feeling the power of their blows in vibrations along the haft. From defence to attack, I spun Nimrod back around in a sweeping strike that caught one of the three in the side of the head. He went tumbling into the others so that they all collapsed in a tangled heap. Lytta was still struggling as I saw Kjatz run past us with two of the guards by his side, leaving the last pair to their attacks, one from the front and one from behind. I flicked Nimrod up and behind me to parry the one from behind with the intent of sweeping back down to block the one in front, but I was just too late. It was a severing blow, aimed at the Serrate's head. I felt everything slow down and then suddenly speed up again. Lytta raised her hilt and blocked the blow. She stood up, blood pouring from her nose, ears and eyes, and in a swift double slash, carved her assailant in twain across the body and slashed his head in two from crown to jaw. The group of three watched the body collapse in pieces and ran as the blood-faced spectre of death stood before them, her blade naked and washed in red. I turned to face the one behind me, but he, too, had run.

"I cannot see," Lytta said.

"Kjatz ran off with his guards. What happened?"

"Ghost dust," she said. "From the Well. It doesn't affect me, but it hurts my host."

I had never heard of this before, but I guessed it disrupted the blood supply in Lytta's body.

"Hold on to me – I'll fly us out of here."

"No! I cannot be seen to rely on your kind." Charming but understandable.

"Go after Kjatz. Cut him off. I will follow as soon as the effect passes."

I looked on into the passage where the Ashai had fled, and wondered how far they had gone. I wasn't going to leave Lytta alone, blind and unprotected in hostile surroundings.

"I can look after myself," she said, wiping dark blood from her eyes and obviously reading my hesitance to leave. "We came for information, Angel, and now it's getting away. If Kjatz can get to the lower roosts, we'll never find him."

I hated to admit it, but she was right. I only hoped I was making the right call, but she was the Serrate after all. I spread my wings and took flight from the arena pit to gasps from the jaded crowd.

Chapter Four

I caught sight of Kjatz and his Ashai running past the entrance gate. He rounded the bend as his guards turned to face me, although to my surprise, they just knelt on the ground and kept their swords sheathed. Cautiously, I overflew them and turned the corner in pursuit of Rasnich's deputy, who was still running swiftly uphill for the tier's edge and an escape into the Low-Nin roosts and their labyrinthine tunnels.

I passed over Kjatz's head with a few feet of clearance between his head and the roof of the tunnel passage, and landed a dozen feet ahead of him. He didn't seem to pay any attention as he came barrelling on, so I shouted at him to halt as Nimrod became a flaming lance. Kjatz stopped and looked at me, as if truly seeing me for the first time.

"Angel! What do you want?"

I was a little incredulous at his question, so I gave the clearest answer I possibly could.

"I want some answers. As does your Serrate."

"She's not my Serrate," Kjatz said dismissively. "This is none of your business, Angel. Go back to your side of the Tether and stay out of things that don't concern you." That was bold talk for a Low-Nin. Possibly the boldest I had ever heard and proof that militancy and rebellion were in the air. Whether Kjatz would have said that in front of other Succae I did not know, but it was revealing and concerning at the same time. If I knew anything of the Succae, it was that defiance and challenges to order only came when there were solid foundations and reasons for it. Whatever Rasnich was a part of clearly had both.

"I care not for your politics or your apparent dislike of your Vod,"

I said as the burly Succae glared at me. "However, a sacred item has been taken from us that needs to be returned. Do you know what I am talking about?"

"I do not!" Kjatz said, and he moved to try and push past me, but I blocked his path. "I say you do, Kjatz. And that you know full well where your master Rasnich is to be found. Before long, the Serrate will have caught up with us, and she will ask the same questions of you in a much more forceful manner. If you want to be gone before then, I suggest you tell me. I am a good listener."

The Low-Nin glared at me and muttered something along the lines of 'not having time to listen to rubbish' before again trying to get past me. This time, I pressed Nimrod's haft against his chest and pushed him back, flames burning holes in his tunic and blackening the flesh below.

"Don't test me, Kjatz! I am on a mission from the Archangel Prince Anael of the Seventh Flight, and I will have answers!"

I could hear the sound of combat from behind us, and I guessed Lytta had nearly caught up.

"Tell me or tell her. Your choice. I am only interested in what has been stolen. Nothing else."

Kjatz seemed to suddenly deflate. "Not stolen," he said. "Just borrowed."

"What do you mean?"

"It will be returned, once the time comes."

"And what time is that?"

Kjatz gave a rueful smile and reached into his satchel. I poked him again with the tip of the lance as he pulled out a bottle from within.

"Just Venii!" he complained. "And I'm not going to throw it at you, Angel, in case you were concerned."

The thought had crossed my mind, but I had my quarry at bay and wasn't overly perturbed. This, as it turned out, was a fatal error, albeit not for me.

I could see Lytta running towards us as Kjatz pulled the stopper on his bottle.

"Until justice is restored, Angel. Until justice is done." He winked at me as Lytta called his name, drank deep from the bottle and within seconds started to convulse as dark blood haemorrhaged from every orifice.

Chapter Five

"I can't believe you just let him poison himself!"

Those were the first words Lytta had said to me in about an hour. "I thought you weren't talking to me?" I said, propping Kjatz's body upright as the cage made its slow ascent. Going down—super fast. Going back up, —not so much.

"Didn't you consider the possibility he would kill himself to prevent being interrogated?" I hadn't. It was not what I understood the Low-Nin life cycle to be. I had understood that toil and progress was the Low-Nin lot until they did deeds to be recognised. I would never have expected Kjatz to sacrifice all he had achieved in who knows how many centuries to protect Rasnich's secrets. Yet here we were with his lifeless cadaver.

It was a tortuously arduous journey back to the Shadow Citadel, during which Lytta continually berated me for my lack of foresight and understanding. Alright, maybe continually is not quite the case, but it sure felt that way. Eventually, as we entered Shadow Square, we settled into discussing the little he had said.

"Exactly what did he say about justice?"

"'Until justice is restored.' 'Until justice is done.' He also said that it was nothing to do with me and that the Rood had been borrowed, not stolen."

"If it was nothing to do with you, then why steal an Angelic artefact?"

It was a good question, and I had no answer to it. At least not one I was comfortable sharing yet, although I was feeling worse and worse about not telling the full story. In truth, there was a very good reason to take the Rood if the scope of its powers of mass control were true.

"Is Karsz unjust?" I asked, only to be met with a withering glare.

"No, of course not!"

"Then why are rebels fomenting dissent?"

"We don't know they are, Angel."

"What about Rukoi?"

"One disenchanted High-Nin does not make for a rebellion."

"No, but thousands of Low-Nin amassing in this square just might do."

"Low-Nin are easily led and just as easily corrected. A body of Highers challenging the Vod and swinging an army of *Jerzay* behind them might be a different matter," she said, referring to the Succae word for hopefuls.

"How do you know that is not happening in those quiet manses we passed through? Rukoi surely wouldn't have thought that he could challenge Karsz alone?"

Lytta didn't have an answer for that, so went back to telling me off as we hauled Kjatz's body up to the steps of the Citadel.

A few hours later, I was back in another vault with another dead body, one I had got to know rather well given I had done most of the carrying of it from the undercity to the citadel. Alright, Lytta had helped here and there, but it sure felt that way. Kjatz's corpulent body, now devoid of the animate blood and spirit within, had started to decay rather quickly, much to the apparent disgust of Lord Ancestral Vachs, who stood as far away from the slab as possible. Also in attendance were the Serrate and Keeper Bibalis from the Hall of Keepings.

"Rain," Bibalis said, confirming what we had already guessed. Rain was a Succae blood drug that had been weaponised and nearly deployed in the recent attempted coup at the renewal of the armistice between the Flight and the Succae. Come to think of it, Karsz had been the target then, too, but I had just managed to disrupt the event and prevent Kjatz's terrible fate being visited on the Succae's leader.

"How did a Low-Nin get hold of such a poison?" Vachs said, clearly unimpressed with the whole procedure. "I thought all that tainted supply had been destroyed." It was true. Much of the poisoned stock, augmented with Angel blood and body parts, had been dealt with, but the idea that a resourceful Low-Tsar like Rasnich couldn't have found a few barrels for later use was far from beyond possibility.

"I hear the Low-Tsars are very resourceful," I said, and Lytta nodded her agreement.

"We must accept that some must have escaped or been entrusted with Rasnich before the plans of the Cabal were activated."

I turned my attention to Bibalis as the Lord Ancestral and his Serrate exchanged whispered words.

"Do you know whose blood ink he was wearing, Keeper?"

Bibalis looked over at Lytta, who nodded to indicate that I was allowed to know this detail. "It is the protection tattoo of the former Marshal, Lord Sarzh. He also bears the marks of the Higher Rukoi and the Low-Tsar Rasnich." These last two were not obvious and had been hidden in tattoos behind his ears. Sarzh had been the leader of the coup on the Succae side. He had very nearly killed me, but thanks to an inventive piece of misdirection by Lytta, I had managed to turn the tables.

"The Low-Tsars are not allowed to give out such marks," Vachs said wearily.

"The Low-Tsars do whatever they want in their own world," Keeper Bibalis said. "These protections are for the Low-Nin's eyes only. They only have meaning among that community which is, of course, where Kjatz would have spent most of his days."

"What does this all mean?" Vachs said, clearly annoyed by the Keeper's statement of an obvious truth.

"We do not yet know, Lord Vachs. This servant of the Low-Tsar Rasnich evaded interrogation. He escaped to the Well before I could question him." Lytta looked at me as she spoke, but opted to leave out a damning indictment of my actions. Small mercies.

"However, the fact that he took such extreme measures—Rukoi's murder and the apparently planned disappearance of the Low-Tsar Rasnich—would seem to indicate a plot of some sort is in motion. I will find answers."

"There is also the matter of your stolen sceptre, Ambassador, and the missing rogue, Malacaz," Vachs said. "Given what has happened and this Low-Nin's seeming admission of knowledge of the theft, it would seem these things are connected."

Lytta looked at me for a response. "I think it is too early to know," I said, "but I deem it wise we remain open to all possibilities." It was a diplomat's answer, but Vachs seemed to find it acceptable.

"Very well, then. I trust you will continue to aid us in the search for this rogue, and in return we will assist you in the matter of your Archangel's missing regalia." It was a statement not a question, so I nodded at Vachs, and he returned the gesture before turning to leave. Then he paused on the threshold as he looked over at the contents of Kjatz's satchel, laid out on the table.

"That's interesting," he said, and walked over to the bottle from which Kjatz had taken his final drink. He picked it up and turned it in his hand as Lytta walked over to him.

"What is it?" she said, stirring Vachs from his study.

"A relic," he said. "This is a Shadowglass bottle. I have not seen the like since we abandoned Khrov during the height of the war. I am surprised it has survived so well." He put it back down and left the chamber as Lytta and I exchanged a glance. A dead city on a dying planet would make a great place to hide and plan a rebellion.

As it turned out, Lytta knew nothing of Shadowglass, which made two of us. Fortunately, Keeper Bibalis did know and was happy to tell all as Kjatz's rapidly decaying body was wrapped and prepared for destruction. With his High-Nin sponsors dead, his flesh would warrant nothing more than being thrown upon a pyre with no ceremony to mark his demise.

"Shadowglass is an alchemist's creation," the Keeper said. "It should really be called Spiritglass, a vessel for spirits held in liquid." Whilst I had not heard of Shadowglass, I had heard of Spiritcraft. This was not unusual in Succae culture, which held that the Necrene Well abounded with all sorts of spirits that could be bound and used to augment everything from structures to weapons, tools to utensils. From what I had seen, however, the practice had fallen into disuse since the Succae migrated from the planet Cerule, mainly for practical reasons. Access to the Well was now tightly controlled in highly guarded vaults below the Citadel, which had not been the case in the days when the Succae had ruled the planet below. Then, it had been freely accessible by all High-Nin, although Spiritcraft alchemy had long been in decline largely, so my dead Succae lover Ischae had once told me, because it didn't work.

"Spiritglass was manufactured in the Well itself. The Necrene blackened specially enchanted glass that caught and imprisoned spirits the Spiritcrafter then bent to a given purpose. There were bottles for war, for love, for growing, and for poisoning," Bibalis said, looking pointedly at the Kjatz's shrouded body. "This bottle was old but unremarkable. The enchantment has long been erased."

"Lord Vachs mentioned Khrov," Lytta said. "Is that where these bottles were created?"

"Yes, Serrate. In the old days there was a thriving trade in Spiritcraft alchemy, especially in the Old Town near the *Kolodesh*."

"*Kolodesh*?"

"The House of the Well," Lytta said. "It used to be at the centre of a temple complex to the old gods."

"The Serrate is correct," Bibalis said. "After Vod Dursc's reforms, it became a marketplace where many alchemists sold their services. Before then, only the Priests of the Old Gods could work such magic."

"So, this bottle came from down on the planet? From Khrov?"

"I would say the balance of probability is yes," Bibalis said. "I am not aware of anyone currently practising such alchemy. I can check the records in the Hall of Keeping for the maker's mark and confirm where, and perhaps when, it was made."

"This practice," Lytta said. "Why do I not know of it?"

"It grew in popularity after your time Serrate, mainly during the war with the Angels."

Bibalis hefted Kjatz's bound body over his shoulder and left us alone to ponder this new information. Kjatz may have escaped interrogation, but perhaps he had inadvertently given us a massive signpost to the whereabouts of Rasnich, although it occurred to me that there was a problem with the Khrov theory.

"How would Rasnich and his followers get down to the planet?" Lytta had a sly look on her face that told me she knew the answer, but that I would have to work to get it.

"Why don't you tell me the truth about your missing regalia first?" I felt uncomfortable, and in the back of my head I could hear Sariel's voice telling me to keep my mouth shut. However, bodies were piling up, Malacaz and his deadly companion were both in the wind, and given the situation, I decided it was time to come clean. Mostly. So, I told Lytta about the White Rood's mythical powers of mass control without going into huge detail of the history of the Flight. I was expecting her to explode, but she just nodded along, which could only mean one thing.

"You already knew?"

"Of course," she said. "We know all about Anael's sacred weapons and regalia, although it was widely believed that not all the stories about the White Rood were true. It's not as if your people keep it a secret, and Vod Karsz has met your Prince on several occasions where much of it has been on display. It would have been foolish for us not to research the powers of the leader of the forces that dislodged us from our ancestral homeland, don't you think? I am sure your Heralds have undertaken similar work about our Vod and myself?" I kept my mouth shut. Honestly, if they had, I would be one of the last to know. "That is why we keep our secrets to ourselves and why Vod Karsz does not carry every item of power he has won. For now, we are at peace, but that may not be the case for ever."

I didn't want to think too deeply about that thought. In fact, my remaining heart skipped a beat at Lytta's words. I knew she was just being pragmatic and that what she said was the truth. It was just that I never wanted to see our two races return to the terrible conflict between us. I changed the subject.

"Very well. I have shared with you. Now, tell me, how would Rasnich access the surface and the city of Khrov?"

"It would be through the Necrene well," she said, and the fact she would share a secret like that with me was reassuring.

"That, surely, would mean they had help from the Vod or one of his inner circle?"

"Not necessarily. I have found that there are several 'way paths' that my kind used to evacuate Cerule. The Low-Tsars were an important part of the co-ordination of that migration, especially for the Lowers. I suspect that Rasnich knew where one or more of these paths could be found. Karsz ordered them sealed after use, mainly so your kind couldn't follow us, but there's no guarantee that such actions were ever taken."

"You think he's there then?"

"I do, but I do not think it is me he is hiding from, although he may have allowed Kjatz to believe otherwise. I think he intended for us to see that bottle and make the connection. I think it is something else that has made him go into hiding. Something connected to whatever plans Rukoi was involved with."

She was talking about rebellion, and I had a bad feeling that it wasn't just on this side of the Tether. Whoever was behind all this had trouble planned for us all.

Whilst we were both keen to get to Rasnich, there were practical issues that prevented an immediate departure. First, it was not possible for me to use the Necrene paths. I had been close to the well before and had felt it draining my life essence away. It was an experience I was not keen to repeat. Neither was it possible for Lytta to accompany me in a flight through space and Cerule's atmosphere, so we would have to travel independently of each other. I was nervous about the vision I had received of dark moons full of hungry ghosts. I wanted to check with Sariel whether the Flight was aware of these satellites, or if it was just my intoxicated imagination working overtime.

We parted company at the moon-side Tether camp and resolved to meet up in three days at the southernmost gates of Khrov city. Lytta said that she believed the nearest useable well path was a good day's travel from the city itself, and she would need time to make that journey. That gave me an opportunity to return to the Princelands and make some enquiries of my own.

Chapter Six

Back on the bright side of the Tether, I headed for the refuge of my Sphere and the chance to do some thinking. I have always found that sailing upon a calm sea under the stars is exactly the right environment for my cluttered mind to achieve some sort of clarity. It was here that I began to unravel the tangled knot my mission had become.

First and most importantly, the White Rood. Kjatz and, by implication, his master, Rasnich, had obviously heard of the theft and possibly been a party to its planning. Did Rasnich still have it? I doubted it. I was still of a mind to say that the Low-Tsar had been a servant of his master, the High-Nin, Rukoi. Had he left a trail for the Serrate to follow deliberately? I was cynical about that, but there was a level of low cunning about it that suited a powerful Low-Tsar. But the questions remained—what did he know, who was he hiding from, and why?

That brought me to Malacaz and Zamalca. I reflected on the drawings in the histories of Scharo's rebellion and the two faces that were portrayed as powers that had been called upon. It was undeniable that the male face looked significantly like Malacaz and the other, Zamalca, an assassin called from the Well who had nearly killed a Succae Spirit of War. It didn't feel as though they were connected to the theft, especially as Malacaz had come to me after the events of the day of unrest in the Landing. The events in Shadow Square and an alignment with the Low-Nin sounded exactly like music to a trickster's ears. Yet I was struggling to see how they fitted in to all this, although it was obvious that if Malacaz could work out how to access the Rood's powers, he could cause a lot of problems. Their place in the vision I had received in Zolorel's house came back to me. If it was to be believed, it seemed they were key players, albeit puppets of hidden higher powers, and at least one of them had wings like mine.

Then there was the mystery of Vasariah, his standing with Anael and the insight and warnings that Saur'Il had given me at the Mausoleum about Kokael and the Irin. The politics of the Flight could be toxic and, in the desire to please the Archangel, sometimes led to ugly and terrible acts. Whatever the ultimate truth was in all that was going on, I had a bad feeling that one—or both—of them were involved.

Finally, there was poor Cassiel, the dead Juvenii, killed by a Lacerate blade and mourned by my best friend Camael, who had since disappeared without a word of explanation. How and why she had been killed was still a terrible mystery, and I felt a pressing need to understand what had happened to her. Had she been involved in the theft of the Rood? If so, why? Was she some sort of idealist whose enthusiasm for a cause had been harnessed by someone with an agenda to sow discontent within the Flight and embarrass Prince Anael? Or was she more than she seemed? An intriguer or a spy? I had a feeling I would need to visit the Juvenii's enclave if I was to learn more about her. If things worked out as planned, I would get that chance soon by accompanying the bearers that took her back to her people.

I saw a squall blowing up on the horizon, and I felt the winds strengthen from that direction. It was a disturbing situation, as I had not built such weather events into my sea of tranquillity. The squall was moving towards my small vessel, rain driven before it, the water frothing and churning as it made a steady progress towards me. I leant against the mast of my sailing boat and watched as the grey mass grew larger. The boat rose and fell in the growing swell and began to take on water as whipped-up waves crashed over the prow. It was a demonstration of power, but by whom, and what did they want with me?

Chapter Seven

She came out of the storm like a dark winged goddess, wreathed in sheets of rain. Her arrival was heralded by the sudden dissipation of the storm, the wind and waves dying down as she hovered in the air above me. It was Kokael, and she was clad in sheer dark blue gauze that clung to her like a passionate lover. Long black hair laced with strands of silver and gold framed her face, a vision of imperious beauty.

"Did I frighten you, Azshael?"

"Not as such," I replied. "The water is not that deep."

"Unlike you," she said with an insouciant grin. It lit up her face and made me smile. I didn't know how she had manipulated my Sphere, and perhaps I should have been angry about that, but at that moment all I cared for was that she might like me and stay a while. She beckoned me to join her and I did, flying up to be next to her in the clearing sky above my water-laden boat.

'Let's fly together," she said, taking my hand. I know a place we can go." Her touch was soft and warm, her smile radiant and enchanting. Together, we flew toward my horizon that, were we to cross over, would take us back to where we had started in a never-ending loop. Or at least, that was what I had expected. However, as we drew nearer that borderline, I could see, in the distance, a strange multihued haze that blurred the edges of my construction. I could hardly believe what I was seeing until I remembered just how powerful Kokael was. She was a Power, possibly even a Throne Power, given her position as leader of the Irin sect, and right now, she was spending time with a lesser power like me. It was intoxicating.

She pulled me closer as we neared the boundary line of what I guessed was her own Sphere, or at least one of her making. My body pressed against hers and I felt a shiver of pure erotic ecstasy run through me. Her form was feminine perfection, curves and lines in perfect proportion. I wanted to tear the gauze shroud away, but what was the point? I could already see the majesty of the bounty of her body in stark relief, and there was something even more alluring about the way it was clad in such thin material.

She laughed as my excitement became obvious, and she flew rings around me before suddenly drawing close, face to face. She put her arms around my shoulders and drew me in for a deep, long, slow kiss that tasted of honey. I ran my hands through her black tresses as her wings wrapped around me

I will admit I was lost in the moment, and to this day I cannot recall every second of the whirlwind that was her. She was the maelstrom, the hurricane that picks you up and tosses you around on her winds. As we passed the boundary, I could see a vast forest beneath the clouds. It was wild, tangled, and untamed just like she who had created it. We headed lower, and a series of great expanses of still, dark water was revealed. Islands dotted the expanses, many with fanes and follies that reminded me of the tombs and temples of the *Pardes* – the great Garden in the old country.

Then we veered away again back over the verdant green forest that stretched as far as the eye could see. It was already perhaps ten times the size of my own Sphere, with no clear end in sight. Finally, a series of clearings came into view and Kokael swooped and dove towards them, coming in to land outside a leafy arbour fashioned from white wood. Inside was a shady alcove formed by ancient trees, filled with climbing plants that created a sylvan bower inlaid with silk and velvet. She turned her back to me and slowly removed the gauze shroud, letting it fall to her feet as she hid her wings. She laid down on the bower and beckoned me to join her.

We made love for hours, gentle exploration turning into intense intercourse. Throughout everything, she was in control, and I was her puppet as she pulled every one of my sexual strings. She mounted me at the end and rode me to the most spectacular Angelic climax I had ever known. We lay in the afterglow, and the inevitable interrogation began. Kokael's ability to charm had been a concern for me ever since she had deployed the power at our first meeting. I knew I had to find an answer when she really turned it on. It hadn't surprised me when she appeared in my Sphere, although the extent to which she was able to manipulate my construct was much greater than I had expected. I was glad she had chosen to do so in my home, however, as it allowed me to create a defence of some kind. I cannot say that it worked completely, but it did provide me with a mental resilience that allowed me to keep some level of my wits about me when her questions began.

The answer lay in my still burning love for Ischae, whose spectre was a regular presence in my living dream. It was not really her of course, just my memory of her made real, and in my own territory, it was easy to transpose Ischae's face over Kokael's. I would like to think I was honouring her memory during the lustful behaviour I had been pulled into, and I wanted to avoid betraying my dead Succae lover. The concentration required to make that happen meant the Irin leader's influence was dampened enough to stop me from drowning in her sea of charm. The task grew harder when we entered Kokael's Sphere, but by that stage, she believed she had me completely in her grip. In many ways, she did, but not completely, which allowed me some room for manoeuvre.

Kokael's questions were subtle to start with; general enquiries to my wellbeing and what I had been up to since she had seen me in Saur'Il's mausoleum. These, I answered with relative ease. I told of my journey to the Vod's court, leaving out Malacaz and Zamalca. Kokael seemed to take everything in without comment, and I had the feeling she knew much of what I was telling her already. She got more interested in the Low-Nin unrest and Karsz's response. I lied about the path that had led Lytta and I to the High-Nin, Rukoi, saying that he had been on a watch list of previous rebels and that we had found him dead. I also left out the *Yurei* attack and our subsequent journey in search of Rasnich. At this point, I thought she was on to me as her questions about what we had found grew in number, and I felt a heightening of her powers of beguilement that called to me to reveal more. It was like a snake uncoiling in my brain, slithering through my consciousness, sliding into my memory in search of its prey – the truth.

I could feel my defences failing so I changed topic and spoke in depth about Lytta. It was a distraction that worked and diverted our conversation. She was intrigued to learn of Zolorel and the house by the lake. I had a horrible sense that I was betraying the Serrate's trust, but I had not been sworn to secrecy, and it was in both our best interests. I also had the feeling that Zolorel was more than capable of looking after herself. I left out my vision, but did go into great and expansive detail on the protocols of the tea ceremony. I could see that Kokael was losing interest, and I felt that ophidian intruder in my mind slowly fade away. But as soon as I thought we were done, she was back in my head again, and this time the topics were the Lacerate and the death of Cassiel.

I felt my mouth spilling words in a torrent, just like the first time we had met. I revealed Master Zhik's revelation that it was an apprentice's work and not a true Shard Blade. I was hoping she would stop there, but she hadn't risen to lead the Irin without the ability to be an effective interrogator, and Low-Tsar Rasnich's name finally came out of my mouth. This is where things got interesting. She didn't ask anything more about him. Nothing at all. It made me think that she probably already knew all there was to know. The only thing I couldn't work out was whether that was because the Irin knew all about the Low-Tsars or whether there was a deeper connection. The way Kokael's interrogation suddenly ended left serious room for doubt.

I awoke back on the beach in my Sphere, my boat pulled up on the shore, safe, dry, and intact. I was alone and had no recollection as to how or when I had returned there. My encounter with Kokael had the quality of a waking dream, and for a moment I wondered whether it had actually happened. Then I realised my imagination was not usually that kind.

I wasn't sure how much time I had lost, but by the pale streaks of dawn light, I guessed it was the day after I had returned to the Garden side of the Tether. That meant I had two days until Cassiel's bearers were due to arrive at the Angel of Death's mausoleum, and one day more after that, I was due to meet Lytta down on the surface of Cerule. It was time to get busy.

Chapter Eight

A return to the Athenaeum was the first task on my list, so I immediately headed for the Upper Landing and the square at the centre of the White Acropolis. Soldiers were out in force, and Lamechial's Legio Alba were predominant among the forces on guard duty. They were heavily concentrated around the Temple of Excelsis and the Herald's Hall. I pulled up the hood of my cloak, keen to go incognito for as long as possible.

At the entrance to the Scriptorium, the watch was lighter, but it was clear that Lamechial had ordered every visitor, Angelic or otherwise, to be stopped for questioning. Thankfully, the scroll case with Anael's seal was enough to convince the rank-and-file soldiers on watch to let me pass without delay, but I knew the story would be different at the entrances guarded by the Legio Alba. I headed into the tranquil halls of the Scriptorium, hoping I could find Sariel at work in one of the writing cells, but other than annoying some studious Cherubs, who gave me less than welcoming glares when I interrupted their work, I came up empty. Keen to avoid further enquiry, I cut through to the enclosed cloister that connected the southern annexe to the Hall of Records and found my quarry sitting by an ornate fountain, head in a scroll whilst eating a rather plump looking piece of fruit.

"Sari! There you are,'" I said as she looked up at me expectantly.

"Well, where else did you think I would be?"

I didn't have a sensible answer to that, so I just said, "We need to talk."

Before long, we were deep in one of the Hall of Records repository vaults where Sariel had been hard at work doing inventory. It was so far away from anyone else that I was confident we could talk without the risk of being overheard.

"Have you found it yet?" Sariel looked at me impatiently.

"No, not yet" I said. "But there are some promising developments."

"Hmph," she said, giving me a doubtful look. "I know what that means."

"What do you mean?"

"I'd say you sound like a Herald, but I know it would upset you. Let's just say you have no idea, do you?"

That's Sariel – straight to the point, and it was a fair one, I suppose.

"This is important, Azsh! You must find the Rood before it falls into the wrong hands. Who knows what mischief could be made by…" she tailed off, looking for the right word.

"Mischief makers?" I volunteered.

"Exactly!"

"Then perhaps you'll help me with some information, and I can get right back on the trail." Sariel looked happy at that response. "Alright then, Azsh. What do you need?"

I talked about the death of Cassiel of the Juvenii and Cam's odd reaction as Sariel shifted uncomfortably on her seat.

"You and Cam go back a long way. Do you know any reason why he would react in such a manner?" She did not respond straight away. I could tell she was working out what to say and choosing her words carefully. For a professional keeper of knowledge, it obviously went against the grain to deceive or withhold information. It was quite sweet really.

"Oh well," she said finally. "I suppose it's not really a secret. Cam spent some time as one of the Juvenii's guardians. He lived for several years on their island after he was wounded in the war."

"I never knew that," I said. I also didn't remember Cam being wounded, but to be fair we had only seen each other intermittently during the conflict.

"So, he would have known Cassiel then?"

"You'd have to ask him. Maybe." I suspected Sariel was not telling me everything, so maybe I was wrong about her reticence to not splurge out the truth.

I decided to change tack. "What do you know about Vasariah and Kokael?"

"Those are very important people. Why do you want to know about them?"

"They have come up in my enquiries," I said nonchalantly.

"Oh really?" she said in a sarcastic tone.

"You know Vasariah has gone missing?"

"When?"

"It's not common knowledge. I just overheard one of Lamechial's captains talking about it. He was meant to be staying in his Sphere after being dismissed from the Trinity, but when he was sent for yesterday, he didn't respond. A Herald was sent to speak with him, but he wasn't there. There's a lot of talk about him being involved in the theft of the Rood, but I don't see how that's possible. He was with the Prince at the height of the unrest. I saw him and his Honores myself."

"I agree. I can't see how the leader of the Honores would benefit."

"Unless there's something we don't know, of course."

"Is there something on that score I should be aware of?"

Sari shrugged. "I don't know, Azsh. I was just saying."

"If you do hear anything, you will tell me, won't you?

"Probably," she said with a mischievous grin.

Things I wasn't aware of was quite a large topic, and it returned Kokael's interrogation and Saur'Il's warning about her to the front of my mind.

"Have you heard anything about unrest at the Trinity?"

"Before this, you mean?"

Sari thought for a moment. "Well, there were rumours that Anael was quite angry with both the Irin and the Honores after all that business with Benazzarr. I heard that both Vasariah and the Irin leader's positions were under review. In the immediate aftermath, anyway."

"Do you think these rumours were true?"

"Well, Darophon came and had words with Narinel about it all. We were all told that there was nothing to it, and any references in the rolls were to be removed. So it must be true. We only do that when the Prince says something that shouldn't have been recorded." I raised an eyebrow at Sariel's candour, although on reflection I don't know why. I had long guessed that the Flight's official records of the past were sanitised versions of the truth.

"Is there any chance you could find out what was written in the rolls before they were... corrected?"

She shook her head. "Not when it comes to the Prince, no. However, if it's just a precis you want, I may be able to find an archivist who saw the original reports."

I wasn't sure I liked the idea that Sariel's enquiries could get back to Narinel and get her into hot water on my behalf, so I told her not to go to any trouble. The idea that both Vasariah and Kokael had come in for criticism was an interesting new development, though. The guardian of Trinity Palace had a lot to lose, but Kokael had even more at stake as the leader of one of the Flight's most powerful sects. I was reminded again that the desire to please the Archangel sometimes led to questionable decisions, but, just like Vasariah, I struggled to see how Kokael could profit from the theft of the Rood. If anything, it had made her situation even more precarious. It just didn't make sense to me, although I now understood why she had emerged from the shadows to take such a personal interest in the ongoing search for answers.

"How much do you know about the Juvenii?"

"Not much. I think they are an odd bunch."

"Well, that explains why Camael went to be among them. He's pretty odd himself."

Sariel laughed, but it was short lived. "I think he went there because his soul was hurting," she said after a long moment of silent reflection. "From what I have heard, their island is a sanctuary of peace and tranquillity."

"I have heard that their kind may be more than they seem."

"That's an old rumour, Azsh. Old Flight hearsay. No one believes that anymore." Except for the Angel of Death, I thought.

"Yet one of their kind was found dead after the unrest, and I have yet to find out why."

"Dead? How?"

"Murdered with a Succae blade." I shared what I knew of Cassiel's death, and Sariel listened intently.

"So, it was the Succae who killed her?"

"Not necessarily. The weapon was made by the Succae, but anyone could have wielded it."

"I can see now why you were talking about those old Juvenii stories," she said.

"What exactly are these tales? I never knew much about them before now."

"Oh, across the ages, there have been various rumours that they are not really the naïve innocents they are made out to be. However, there's never been any real evidence that they aren't, so I have always thought it was just idle talk."

"What do people think they are then?" I thought back to Saur'Il's revelations about the evidence that Cassiel had trained with weapons.

"Spies, essentially, but ones who could be denied, as they are not actually members of the Flight."

"Surely an Angel is an Angel!"

"True. The most ominous of the rumours were that they were meant to spy on the Flight itself. Like the Irin and their witch of a leader."

"What have you got against Kokael?"

"I wouldn't trust her as far as I could throw her. She's devious and cunning, and I don't think she cares about anyone who isn't one of her own."

I felt an instinctive need to defend Kokael, but thought better of it. Frankly, Sariel was probably right.

"Do you believe those tales?

"Not entirely. Yet there's one thing I do know about the Flight. Everyone serves and everyone gets used, one way or another. I expect the Juvenii are not exempt."

It was a cynical view but hard to argue with. I decided to move on to a different topic.

"Do you know if the Thrones fully charted Cerule and its moons before we built the Garden shell?"

"That's an odd question to ask! What do you mean 'moons'? There's only one moon. Well, come to think of it, there are two but the other one is dead and frozen."

"Are we sure?"

"Well yes. Why do you ask?"

"I had a strange vision when I was down the Tether. It suggested there were four moons in total."

"How odd. I only know of two, but you can look through the Throne Pilot's charts if you like. They are on display in Registry Hall."

Sariel led me to the heart of the Scriptorium, which was quieter than the last time I had been there. Academic calm had been restored now Lamechial and his troops had left the building. Registry Hall was a library and administration hub that was open to the Flight and the Bonded. Long reading tables were available where visitors could spend as long as they liked in quite consultation of the vast number of scrolls, books, and tablets that Narinel and his archivists curated.

On this day, it was almost empty, and Sariel led me to the Archivist's Seat at the end of the Hall. Banners hung to the left and right of a wooden throne that was flanked by three seats on both sides for the Archivist's Council, which met occasionally when matters of protocol, law and proclamations from the Prince needed to be debated. Narinel and his council, usually selected from among the lesser Heralds had little actual power. It was their task to ensure the accurate and effective dissemination of information sent from the Herald's Hall, who, in turn, received the Archangel's commands from the Archangel's Privy Council, led by Darophon, the Herald Prime.

Secured under glass in a rectangular display cabinet was the Pilot's map of the planet Cerule and the wider celestial array within which it lay. Sure enough, there were two moons marked on the map, which had been drawn long before Karsz and his people had abandoned the planet itself for its satellite moon. Scarpe, the moon they had retreated to, was clearly far larger than the dead and frozen one that sat slightly higher in the planet's orbit. I thought back to my waking dream and realised it was not accurate. In my vision, the order of the moons was reversed, like looking at a reflection. The evidence seemed to suggest that this had been the product of an overactive imagination rather than a genuinely prophetic vision. I felt a bit stupid until Sariel said, "This is interesting." She pointed to two small red clusters of three red dots that were faded and barely visible. "I wonder what that means."

I was about to ask Sariel to make some enquiries when the sound of voices came from the entrance lobby, one of which I immediately recognised. It was Darophon, and he was flanked by two guests who I immediately recognised—the leaders of the Bonded, Charomos and Aethi.

Charomos was tall, dressed in white robes fringed with grey bands. On his head, he wore a headdress that framed a stern but handsome face with deep grey eyes that evoked a sense of deep-set wisdom. To his right stood Aethi, a beautiful female in a flowing green dress that hugged a statuesque form. Long golden locks, tinged with russet flecks, flowed over her alabaster skin, and wide green eyes drew you in to a high cheek-boned face and a smile that was warm and welcoming. Copper bracers fashioned as snakes coiled around her arms and legs, and spoke of the field and the earth. Both bore golden staffs that were as tall as they were. His was crowned with a set of scales, whilst hers was topped off by a stylised Bull's head.

"Ambassador Azshael," Darophon said in his warm, resonant tone, "what an unexpected surprise."

"Likewise, Herald Prime. I was just catching up with Sariel after a command from the Prince relating to the Red Roof Inn in the Lower Landing."

"Yes," Darophon said. "I understand you have made it a Flight embassy now. I am surprised you didn't think of that before, given the amount of time you spend there."

I smarted slightly. How Darophon managed to know everything so swiftly, I had no idea. All I could think was that he spent every spare minute reading reports.

"Any news from our friends on the other side of the Tether?"

"There are some promising leads but nothing solid so far." Darophon nodded and didn't push me, although I was certain that had we been alone, I wouldn't have got off so lightly.

"So, this is the Ambassador to the Succae," Charomos said. He sounded avuncular with a warm smile that was immediately engaging. It was a surprising contrast to his initially cold demeanour.

"I hope Malacaz hasn't caused you too much trouble?"

"Malacaz?" I said, feigning ignorance.

"Yes, the trickster Malacaz. I understand he was in your company a couple of days ago?" Darophon's face betrayed nothing, but his eyes narrowed. Clearly this was one report that hadn't got back to him.

"Oh, yes. He was among a group of rogues that were causing trouble at the Red Roof Inn. I had a word with them and then Lamechial and his soldiers burst in and arrested them."

"Really?" Charomos said with a thin smile. "Malacaz evaded captivity, so I thought he had perhaps sought your protection?"

"He said something about that," I said evenly. "I told him to look elsewhere."

Charomos shrugged and turned to Aethi. "I suppose we were misled then, my dear. Forgive me, Ambassador. We had received reports that Malacaz was seen on the Succae moon in your company, then vanished, and is now being hunted by their forces." I didn't know what Charomos's game was or how he had come by his information, but I had cast my die and had no choice but to perpetuate the lie.

"There is a hunt taking place, but not for some stray and inconsequential rogue. I would counsel you not to listen to rumours. However, I can understand your concern. He betrayed you, didn't he? Led us right to you and forced your abdication to be Bonded under Judgment?"

Charomos didn't rise to the bait, but I saw Aethi's smile disappear. I could also tell that Darophon was unimpressed with my less than diplomatic needling of the leader of the Primogi.

"You're right of course, Ambassador," Charomos said with a rueful look on his face. "I was only going to say that I would be careful if I were you. A trickster denied can be a dangerous enemy, as I found out to my cost."

I said nothing as Charomos gazed at me for an uncomfortably long time. I stared right back at him. Then Darophon broke the silence and steered his guests back into the Hall. Charomos smiled and took Aethi by the hand, nodding at me in a gesture of respect.

"What was all that about?" Sariel said after we were left alone in Registry Hall again.

"I really don't know," I said, but I was suddenly suspicious of the former god of justice and his earth goddess paramour. I had no idea what our exchange had meant, but I was sure it had been a deliberate power play in front of the Herald Prime.

Chapter Nine

I left Sariel at the Scriptorium, having asked her to find out more about the notations on the Pilot's map and to send word to the Red Roof as and when she had answers. I had to admit the encounter with Charomos had left me feeling unsettled. It was true he had a connection to Malacaz, but I had thought that tie would have been long severed by the rogue's betrayal of his master. Charomos had surrendered to judgment without fear or resistance, and now I wondered why? In the usual arrogance of the Flight, it had no doubt been assumed that he had been intimidated into surrender, but that might not have been the real reason for his enthusiastic embrace of the wisdom of Excelsis. Some gods were pragmatists and surrendered because they realised the odds of survival and a successful resistance were slim. Others chose the same path with no intention of honouring their Bonded pact. These rare deities were devious and cunning, believing it was only a matter of time before they could escape and tread a path back to glory. Could Charomos have been playing the long game? If so, what was it, and could his former nemesis, Malacaz, who had played the part of his apparent betrayer be involved? I didn't like the thoughts that were suddenly running around my head.

I decided to check in on my friends from the Inn and headed across the Athenaeum to the Temple of Excelsis. Here, I spent a good hour being irritated by the indolent intractability of the Legio Alba, who refused to allow me to enter the Temple's underground gaol. Most galling was their refusal to take the Prince's seal as proof of a warrant of passage. I could feel myself getting angry, so it was most timely when Captain Galaeal came to my rescue.

"Ambassador Azshael," he said, giving the winged meatheads I had been arguing with a reproving look. "I am sorry you have been delayed. How can the Legio be of service?" I was about to say the Legio could fly face first into a mountainside, but I managed to stop myself.

"I would like to check on my embassy staff, Captain. Given their status, they should be liberated and restored to the Red Roof immediately." Galaeal gave me a look that told me I was overplaying a weak hand.

"You have a release warrant for these individuals I presume?" I didn't, of course, but it was worth a try. I muttered something about paperwork being in progress.

"I would need warrants to release them," he said, "but I see no problem with you visiting them in the cells."

The two dum-dums looked at the Captain as if to say he was overstepping his authority and stayed stock still. "We were told no admissions except on the Commander's own authority," meathead one said. Galaeal lent in close and said in a low, menacing tone, "I am the Commander's authority. I hear Vigil Keep is exceptionally remote, cold, and dull presently, but desperately in need of more extra vigilant guards. Perhaps you would like me to use my authority to send you both there?"

Meathead one and two looked at each other and stepped out of the way.

The Temple to Excelsis was a surprisingly simple affair. On ground level, it was an open space with a sunken grotto at the centre, within which seven Spheres could be accessed. These were devotional spaces and reminders of the Golden City. Before the war, Excelsis's temple had been a busy place, but since the armistice, it had grown quieter, and the ceremonial fires that used to burn bright in their braziers were allowed to burn low before being stoked back into life. It seemed to me that the inertia of the situation we had found ourselves in, stuck in an existential dilemma, meant that many members of the Flight did not want to be reminded of our home and past glories.

That dilemma also went to the heart of a wider question. Was Excelsis itself a power worth following at all? Given that many

Angels had died in its name during Duma's Rebellion against Excelsis's rule, it was a topic bound to set off passionate debate on both sides of the argument. In the end, we followed the Heralds, who followed Darophon, who obviously still believed in the Anael's leadership. It was a discipline that had endured since the armistice, but every now and then, you could feel it waver as prolonged indecision gradually ate away at our certainty in the rightness and morality of our mission. I didn't pretend to have any answers, and I didn't envy our Prince the burden of command, but sooner or later, he would have to decide our onward path, and the day of reckoning would come for us all.

I followed Galaeal past the grotto and into the rear of the Temple, where the entrance to its subterranean heart was guarded by more of the Albans. These seemed to be more respectful of the Captain's command and immediately allowed us to head down wide white steps made of stone. Torchlight flickered in the dark passages we followed for a short time before arriving at more steps that led down to a wide cavern with gates that led to the temple gaol.

On the other side, cells were packed with those the Legio had detained. I recognised various faces of the Bonded who lived in the same district as the Red Roof Inn. The area attracted former deities and demigods who had surrendered to judgment at one time or another. Most now lived quiet lives, restored to a purpose in keeping with their roles within the cultures that had once worshipped them. There were gods of the elements that shaped water, air, earth, and fire for practical and decorative purposes. There were also gods of different trades; potters, weavers, masons, gamblers, smiths, and more, whose blessings and craftsmanship were still sought after. They had all been stripped of their powers, so what remained was of no threat to the Flight. Or that was the idea, anyway. They all looked out at me with sad and sullen faces from behind the bars of the cells they were caged in. I guessed many of them had perhaps forgotten that they were captives, and it was only now they truly understood what being Bonded really meant. All in all, it was a depressing sight.

I found Ysabeau languishing in a cell with a large older woman whose short spiky black hair stood up on end as if she had just come in from a lightning storm. She wore a dark green shroud decorated with jet and emeralds whose facets sparkled in the torchlight.

"Azsh!" Ysabeau leapt to her feet. "Look, mother! It's Azshael." I was slightly taken aback. Ysabeau's mother was not actually her mother. More, they had formed a familial relationship in self-interest. Mother ate souls to maintain her existence and Ysabeau needed to dip her hair in their blood to survive. It had been a murderous trade, marked by Ysabeau's beguiling beauty and the golden voice of a landlocked siren. I had never seen Mother in any other form than her real one; a ten-foot-long emerald spider that wove strings for the various instruments her 'daughter' played like a virtuoso.

"Have you come to get us out?" Ysabeau said, her red tresses looking duller than I had seen them in some time.

"I'm working on it, Ys, but no, not yet. I just wanted to check in on you all and make sure you are alright." Ysabeau related a familiar tale of rude treatment by Lamechial's Legion. and that a very brief interrogation had been undertaken. I am, of course, paraphrasing; when Ysabeau gets going it's hard to get her to stop, so it was a good few minutes before she ran out of steam. In that time, I looked around for the Hyenae, but saw no sign of them. Once Ys had finished her tale of outrageous treatment, I asked where they were.

"They were taken beyond the iron gates a day ago," she said, pointing deeper into the gaol complex. I thanked her and headed that direction, assuring her I was working to get them all released as soon as I could. That probably meant a few more days at least, but that was likely the best I could do. I expected the Prince would keep the more powerful of the Bonded locked down until the Rood was returned.

The Iron gates to the deeper prison were guarded by ten of the Legio's larger specimens, but Captain Galaeal once again proved invaluable in getting me past them. On the other side, the atmosphere was oppressive, and I could feel a brooding malice radiate from those held behind these thicker bars. I found the Hyenae fast asleep but in separate cells. Mama Feast's snoring could be heard from dozens of paces away, whilst Papa Famine whimpered as he seemed to convulse in his slumber. I thought about leaving them be, but I had come this far, and it was only right that they knew I was doing what I could to speed their release. I opted to wake Papa first and tapped gently on his cell door. One dark brown eye opened, and then he was on his paws as if he had been awake all the time. "Azshael!" he exclaimed, and I looked over at Mama, expecting her to also come alive. However, the matriarch of a thousand tribes of snickering, slavering, murderous pups snored away, blissfully unaware. No doubt lost in a dream of the time she and her subservient mate had ruled the fates of many.

"Is Sylvenell alright? I heard they were going to burn the Inn down!"

I reassured Papa and brought him up to date with recent events. He looked relieved at the news of Syl's safety and the Inn's newfound protected status.

"Mama t'inks if it weren't for them bad folk being under the Red Roof when the soldiers done come, we wouldn't be here now." I thought about disabusing Papa of that notion, as I really didn't think it would have made any difference, but decided against it.

"All this time, that wolf been licking his lips like he swallowed an antelope whole."

I looked over my shoulder towards the back of the heftily reinforced prison cell, and saw a pair of familiar dull, yellow eyes alive in the dark staring back at me. It was Marok the Wolf, one of Malacaz's erstwhile companions. I looked around for the others who had been in the Inn with him a few days ago, but I couldn't see them. After promising Papa I would work to get him and his wife released as quickly as I could, I decided to visit the wolf in his den.

Marok yawned as I approached his cell, but then stood up and dusted himself down. "Well, if it isn't the Angel of the Inn. Come to gloat at the fate of an old wolf, have you?"

"Not really Marok. I just wanted to make sure you were alright."

Marok laughed, a deep rumble that sounded sarcastic at its tail.

"I don't do well in small spaces, but your kind already knew that."

"Perhaps I could do something about that, Master Wolf. If you are willing to help me."

Marok eyed me cautiously. "Help you? What do you think I can do to aid someone like you?"

"I suspect it won't surprise you to know that Malacaz has gone missing?"

Marok chuckled. "Feeling used, are you, Ambassador?"

"No more than you," I said evenly. "Malacaz isn't behind bars, is he? That's you and the others, isn't it?

Marok looked away, and I knew I had hit a nerve. The thought had been banging away in the back of my head that Malacaz was not a leader type, but Marok very much was. He was also an animal shape changer, same as Virdae, the carrion queen and Flynx, the fox spirit. I wondered now if Malacaz had bent one to his service and got the others as well.

"I was sorry about what happened to Virdae."

"You didn't know her!" Marok growled in anger.

"No, I didn't, but I also didn't like what happened to her, and if I could have stopped it, I would have done so." Suddenly Marok looked his age. Ancient and tired. "It's too late now," he said in a hushed tone. "She's gone."

"What about the others? Where are they?" The old wolf shrugged and walked away from the bars. "I don't know, Angel. That's your business."

I let him wallow in his anger and misery for a moment as I thought about what had happened at the Inn. Would I have been so ready to help a trickster if Virdae's death hadn't happened? I suspected not. I had got carried away in the moment and made a poor decision. That made me wonder if Malacaz had, in some way, influenced that moment. Had he banked on me making the choice I had, given appropriate motivation? It was a big gamble on Malacaz's part, but my disdain for other members of the Flight wasn't exactly a big secret. It was a very trickster thing to do, and just the sort of crazy plan he probably believed he could pull off.

"What did he promise you and the others, Marok?"

Marok folded his arms and shook his head, but said nothing. "Something about big changes where you would be treated with more respect perhaps? A new way of life under a different leader?"

The old wolfman shifted uncomfortably, and I knew I was on the right track.

"What did he tell you? Who was he working for? Was it another Angel?"

Marok came back to the bars and was about to say something when a strange noise came from his mouth. I was about to ask him to repeat himself when I saw the tip of a thin blade emerge from his throat. His last word died with him at that moment, and then Kaualakoo was on me.

Marok's body slumped forward and slid down the bars of the cage. His assassin was inside the cell and thrust two long, thin daggers through the bars at my face. I just managed to spin away from the first one and brought my left hand to up to block the second. It pierced flesh and went straight through before he twisted the blade and yanked it back toward him, pulling my impaled hand with it. I could hear shouts behind me as Galaeal called his guards to come to my assistance.

Calling Nimrod to take the shape of a mace, I blazed with a flash of bright light, pulled my impaled hand back toward me and swung the mace down in a heavy blow on the exposed haft of the assassin's weapon. It did the trick, breaking the dagger blade away from the handle and ending a potentially deadly and extremely painful tug of war. I leapt back from the cell bars and scoured the dark shadows of the interior in search of my attacker as Galaeal arrived at my side, closely followed by Legio guardsmen armed with shields and spears. Galaeal moved to unlock the cell doors, but I told him to wait. "He's in the cell now," I said. "Let's not give him an opening to evade us."

Galaeal nodded and turned to his guards. "Fetch light. Let's banish all the shadows in there and give our quarry no place to hide."

No sooner had the command been given than Kaualakoo smashed into the cell door with an almighty crash. The bars held, although dust fell from the walls into which they were embedded as shadows coalesced around Kaualakoo, and he vanished again. Galaeal ordered me to get behind him as he and his soldiers locked shields and levelled their bright and shiny spears in his direction.

"Surrender, assassin!" Galaeal called out. "Or die!"

There was no immediate response as Legio guards used their

auras to bathe the cell in radiant light to reveal Marok's killer hiding in the ceiling space. He was desperately trying to hack a hole above himself, but his efforts were too little too late.

"Give it up, Kaualakoo!" I said, "there's nowhere for you to go." As the Legio moved in, he dropped to the floor and threw down his bandolier of blades. Galaeal unlocked the cage as Angels closed in on him from all sides. It was then a blade leapt into his hand from somewhere hidden in his sleeve, and without a second thought he stabbed it straight through his own left eye. He shuddered for a moment, then fell forward to lie motionless on the cell floor.

We all took a breath, not quite believing what had just happened. I was stunned that Kaualakoo would kill himself rather than be captured. What secrets were he and Marok keeping, and on whose behalf? Galaeal moved to the motionless assassin's side, and as he did so, I recalled that the trickster was also a demigod and a master of deception and death. I was about to call out a warning when the dead suddenly came to life and buried two blades straight into Galaeal's chest. It happened so fast the poor captain was completely taken by surprise. He staggered backwards as Kaualakoo leapt vertically and came down among the surprised guards, sweeping through them like a small tornado. I saw holes punched through wings, faces slashed and vicious kicks that sent Angels sprawling. He was through the cell door and into the passageway as I commanded Nimrod to take the shape of a javelin. It transformed in a split second, and I hurled it with all my might down the central passageway after him. However, it hit nothing but the wall at the turn of the passage and clattered to the floor. I called it back to my hand and charged up the stairs with Galaeal's guards in tow, but Kaualakoo was gone or had hidden himself back in some shadowy spot. I returned to Galaeal's side as more Albans were called from the Iron Gates to assist in the search. He stared up at me with open eyes whose light had been forever dimmed.

A while later, Lamechial stood over his dead captain's body, his fists clenching and unclenching in a display of contained anger.

"Who did this?" he said quietly. Legio troops stood nearby, but I knew his words were meant only for me.

"His name is Kaualakoo. He is one of the Bonded. A rogue who was once a god of assassins."

"If he was Bonded, how did he still possess such deadly powers?" It was a good point and something I had also been mulling over. The Bonding process was meant to deny the subject of most of their powers, but that, of course, was relative. On balance, I had to agree with Lamechial that the assassin's abilities were surprisingly potent for one of the Bonded.

"Find him, and if he is still in these halls, bring him to me alive, if possible," the Commander said, turning to his troops. "However, take no risks and if you encounter resistance, kill him." Over the next few hours, light was brought to every place of shadow to flush Kaualakoo from hiding. I assisted in the search, but I had the feeling it was an exercise in futility. The rogue was gone, at least for now, but the questions remained. Who was he working for, and what secrets were they protecting? I had a feeling the answers lay on the surface of the dying planet below. First on an island of innocents and then in the dead city of Khrov. There were enough questions. It was now time for answers.

Part Four

Chapter One

I had a matter of hours in hand before I was due to head to the Mausoleum and rendezvous with the Juvenii party sent to take Cassiel's body home. However, Lamechial's observations about Kaualakoo's apparently undiminished powers were weighing heavily on my mind. It made me wonder what the limitations of being Bonded were, and why we hadn't seen such behaviours before? There was also the issue of Marok being silenced by one of his own, although that assumption seemed now to be on shaky foundations. I had a growing suspicion that Marok might have been the odd one out in that gang of thieves for whom honour and loyalty were nebulous concepts that could change with the wind and the tide.

I decided to call on Sariel's help once more and returned to the Scriptorium in search of my favourite Cherub. I found her exactly where I had left her in the Registry Hall, where she was lying on top of the celestial map cabinet, surrounded by scrolls and books. I could see she was sketching her own smaller map based on the much larger pilot's map and then checking on other scrolls around her that she had secured in place with golden inkpots.

"Have you found it yet?" she asked without looking up as I entered the Hall.

"No," I said. "And you constantly asking me won't make me find it any sooner."

"What about your promising leads?"

"They're still promising. Just waiting for me to get to them is all."

"Oh, I see," she said, and was about to go on when she looked up and saw the grim look on my face. "What's wrong?"

"Captain Galaeal is dead," I said, and the last word caught in my throat.

"Dead? How?"

"He was killed in the Temple gaol by an assassin who should have been under lock and key. I need your help, Sariel."

Soon we were gathered in the middle of four long reading tables I had pushed together whilst Sariel had headed off to the vaults and roped in five more Cherubs to help gather records on the group of rogues that had caused Ysabeau such distress on that cold, fateful afternoon in the Red Roof Inn.

"What are we looking for, Azsh?" Sariel said as various reports, scrolls, books, and tablets arrived at our tables.

"I'm not sure. Anything odd. Any connections between them all and any known associates."

Sariel nodded and briefed her other archivists to separate the stacks by individual. Before long, we had a pile each for Flynx, Kaualakoo, Malacaz, Marok, and Virdae. I also asked Sariel to check for records on Zamalca and the two Primogi, Charomos and Aethi.

Valuable time ticked past in the digestion of dense reports that on an initial look, told me nothing new. Then Sariel made a breakthrough.

"He's a Traveller!" she exclaimed.

"Who is?"

"Kaualakoo," she said, handing me a scroll. The contents were a report on the demigod of assassins written by the Irin when he had surrendered to be Bonded. It had long been assumed that the process of judgement was infallible, but the Flight sometimes encountered entities in different places who we thought we had already defeated. Consciously or unconsciously, these deities existed in multiple universes living multiple lives, but at their core they were one and the same. There were always other places, either to escape to or exist in as long as they had worshippers willing to sacrifice for them. The evidence that Malacaz had been involved in Scharo's rebellion in a world different from his own and now Kaualakoo's status as a Traveller opened a new set of possibilities, as did the fact that the report came from the Irin.

"I didn't know the Irin were responsible for Bonding."

"They don't facilitate the process," Sariel said, "but they do talk to every fallen power that becomes Bonded. The High Watcher and the Irin's leader are responsible for documenting any potential threat to the Flight."

"Potential threat? I thought the whole point of Bonding was to curtail their powers."

"It is! I think the fact-finding is to prepare for future encounters with a splinter of that power."

For the rest of the day, Sariel and her team pored over documents looking for more connections, but as shadows lengthened and lamps were lit, further leads seemed elusive. Marok, Virdae, and Flynx seemed to be a group unto themselves and there was no evidence that they were Travellers, but Marok had a connection to the goddess Aethi, and she in turn had been identified as a preserver of nature and protector of the earth in the various pantheons we had encountered. Aethi's nature had been passive and unthreatening so records on her were sparse, but she was another Traveller. I was beginning to think we were homing in on something, but what it all meant, I wasn't sure. Had Aethi somehow got Marok involved with Charomos's trickster? If so, for what purpose, and was the jaded god of justice involved? I was missing parts of the puzzle, and an overall picture was still to come into focus.

Sari agreed to continue searching the records with her team as I prepared to depart, and she walked with me back to the Athenaeum square.

"Oh, by the way, I found out what those annotations on the pilot's map were."

"You did? What do they mean?"

"They are what's called energy anomalies."

"Anomalies?"

"Yes. Things that were detected on arrival and marked for later examination."

"What kind of things?"

"No one knows. That's why they are anomalies. They are oddities in space and time that need further exploration. It's just that no-one has explored them yet."

"Is anyone going to?"

"It's a Privy Council matter. I suspect the war kind of got in the way and everyone forgot about them."

"So, there could be hidden satellites then?"

"Hmm. I'm not so sure about that, Azsh. I think the Powers would have seen them during the construction of the Horta Magna. It's more likely they are debris fields, asteroids, gravity wells or some such. There are a lot of things that count as anomalies."

"Can you raise it with Narinel?"

"Do I have to?"

"I just have a bad feeling about this."

"Alright. I'll mention it, but I doubt Narinel will think it's a pressing matter."

That's because he hadn't seen what I had seen - thousands of hungry ghosts falling from space.

Chapter Two

It was late in the afternoon when I arrived at the House of Saur'll. The gardens surrounding the Mausoleum were still sparkling with ice and the chill winds only added to the building's unwelcoming and brooding presence.

In the gardens below, I could see a group surrounding the statue of the Herald Chorael, the first casualty in the war with the Succae. His history was one to divide opinions. To Flight loyalists, he was a fearless and loyal supporter of the Prince who had sought an accommodation with the Succae and had died a valiant death trying to deliver them to judgment. To my mind, Chorael was like many of the Heralds, an arrogant fool who had been stupid enough to demand the Succae surrender without any attempt to understand them or negotiate. In return, the Succae had sent back their answer in the form of his severed head. I suppose that however you looked at it, his was a tragic and pointless death, but the fact that he had become a mournful symbol of some supposedly heroic act generally turned my stomach. Like most Heralds, he had been a scheming politician who had sensed a chance for recognition and advancement, and his hubris had caused his stupid head to be separated from his stupid body.

I came in to land in the frozen garden at a respectful distance from the group, who were wearing long grey and white hooded robes. They were taking turns to lay small wreaths made of bright flowers at the base of the statue, where a white feather had been placed in a devotional gold bowl at the bottom of the plinth, each of them kneeling in turn and saying quiet words of prayer as the tributes were placed. I guessed these had to be the Juvenii bearers, and they were saying words for Cassiel.

I was about to join them when I heard a whistle coming from the steps of the Mausoleum. I looked over and saw a tall, slender figure also dressed in grey robes, face hidden by their hood. But I immediately knew who it was. In their right hand, I saw the red spear named Revelation. At their belt, a golden sickle, and beneath the hood, amber eyes sparked with a warm glow.

"Pell!" I said with surprise and no little warmth and enthusiasm as I flew to her side. The young faces of the Juvenii turned to look at us, but Pell turned away and walked inside the shadows of the colonnade.

"It's Pellandriel to you, Ambassador," she said quietly as I walked behind her into Saur'Il's hall. I could tell our friendship had cooled.

"I haven't seen you for some time. Where have you been, Pell?"

Pellandriel pulled down her hood, and where long copper tresses had crowned a face of exquisite beauty, now only a shaved head and gaunt visage greeted me. It was a shock, and I could see my surprise had been noted.

"Where do you think?" she said, looking over at the Juvenii. "Thanks to you, I have been in exile."

Until quite recently, Pellandriel had been a power and probably the highest ranked female in the Flight. She had saved me from assassination and bought me valuable time to intervene in the cabal's plans to wreck the armistice and poison the Succae's Vod, Karsz. It had come at a price and cost her both her position and influence, even though I had appealed directly to Darophon at the time. I now thought I knew where she had been since the Privy Council had stripped her of rank and status as guardian of the Sky Gate, our only way back to Excelsis and the Golden City.

I reached for her to offer a comforting embrace, but she shrank away, looking annoyed. "Stop it, Azsh," she said. "I don't need or want your pity." Given we had once been lovers, albeit many years ago, I felt the cold winds of rejection keenly and self-consciously stepped away from her, wrapping myself in my wings. She turned away from me and looked back out at the frozen garden where the Juvenii were finishing the process of paying their respects.

"For Cassiel, I suppose?" I said, trying to fill an uncomfortable silence.

Pell nodded and said nothing straight away. Then she spoke up. "We should have been gone from this place hours ago, but the Angel of Death insisted the proper protocols were observed before we left." I silently thanked Saur'll for finding a way to keep his word and delay the bearer party until my arrival.

"What are you doing here anyway?" she said, and I knew I would need to tread carefully to avoid sinking any deeper in Pell's estimation. "I am bound by the Prince's command. Cassiel's death was no accident."

"I didn't think it was," Pell said sharply. "Murder is never an accident, unless it was a case of mistaken identity, and they killed the wrong Angel?" Pell let that thought hang there, but I said nothing in response as the winds changed direction and whipped our cloaks around us.

"I presume Anael has you running around with the Succae?"

"Yes. Something like that. Pell, I would like to return with you to the Juvenii enclave."

"Whatever for?"

"I need to understand their ways. I agree with you that Cassiel's death was obviously no accident, but I have reasons to believe she was no innocent either."

"What do you mean by that?"

"I mean, her body was found in the Lower Landing, and there is evidence she may have been more than she seemed to be."

I could feel the frost between us grow even colder.

"You have the Prince's warrant to travel to the Juvenii island?"

"I do," I said, slightly bending the truth of the seal I was carrying.

"Then I suppose we can't stop you, but I can tell you now, you're chasing feathers. Cassiel was no spy or intriguer. I don't know why she went to the Landing, but I think she was probably murdered by the Succae for seeing something she shouldn't have."

I wanted to correct the assumption that it had been a Succae who had killed her, but I bit my tongue as I had no actual proof. Just a growing suspicion that the Lacerate blade had been used deliberately to point the finger at them. As for the idea that she had been silenced as a witness to something she shouldn't have seen, given Marok's recent assassination, it certainly couldn't be ruled out. Someone was cleaning up a messy trail and perhaps it had started with our unfortunate Juvenii.

"It is a possibility I am open to," I said.

"Are you investigating her death?"

"That is not my mission, Pell, but I will do what I can to get to the truth."

I saw a strange look cross Pell's face, but it was there and gone in a flash and I didn't know what to make of it. She called her Juvenii charges in from the garden and didn't say another word.

Chapter Three

We flew through space together, falling from the Horta Magna like a cascade of silver tears. Many of those had been shed as Cassiel's body was presented to her bearers by Saur'Il, prior to being wrapped and bound by the Mausoleum's Keepers in the white shroud that would be the last raiment she would ever wear. I will confess that some of those tears were mine as I watched Pellandriel hold Cassiel in her arms and whisper soft words of sorrow and regret. It was clear, from the sorrow of the Juvenii who had come to take her to her resting place, that Cassiel had been a popular and valued member of their community, and the pain of her sudden death was raw and real.

As we descended, with Pell in the lead and the young bearers tightly packed in a flight group, each with a hand on the silver coffin in which Cassiel's body had been placed, I followed in train. As we travelled the relatively short distance into the planet's atmosphere, I found myself trying to see any sign of the hidden moons that still haunted me. For a moment I thought I could see a swirling darkness in the distance beyond the Succae moon. It was almost as though there was something blacker than the darkness of space itself there, but the more I stared at it, the more I was convinced that it was my imagination playing tricks on me.

Looking away to the planet below, I could see the signs of the massive storms rolling across the surface, no doubt leaving terrible destruction in their wake. There were also signs of magma leaking into the oceans as the planet literally bled from its core. I had no idea how long Cerule would take to die, but the process had clearly begun and was beginning to show an acceleration and steady decline.

Pell was our pilot, and she raised her hand to halt our progression. She had planned to take a direct trajectory and make entry above the

Juvenii island enclave, but a fast-moving tropical storm gave her cause to wait. The depression looked to be on a direct course for island landfall, but as we watched, it lost momentum and separated into a group of three smaller storms that then raced away from each other.

Darkness gave way to light as we passed into Cerule's atmosphere, and we were immediately drenched in warm rain and enveloped in thick clouds. Strong winds buffeted us as we passed through the clouds and into a vivid azure blue seascape that was translucent and teeming with aquatic life.

In the distance, I could see not one but a chain of six tropical islands of varying shape and size come into sight. A haze hung over them, and I recognised that the same Throne wards that protected the Horta Magna had also been deployed here. The largest island was at the centre of the group, and was maybe fifty miles long and around twenty miles in diameter at its widest point. The others spread out around the central isle in a semi-circle and were substantially smaller, varying from about half that size to just a few miles in length and width with varying levels of vegetation and cover. The most verdant island looked like it sat a few miles outside the protective aura, and I could see it was still taking shape, the waters on its western side steaming and bubbling as magma leaking from below was now extending the landmass.

Pell flew towards the central island, and as we got closer, I could see a settlement nestling amid a forested hillside and a small set of docks around which small fishing boats with colourful sails bobbed on the bright blue surface.

Stone buildings dotted the hillside, and an array of smaller wooden huts lined the beach. Cerule's incredible inherent luminosity bathed the sea and the island itself in a warm glow, and as we passed the Throne's wards, the winds died down, replaced by a fragrant breeze that was a tonic for the body and soul and put a smile on my face. The aromas were exotic and refreshing, and delivered a tremendous sense of wellbeing. Nestling in the hillside above the seaside village stood the shrine to Excelsis, a smaller though exact replica of the temple in the White Citadel. Here, a group of the

Juvenii's guardian Angels awaited us, robed in white and gold.

Pell landed in front of the shrine, and her Juvenii bearers followed behind, touching down gently with their precious cargo. They lifted Cassiel's coffin on to their shoulders as Pell walked forward and knelt in front of a tall female Angel with long white hair who bore a silver staff that was intricately decorated with images of doves. I had heard of the Throne power, Jophael, but never seen her this close up close before. She had been the Prince's advocate and closest advisor at the signing of the original Succae armistice, and had a formidable reputation for wisdom and graciousness. It made perfect sense that she would be the guardian protector of the Juvenii.

"Rise, bearers," she said, her voice a sonorous sound that sighed on the breeze.

From within the shrine, a bell started to toll, and the hillside was suddenly alive with Juvenii who raced to join a growing throng of several hundred others. It was a strange sight to see all these young Angels, their beautiful, innocent faces brimming with curiosity and guileless interest. I felt a strange pang of regret for that which I had lost. I must have been like them in some distant age long ago, but if so, those memories were lost and gone. Instead, here I was, a complex and tortured soul with far too much blood on my hands. I was suddenly hit by a rush of emotion and thought I might break down in tears, but I felt small hands sliding into mine, and the eternal optimism of youth saved me as they led me forward to the shrine of Excelsis for Cassiel's funeral rites.

The ceremony was led by Jophael in the shrine's inner sanctum, deep in the heart of the hill. A circular processional led down into the ceremonial space. Great cauldrons lit up the chamber and bathed the walls in red and yellow. Shadows leapt and danced, and the air was heady with the smell of ritual incense. It was a moving experience as Cassiel was taken from her coffin and laid on top of a central altar. The Keepers at Saur'Il's mausoleum had done an amazing job of restoring her body, and to my mind, it looked like she was simply asleep. I fought off a mad impulse to rush to her, shake her awake and tell her to breathe again, live again, return to us whole and renewed. It was a beautiful dream, but I knew the reality was that she was gone from us and would never play among her friends here again.

Voices were lifted in song and reverberated around the walls. There were mournful songs to allow the melancholy to flood out and vibrant hymns to entreat Excelsis to return Cassiel from the fires of creation. She had earned such love and respect; surely this was the least that could be expected. That's when I was brought out of my reverie. I had reached the point where the trust I had previously given to Excelsis without conscious thought would now be judged by deeds and actions. In that moment, I caught a glimpse of the terrible dilemma that the Archangel Anael was facing and felt nothing but sorrow. I drifted away before the final commission of Cassiel's body into fire was made. I had seen enough Angels make that return to fire and didn't want to see any more.

As I headed outside, I took a breath of the warm evening air and tried to find a level of peace within my troubled mind. Waves lapped up against the sandy shore as I walked along the beach where primitive but solidly built wooden huts nestled at the edge of a verdant forest. There was an undeniable appeal about the Juvenii's apparently simple lives, and I wondered whether it would be good for me to volunteer as one of the island's guardians for a spell. Then I spotted wide yellow eyes in the forest edge, and a great leopard emerged and padded toward me. It looked like I had finally caught up with Camael, or he had caught up with me.

Chapter Four

"What are you doing here, Azshael?" Cam said as he transformed into his Angel form. It was hardly the warm greeting I had expected from my best friend.

"I could ask you the same question, Cam. Why have you been hiding out here?"

"I haven't been hiding."

"Well, you didn't tell anyone where you were going either. You just stormed off without a word of explanation!"

"You think I owe you anything?"

"No, but I thought you were my friend!"

"Well, maybe I shouldn't be. Not after what happened to Sylvenell," he said, referring to Syl's transformation to help deal with the Halokim assassins sent to the Red Roof during Benazzar's attempted breaking of the armistice.

"You still blame me for that? I never asked Syl to do what she did. That was her decision and her choice alone. She acted to save the lives of those she loved, Cam. Yes, it was a sacrifice, but I know she would do the same thing again in a heartbeat."

Camael looked at me with a face full of anger and pain. "You should leave, Azsh. There is nothing for you here. Nothing at all."

I felt anger and resentment boiling up inside me. "You don't get to order me around, Camael. I bear the Prince's warrant."

"Like that matters! It's meaningless here, Ambassador." He laced mention of my title with a dose of sarcastic venom.

"Fine! Then why don't you answer my questions, and I can be gone sooner rather than later?" Cam folded his arms and sighed deeply. "Go on then. What do you want to know?"

"Cassiel. Who, or rather what, was she?"

"A Juvenii. Next?"

"Just an innocent who happened to be murdered by a very specific and rare Succae weapon. Do you know how valuable even one of those blades is to the Succae? This was no accident."

Camael glared at me and looked uncomfortable. "I am fully aware of how she died," he said.

"Do you know why she was in the Landing that day?"

"I do not," he said, and I could see his body tense up. Cam was many things, but a good liar was not one of them.

"Why are you lying, Camael? This is me. Azsh. I am your friend first. Just tell me what you know!"

"I have!" he yelled and the ground shook at his intensity. Exotic birds startled from their evening roosts burst into the sky in a flash of myriad colours. The fierceness of his reaction took me by surprise. It was as uncharacteristic as his outburst of sorrow when Cassiel's lifeless body had been found. I had the option of backing down and calming the situation or going back at him with everything I had. I chose the latter.

"I am not a fool, so don't try to treat me as one. I won't be lied to! Not by my best friend and not to my face! You knew I would come looking for answers. You said as much to Saur'll when you took Cassiel's body to the Mausoleum. So help me now. Help me understand what happened."

Camael looked back at me with a face of stone. He snarled and spread his wings, shooting into the night air. I was set to pursue him when a voice from the shadows called my name and stopped me.

"Azshael. The Prince's ambassador to the Succae." It was Jophael, and what she said in her soft, lyrical tone was more a statement than a question.

"Protector," I said, falling to one knee. She laughed and it was like the sound of sonorous bells ringing in the distance, instantly enchanting and beautiful.

"I am no Archangel. You may stand."

Even at my full height I was looking up at 'The White Lady'.

"I understand from Pellandriel that you have come to see the Juvenii colony and see our ways for yourself?"

"That is correct, Lady Jophael. I have also come to ask questions about the tragic death of Cassiel. I want to understand how she could have got from here to Asuriel's Landing and why she was murdered that day."

"It is my understanding that you are not tasked with investigating her death, Ambassador. So why are you asking such questions?"

"Cassiel's murder was not the only crime committed that day. An important piece of the Prince's regalia was also stolen, and I have been tasked with assisting in its recovery."

"You think Cassiel was responsible?"

"I have no opinion one way or the other. I am gathering evidence and following where it leads me."

"Yet you are here now. And it would seem you are upsetting the harmony of this island at the same time."

"I apologise if that is the case. Camael and I have known each other for a long time and emotions can sometimes run high between us. I promise to be more circumspect in the future. You must know that the last thing I would want to do is to bring this island any more trouble."

Jophael paused and looked down at me, golden eyes seemingly piercing my core and weighing my soul. "I believe you, Azshael. Let me take you for a tour around the island and see if we can answer your questions."

We took flight and talked as we flew. I could tell 'The White Lady' was troubled by my arrival. We talked first of Pellandriel, and I explained what had happened to her after the events of Benazzar's conspiracy to break the armistice with the Succae. It was obvious Pell had never spoken of this, and I could tell Jophael was not too impressed with the so-called justice she had received from the Heralds, and ultimately, Prince Anael himself. She had arrived here broken, and it seemed the Juvenii's island was slowly restoring her back to the glorious Power she had once been.

As we flew over the dense forest hillside to crest over the hill of the Shrine of Excelsis, we talked about Camael. It seemed that his and Pell's stories were similar in many ways. As Sariel had told me, he had come to serve as an island guardian in the dying days of the war. He had been injured by a Necrene weapon, and his wound had festered. Among her other skills, Jophael was a noted healer, and she had tended to his wounds. Here, his body, as well as his troubled mind, had been restored.

"He seems very angry and defensive now," I said, as below us, snaking trails revealed occasional groupings of huts and lodges where the warm orange embers of fires sent up occasional sparks like so many fireflies in the night.

"Camael was a mentor to Cassiel. He has found her death hard to bear." He wasn't the only one, I thought.

"Mentor? In what way?"

Jophael landed on a strand of beach where the waves gently washed up on sand so pale it gave off a luminescence that chased away the shadows.

"Cassiel was quite the adventurer and keen to learn new skills. Camael taught her everything from rock climbing to flying by the stars. That sort of thing."

I sat silently for a while as I evaluated Jophael. She seemed honest enough and was reasonable in tone and demeanour, but I have a natural suspicion of authority and I wondered if I could really trust her. It was time for some more direct questions.

"How do you think Cassiel got to the White Citadel?"

"I honestly have no idea. The Juvenii are not imprisoned here. They can come and go as they wish."

"Some of the Flight think that Cassiel was an intriguer. I presume you would know if that was true?"

Jophael turned and looked at me. "Yes, I would think I would. Of course, you also know everything about every one of your acquaintance, I presume? Their secrets, inner thoughts, and motivations?" I felt a rueful grin spreading across my face. It was a clever deflection but a deflection, nonetheless.

"So the fact Cassiel was found dead in the streets of the Landing came as a complete surprise?"

"Yes, it did. I don't know why she went or how she got there."

"I can tell you she was involved in something, Jophael. The weapon that killed her would not have been used idly."

"A Succae blade, I understand?"

"The weapon yes, but not necessarily the hand that wielded it."

"But you would say that, wouldn't you?" I felt my hackles rise.

"You are the ambassador to the Succae, and you know them well, do you not?"

"That is true, but that doesn't mean…"

"And from what I hear, you like them more than you like your own kind?"

"That is not fair or true, Jophael. I fell in love with a Succae woman, but many of their kind have also fallen to my spear."

"As have many Angels."

"Those that tried to kill me, yes. They got what they deserved."

Jophael fell silent for a moment as we watched the green luminescent waves wash up dead seaweed on the shore. A pair of sea turtles that looked like their shells were seared crawled out of the sea to lie exhausted on the sand. They began to attempt to bury themselves, but the effort was too much, and they both lay there, only the movement of their eyes showing they were still alive.

"Hiding in plain sight," Jophael said, before standing up and going over to them. She knelt beside them and ran her hands over their shells. They were both suffused in a soft white haze and when she stood up again, they went back to digging themselves to hidden safety beneath the white sands. "I am sorry I can't be of more help to you, Ambassador, but I must agree with Camael. There is nothing for you here."

She was about to take flight when the memory of Saur'll showing me weapon calluses on Cassiel's hands came back to me.

"You said Camael was a guardian, and now Pell is too. Exactly what are you all protecting this enclave from?"

"The unknown," she said and then she was gone into the pale night sky.

I sat on the beach for the rest of the night until the day luminescence lit up the blue sea with a sparkling brilliance that was both dazzling and beautiful. I suspected Jophael had left because she was getting uncomfortable with my line of questioning. Were her answers an attempt at subtle sophistry or did I just have trust issues with Angels in power? Jophael's reputation was one of truth and fairness, but I had heard other senior members of the Flight, who had turned out not to be, called that before. Still, I could not see her as someone who would deliberately deceive one of her own kind, but her blunt and cold evaluation of my history, informed as it probably was by Pell and possibly Cam, too, seemed strange. I was obviously asking uncomfortable questions, and it felt like I had turned over a rock to reveal a pit of angry snakes who didn't appreciate being disturbed. There was something going on here, but for now I didn't know what, and my time was running short.

Morning on the Juvenii islands seemed to be a hive of activity. Fishers pushed out their boats and headed out in search of a catch, whilst others worked verdant loam. The youngest sat with their mature guardians and listened to their stories and teachings. Everywhere I went, I was greeted with warm welcomes and guileless smiles, at least from the Juvenii. Their guardians, who carried simple spears and wore daggers at their sides, were less enthusiastic, but certainly not hostile, and they didn't stop me from snooping around. I found no obvious martial training ground and no armoury or forge to manufacture weapons and armour. It looked as if the rumours of a school for spies had been somewhat overblown, and I started to feel a bit foolish for having believed them in the first place. I was about to fly back to bid farewell to Jophael when one of the younger Juvenii ran up to me and grabbed my arm. I looked down as she pressed a round metal item into my hand.

Squinting up at me she said, "I was told you should have this." Then she ran off as I looked down at the item I had been given. It was the mark of Vasariah's Honores. As I watched her run into the woodland and then take flight, I saw movement in the canopy. It was Pell, and as our eyes met, she suddenly took flight and shot past me toward the sparkling sea. I followed the trail of her red spear, Revelation, blazing with golden light and charting a course out past the island wards and across the deep ocean, where dull red magma blossomed in the depths like so many roses planted in an underwater garden. We were headed for the island mass that was still taking shape I had seen on the way in. For a moment, I wondered if Pell and Camael disliked me enough to silence me permanently, and whether I was being led into a trap. I couldn't believe that of two of my best friends, if indeed they still counted as such, but then paranoia had become a constant companion since Ischae's murder. However, two Powers against one unofficial Ambassador was not good odds. I called Nimrod to take shape. I supposed I was about to find out exactly where I stood, and maybe something else. I clenched the coin in my hand and followed Pell's trail to the eastern side of the green isle where the sea boiled and churned, shrouding the new landmass in a steamy haze.

Chapter Five

Pell waited for me to catch up. We were high in the sky above the island's centre, which was dominated by a massive hill that had to be about two thousand feet above sea level. It was densely covered with plant life that was a riot of colour. It was supposed that due to the exposure to the Necrene well, which had once been housed in the planet core, all life was tainted, twisted, or born mutated if it could take hold at all. Clearly, however, the well's relocation with the Succae had allowed Cerule's biosphere to repair. It would be a short-lived victory for nature however, as the violent seismic activity that had birthed this new land was evidence of the beginnings of the death throes of a world that would slowly tear itself apart from the inside. Eventually, the heart of the earth would falter and the incredible natural energy that gave the planet life and light would fade away to leave a cold, dead husk.

"I'm not sure about this," Pell said as she looked down at the island nervously.

"What do you mean? Why have you brought me here, and what's the meaning of this coin?"

"Cam found it on a chain around Cassiel's neck."

"What? When?"

"When he took her body to the Mausoleum. You know what it is?"

"It's the mark of the Legio Honores. I know that much. Why would Cassiel have it around her neck?"

"She was working for them, Azsh. Well not for them, but for their leader." I suddenly remembered what Sariel had said about Vasariah not reporting for duty and being absent from his Sphere.

"Is Vasariah here?" Pell would not meet my eyes, and I suddenly had a very bad feeling. "What's going on here, Pellandriel?"

"It's Camael. He's very angry. I don't know what he's going to do!"

"He has Vasariah?"

Pell nodded and looked utterly miserable. "It's alright, Pell. You did the right thing telling me. Take me to Cam and let's see if we can all have a reasonable conversation."

Pell led me down to the island itself and we passed over the top of the great hill, descending towards a lagoon where the waters were churning and roiling. Pell landed and pointed to the entrance to a dark sea cavern obscured by hanging vines and other vegetation that looked heavily overgrown. The sea was cooler and calmer here, but it was the only thing that was. I was very definitely on edge after my earlier encounter with Cam. I really wasn't sure that the Camael we were about to meet was the same one I had known for more years than I cared to remember. His emotions ran deep, but I had never known him to let them get out of control as it seemed they now were.

"Stay here, Pell. Let me handle this," I said, trying to sound more confident than I actually felt. Pell shook her head. "No way, Azsh. I won't let you face him alone." I was going to protest but realised I had hoped she would say that. I was far from certain we'd be enough to stop Camael if things turned nasty.

Inside the dark cavern, the waves crashed against rocks, sending spumes high into the air. I could see Cam sitting alone on a rocky promontory. It looked like he was asleep or meditating, and I landed a few dozen feet away from him, with Pell behind me. His eyes opened and he stood up, and looked surprisingly calm.

"Why did you bring Azshael here, Pellandriel?"

"You know why," Pell said. "We've gone too far, Camael. Maybe Azsh can talk some sense into you, and maybe you'll listen to him!" Cam looked at me expectantly. "Go on then, Azsh. Talk sense to me."

"Where is Vasariah?"

"He's around. For now."

"What's going on here? Did you abduct him?"

"I brought him to justice!" Cam said, shouting the word 'justice' so that it echoed around the caves.

"Whose justice? Yours?"

"Why not, Azsh? You've been saying for years that the Heralds can't be trusted, so what would you have me do? Take a murderer to them so that he can use his position, power, and connections to wriggle free? No! I will not allow that to happen this time!"

Anger was coursing through Camael. I had never seen him so agitated.

"Alright, I hear you," I said placatingly. "Why don't we all calm down and discuss what's happened here. Pell said that Cassiel was working for Vasariah. Is that right?"

"He used her, Azsh. Recruited her for a devious task. She would never have done it if she had known the truth. He must have lied to her."

"She stole the White Rood?"

"No," Pell said quietly. "Not exactly."

"What do you mean?"

"Vasariah asked her to try and steal it, but she never got the opportunity."

I was already getting lost, and Cam picked up on my furrowed brow and confused expression. "This is pointless," he said. "Speak to Vasariah himself and let him tell you what happened. Then we can decide what to do with him. I wanted to leave you both out of this but we're all in it together now. Just know that Vasariah put Cassiel in harm's way and is responsible for what happened to her."

Cam led us deeper into the cavern and the further we went, the hotter and steamier it became. Finally, we arrived at a grotto where geysers erupted violently, spattering the walls with sulphurous spray. In the centre of this volatile lake was a strand of black rock where a broken Angel lay motionless.

"Did you kill him, Cam?" I said incredulously.

"Not yet," he replied ominously. "Not to say he doesn't deserve it or that I won't send him to the fires that burn beneath these waters. Go, Azsh. Go and talk to him. All the lies have been crushed out of him. We already had that conversation."

I flew to Vasariah's side, and was relieved to see his eyes flicker with life. It was clear, though, that he was in a bad way. His wings had been pounded, and I guessed that every bone in them had been broken. His arms and legs also lay at odd angles, and whilst I was certain his body was in the process of healing, it would be many hours before he would be able to stand or fly again. For now, he was at our mercy.

"Aren't you going to ask me if I'm alright?" Vasariah whispered and then laughed incongruously.

"I can see you are not," I said with some sympathy. He had to be in agony.

"Camael knows how to break an Angel. Even a Domini like me. As he was pounding my wing bones into dust, I realised how stupid such titles are in the final event."

"What happened with Cassiel, Vasariah? Cam says you're responsible for her death. Give me something to work with, and I'll do my best to get you out of here alive."

"I didn't kill her, but I did ask her to do a task for me."

"How did you know her?"

"I was a Guardian for a time during the war. Like Camael, I was a Protector of the Juvenii islands, but unlike him, I saw an opportunity to harness emerging talent. We had already taken so many losses by the time I came here; I just thought it would be wise to make provision for the future."

"You trained her to fight?"

"Yes. Her and a few more like her. All this talk that these Juvenii don't want to fight is a lie. They are Angels born of fire just like us, and fire rages and consumes. It's what we are, and you can't escape your nature."

"Was Jophael aware?"

"No! She would never have consented to such behaviour. I tried to convince her that sooner or later we would all be fighting for our lives, but she wasn't convinced. I think she had me promoted away as she thought I was a danger to her charges."

"What did you ask Cassiel to do?"

"I asked her to test the Trinity's defences, or at least that's what I told her."

"You deceived her?"

"It was a white lie, a small deception. It wouldn't have mattered to her if she had known the truth. I was just trying to protect her!"

"So what was the truth? You told her to steal the White Rood?"

"I did, yes. She was enthusiastic to put all that both Camael and I had taught her into practice."

"What happened?"

"She got there, and it was already gone. It had already been taken."

"Do you know who took it?"

"I have my suspicions, Azshael, but no proof."

"Tell me."

"You need to understand, it was just meant to be a warning."

"A warning to whom? The Prince?"

"Yes. He's become very difficult to deal with since all that business with Benazzarr. He sees plots and plotters everywhere. He threatened both me and the leader of the Irin with consequences if anything like that were to happen again."

"Kokael?"

"Yes. Her. We were both dressed down at the same time in front of the Privy Council. He seemed to find it amusing to make us look small. I didn't take it well, and nor did she."

"You think she hatched the same plan as you did but just got there first?"

"Yes. The Rood was her idea. She said it has the power of command, which means it could directly threaten Anael's primacy. She said that if another were to rise and all the Flight's Legions were to fall behind them, Anael would have no option but to relinquish command of the Seventh and step down. The idea would be to remind him that he wasn't all powerful and that his own position could also come under threat."

"She told you to do this?"

"No, not exactly, but she put the idea in my head. It would never have occurred to me on my own. I am a soldier and have little taste for such intrigue."

"Yet you went ahead and planned to use a Juvenii to infiltrate the Trinity under a false pretence to steal the Rood and hold your Prince to ransom! That sounds like a lot of intrigue to me, Vasariah! It also made Anael even more suspicious of your competence. It cost you your command, exactly the opposite of what you had set out to achieve!"

"I regret what happened. It was stupid, I'll admit that now. I was just so angry with the way I had been treated. I wanted to make the Archangel think again, and if I had held the Rood, things might have been different."

"How's that?"

"Anael would have sweated for a while, like he is doing now, and then I would have returned it and been seen as the Angel of the hour. Or I could have used it. I won't say I wasn't thinking about that possibility."

"You would have deposed the Prince?"

"No! I would have made him swear to treat his soldiers with the respect they deserve. That's all."

I wasn't entirely sure I believed Vasariah, but then I'm not certain he believed himself either. It was a moot point, given that the Rood had never fallen into his hands.

"How would this other thief have made it past your guards? I can see that Cassiel might have got in whilst you and the Honores were following the Prince, but how would Kokael or one of her Irin have managed it?"

"She has many agents on both sides of the Tether, Azshael. She also knows the Trinity inside out and would know exactly how to avoid our patrols. The Irin were brought in after that attempted coup, and I was told to follow their lead. They enhanced our watch on the perimeter but at the expense of the inner guard. I now think that was deliberate." This was new information and painted things in a different light. "Was that before or after the Prince's reprimand?"

"After. I believe she convinced him of the need to improve the Trinity's security."

I had personal experience of Kokael's ability to enchant and beguile, but surely a Prince was immune to such charms?

"Do you know what happened to Cassiel? Why was she wearing your mark around her neck?"

"I don't know. I suspect she fell afoul of the real thieves somehow. I think she was silenced, although I don't know why. She was wearing the mark of the Honores as insurance in case she was caught. I knew she would be brought to me first in that instance. I marked the Rood as a precaution in case something went wrong with that same sigil. Cassiel knew I would never have asked for her help if I'd thought she was in any real danger. I swear that on my life, Azshael." It was a poor choice of words given the situation.

Chapter Six

"He didn't kill her, Cam." If thunder had a visual appearance, it would have looked like Cam did at that moment. "But you already know that."

"He's responsible for what happened!"

"Partly, yes, but she wasn't forced to go! She made that choice for herself."

"She was misled. She was lied to, and he's the one that did that."

"I don't agree with what he did, but I also don't think he should die because of it!"

We stood there glaring at each other, and I could tell Pell agreed with me, but then she probably had all along otherwise I wouldn't have been there. Cam refused to look me in the eye, and in that moment, I saw the truth—that he blamed himself. The question was how to say that to him without getting Vasariah, or even myself, killed in the process.

"Jophael told me Cassiel was adventurous and outgoing. I know you all loved her for that. You Protectors are all Powers, and I am sure she looked up to you and wanted to be just like you, and there is nothing wrong with that. You showed her a life beyond the enclave, and I think she was taking tentative steps toward that. Vasariah took it one step further because he's a soldier, and that is all he knows how to be."

"It was a step too far though, Azsh," Pell said.

"Maybe it was, but I believe him when he says he never thought any harm would come to her."

Cam snorted derisively. "Care? He cared about himself and only himself. He was happy to sacrifice her to safeguard his position and power."

"If that's true, then why did he make provision for what would happen if she was caught in the Trinity Palace? That's why she was wearing his order's mark around her neck. I think he cared about her as much as everyone else here did."

Cam looked away, and I could see the misery and conflict on his face. He had been able to focus his rage on Vasariah when no-one was arguing with him, but now the situation was growing more complex. Simple truths are far easier to believe than ones that are made ambiguous with nuance. The truth is often a fluid and malleable thing, and can easily slip out of one's grip. That's what I saw Cam coming to terms with now.

Cam suddenly took flight, but away from where Vasariah still lay broken by his rage. Instead, he headed back into the interior and toward the surface.

"Do you think I should go after him?" Pell asked.

"No. Leave him be. I have said all I can for now. If he is going to kill Vasariah, there's not much we can do to stop him. I hope I have given him pause for thought and seeded enough doubt. He blames himself as much as he does Vasariah, but neither of them plunged that blade into Cassiel's chest. They were just trying to help her find her true path."

"Do you really believe what you just said? I would have thought Vasariah was exactly the sort of Angel you detest!"

I thought for a moment, but not about that. It was that image of someone killing a young Angel in cold blood with a devastating weapon. In my mind that was an act of madness, and I was still at a loss to think what threat Cassiel had truly posed to her killer. Of course, it wasn't really about Cassiel, it was the White Rood itself.

"Vasariah said the Rood was marked?"

"Yes. From what we know of Cassiel, I doubt she would have given up when she found the regalia was missing, or maybe she was looking for Vasariah to let him know. It might explain why she was in the Landing and how she managed to find the Rood in the hands of a bunch of killers that day."

"They killed her before she could raise the alarm?"

"It's certainly plausible. She was only streets away from Cam so maybe she was trying to find him and let him know what was going on."

"How awful. Poor, poor, Cassiel."

I found Cam atop the great hill at the centre of the island. He was sitting still, staring out over the sparkling blue waters that were so clear you could see the glittering coral formations on the seabed.

"Don't say anything," he growled at me, yet the edge was gone from his voice, and I sat there quietly for a while, waiting him out.

"Who do you think killed her?"

"I have my suspicions, but I can't yet see the connections. Trust me, Cam, I will find out."

"And when you do, you'll let me know?"

"I will. I promise. If you promise not to fly off the handle again."

"If you tell me who they are, I can get you swift answers."

"Of that I have no doubt, but there could be much at stake here. In the wrong hands, the Rood that Vasariah told Cassiel to acquire could be very dangerous. It may already have been used on that day in the Landing. It could turn Angel against Angel and usher in an age of chaos akin to our tribal wars and the Fallenstar's rebellion. I can see why Cassiel would have been very motivated to stop that happening, and why someone with the right vested interests would have been willing to kill her. I suspect whoever killed Cassiel was a soldier and not the leader. It's them we need to find."

"You live in a complex world."

"Sometimes, Cam, there are no easy answers."

"I will let Vasariah live," he said finally. "For now."

"I think that is wise. As a matter of interest, did you teach Cassiel about hunting and tracking?"

"Of course I did."

It was the answer I was expecting, and I felt another piece of the puzzle potentially slotting into place. Now the question was who she'd been with that day, and what had happened. I had a feeling that the answers to those questions lay with the Low-Tsar Rasnich, and it was high time I got underway on the long flight to the dead Succae capital of Khrov.

Chapter Seven

My flight to the plains of Khast was long, arduous and quite harrowing. I saw lots of evidence as to how Cerule was moving into its last phase of existence and all the biosphere was being impacted as a result. Life on Cerule had been sustained by a remarkable bioluminescence, or planet shine, that emanated from within its core, lighting and warming the surface and helping to sustain a wide array of life. The Necrene well brought by the Succae had fed off this planetary lifeforce, and there had been a strange effect as anti-life met with superpowered nature. Rather than diminishing its power, the Necrenic energy had made the living biosphere work even harder at its task, and the world had flourished.

It had been the war between Angel and vampire that had forced Cerule into decline, and as our powers clashed, the Succae war machine had pulled more and more life from the planet, harnessing Necrenic force as a resource. As our Powers tried to deny the Succae their dark energy, so more of the world was razed and drained of life. When the vampires had abandoned the surface, the well's removal to the Scarpe moon had spelled doom for the world they had called home for centuries, and without its symbiotic powers, the planet's core had started to decay and die.

Cerule's four large continents were similar in shape and size, and as I passed over the southern landmass, I could see the red scars from violent eruptions in the tectonic plates that had breached the surface, setting fire to vast swathes of territory. Miles and miles of woodland had burned down, and even at my high elevation, the air tasted of bitter ashes. I knew the life below that had survived would now be compromised by the destruction of the environment, and the resulting impact on the natural order would lead to death and extinction of valuable species. The same had happened with the arrival of the Succae, of course, although their civilisation had largely been restricted to the northern continent where all life had been tainted, twisted, or destroyed by the dark energies of the Necrene well. Now, however, all life was under threat.

I could bear it no more, so I headed out of the atmosphere and into space where travel would be faster and cleaner. The Succae had originally settled in the centre of the continent and spread out from there. Their capital, Khrov, was a grand fortress city located in the centre of a vast steppe known as the Khast plains. It was strange to see other regions of the planet from above, still brightly lit whilst this continent was shrouded in inky black shadow, dark, cold, and foreboding. As I entered the atmosphere, I was hit by icy cold winds and a deathly stillness in the air. It had been several years since I had been here, and unpleasant memories suddenly flooded back.

Khrov itself was a solid bastion surrounded by great black basalt walls. Imperfections in the rock gave them a speckled look, and as my radiance caught them, they glittered faintly like diamonds in a coal face. As I landed before the sundered gates at the southern end of the city, I took stock of the place as it was now. Khrov waited quietly for a people who would never return. The great statues of the original Vods that dominated the skyline still towered over sharp, angular buildings that were squat and ugly, at least to my mind. They were also broken, having taken the brunt of the Flight's cannons of destruction in multiple sieges and assaults on the Succae capital. As with all Succae settlements, what you saw above ground was only half of the story, and I knew a vast subterranean undercity lay beneath Khrov's densely packed streets. A great rumble split the deathly quiet and I felt the ground shift and shake around me. An earthquake split seams in the ground along old fault lines, and I heard a great crashing sound from within the walls as already weakened structures finally gave way and collapsed.

"Look what you did," came a voice from the shadows, and Lytta materialised out of the gloom. "Not guilty," I said. "Nowhere near powerful enough to have done that." I pointed to the remains of the great southern gates, which had collapsed in on each other and, even under the power of the quake, remained stubbornly upright. Sagging but somehow still standing, reminiscent of a pair of drunks who only had each other to rely on for support.

"Have you been here long, Serrate?"

"Half a day or so," she said nonchalantly.

"Any sign of our fugitive Low-Tsar?"

"I was waiting for you. I didn't want you getting lost in the alleyways of the old city."

"I would have thought he'd be in the undercity."

"The undercity is largely impassable now. There has been much disturbance in the ground around here, and large parts of what was once above ground has now fallen below." As if to punctuate her point, an aftershock shook the area and the 'drunks' collapsed. Lytta stepped neatly out of the way of being buried beneath one. It was remarkably smooth for what I thought was a narrow escape.

"So where, then?"

"I think the area around the *Kolodesh* would be a good place to start," she said.

As we made our way toward the grand market in the centre of the city, I soon saw for myself the terrible and widespread destruction that seismic events had wrought in the recent past. Vast sinkholes had swallowed entire streets, and the black scars of great rents in the ground ran down once busy thoroughfares. The remains of buildings whose sides had caved in now teetered on the edges of jagged precipices. The damage seemed to be most noticeable on the outer edges of the city, although only the southern walls had been undermined so far.

Khrov was unlike Scarpe. Its narrow streets were hemmed in by grey stone buildings interlinked with twisting alleyways, and the closer we got to the centre of the town and the old quarter, the more labyrinthine it became. It was oppressive as the buildings closed in around us, their dense and sharp angular construction casting everything in shadow. I took flight to take a look from above and what I saw had a chilling resonance.

The centre of Khrov was dominated by the great temple to the Succae's old gods. It was a huge square building of black stone with sloped sides that dwarfed all the structures around it. Only the four statues of the ancestral Vods that stood their eternal silent vigil around its corners were taller. I recognised the impressively detailed representations of Karsz and Dursc, but not the others. Ischae had once told me their names, but as they were now consigned to history and, therefore, of academic interest only, I hadn't committed them to memory. Around the Black Temple's base, great steps on each side led down to a series of small squares strewn with debris from where tall, wide stone walls had once partitioned them. The building had subsided to the right, and whilst its structure was not the same as the one in my vision at Zolorel's house, I felt an instinctive shudder of recognition run through me. There had to be a connection.

"Anything?" Lytta called to me from below as she paused in front of a wide arch leading to a covered alleyway.

"I don't know," I said, at a loss to explain something I didn't fully understand myself. "I think we should be cautious." Lytta frowned at my singularly useless choice of words and stated the obvious. "I thought we were being that already." Then she marched off and was swallowed by the darkness. Feeling a little foolish, I dropped to the ground and followed the Serrate on into the dark black heart of the Succae's dead city.

We emerged into the southernmost square of the temple plaza and stood in front of the broken steps. It was an awesome structure, a brooding monolithic hulk. Somehow, the stone of which it had been constructed was darker than the darkness around it, so it sat in stark relief against the sky above, blacker than black. Lytta knelt and ran her hand along the steps. She whispered something under her breath, and tendrils of blue light emerged from the stone and wreathed around her fingers. It was already quiet, but now I felt my senses heighten as the world came into sharp focus around me. The tendrils lengthened as they flowed from Lytta's hand over the steps and up towards a tall and wide pool of darkness that I took to be the entrance to the structure. "What is that?" I asked, my voice barely a whisper, lost in awe.

"Blithe spirits," she said, as if that was an explanation. "Old friends from the Well, here to help us now."

"Spirit scouts?"

"Of a sort, yes."

The lights sped away from Lytta's hands and disappeared into the temple's interior. No more than a minute later, she turned to me with fangs bared.

"Trouble," she said, and raced up the steps at a sprint.

Chapter Eight

In the surprisingly tight confines of the narrow temple lobby, I increased my aura to shine a light on the interior. Lytta had paused at the end of the passage, and the blue spirit lights were circling like fireflies around a campfire. The chamber beyond looked vast. A grand temple floor supported by great square columns of pale grey stone.

"What's happening?" I asked, as there was no obvious sign of trouble.

"This way," she said, drawing both her long and short swords and bathing us both in a soft blood-red glow. Lytta stalked across the wide temple floor inlaid with a mosaic of the ancient gods and goddesses the Succae had once revered in a rapacious antique age of conquest and enslavement. Even as artistic interpretations went, they looked like cruel and merciless beings. Lytta led me up the steps to the centre of the chamber, where a great stone slab waited on a wide plinth. From the rivulets and indents carved on the surface, I could tell it had once served as a sacrificial block. She sheathed her blades and bade me join her.

"Push," she said, and together, we put our shoulders to the heavy stone. It moved with surprising ease, hardly making a sound as the block slid sideways to reveal steps descending into deeper darkness.

"What's down there? What did your spirits see?"

"Ghosts," she said simply. "More ghosts."

"Like the ones at Rukoi's manse?"

"I'm not certain. Are you ready, Angel?"

The answer to that was no, but there was no time to get ready, so I just nodded grimly as Lytta disappeared into the darkness, her carnelian blades lighting the way ahead.

The steps took us down about fifty feet into a narrow passageway with decorated walls. The colours were vivid, and in the shadows cast by my aura, they seemed to animate and come to life. I didn't have time to take it all in, but it looked like a Succae history in a complex interlinked series of narratives. After a few hundred feet, the passage turned sharply and emerged into the upper level of a grand vaulted chamber with tiered rows of steps arranged in semi-circular formations to our left and right.

"Douse your light!" Lytta said to me sharply, and I quickly obeyed. We were in the gallery, about fifty feet above the floor of the chamber below. It looked like a receiving hall, and the floor was packed with hundreds of Shadowglass bottles. At the far end of the chamber, I could see a Succae male surrounded by a red haze which appeared to be repelling attacks from a pack of luminous entities. Like the wraiths that had attacked us in Rukoi's home and presumably brought about the former High-Nin's demise, these creatures phased in and out of corporeal form.

"Is that Rasnich?" I asked Lytta quietly as we both knelt and took stock of the situation. "I think it must be," she said. "He's using blood magic and Spiritcraft to create a protective ward. Look." Lytta pointed at the Shadowglass bottles closest to where Rasnich was standing. Tiny blue lights lit up inside them and would depart for the ward, where they were absorbed into the red haze around him. The creatures leapt at the ward, which flashed as their attacks were repulsed.

"I think his time is running short," Lytta said. "The ward is diminishing. I don't know how many spirits he has left to call on from those bottles, but my senses tell me not many remain, and he is running low on blood with which to manipulate them."

The creatures attacking Rasnich were canine like quadrupeds with long, emaciated bodies, elongated snouts, and maws full of sharp teeth. The loose skin stretching over their skeletal frames was leprous and oozing with dark discharges of ichor that dripped from their bodies to hiss and smoke on the stone floor beneath them.

"What are those things?" I asked.

"Tindalae," she said, and the wariness in her voice was obvious.

"Daemon guardians from the Well. They are sometimes used as hunters and trackers. In this case it looks like they have found their quarry. They are hard to fight, especially in these numbers. If the whole pack turns on us it could be an interesting contest." Interesting for her, perhaps, but give me dull contests any day if it keeps my wings intact. There were ten of the beasts, but so far, they were showing no sign of having seen us.

"How do we fight them?"

"Carefully," she said. "Your light may blind and disorient them, and fire should prove potent in terms of harming them. However, we should be cautious. I see the pack but not the hunt master. They must be around somewhere." She had a point, and I had the strong feeling that we were looking for Zamalca and her twin, Malacaz. The question was, if not here, then where were they?

"Let's get down there and try and split the pack. I have an idea." Lytta told me her plan, which I thought was risky, but in the absence of anything else, would have to do.

She headed round the banks of seating on the left side of the auditorium whilst I took flight towards the right. I waited for her cue, and we both dropped to the ground simultaneously. The Tindalae initially paid us no mind, and it was only after Nimrod was wreathed in Angelfire that I got their full attention. They all became translucent, taking their spirit forms. To my mind, they looked even more frightening, corrupted canine entities whose eyes burned with bright yellow flame. They spread out around me as I brandished my spear. In their discorporate forms they seemed unafraid of my fire, and I sensed a malign group intelligence controlling the pack.

"Look for an alpha," Lytta shouted helpfully, but on initial inspection I couldn't make out any differences between them. In a sudden shift, they became corporeal and lunged forward. I took flight as they leapt at me, snapping, slavering, and growling in a strange high pitch that pained the ears. As I passed over the pack, I stabbed down and speared one of them through its open maw, down into its throat and out of its neck. It yowled and twisted on the haft as fire immolated the beast's upper body. I could see it trying to shift to its spirit form, but Nimrod had it pinned to this plane of existence, and within seconds, it had gone still. Its spirit fled from the now inert form only to be pounced on by the Sixth Succae Spirit of War. Colours and shapes blurred in a sudden motion, as Lytta's true form became manifest, a many-legged rainbow tigress with a draconic tail flying tattered banners behind her. She had left her host body, and in a swirl of many colours, swallowed the Tindalae daemon in a single bite. She swiftly returned to her host, and picked up one of the empty Shadowglass bottles from the floor and regurgitated the unfortunate captive soul into it, deftly replacing the silver bottle stopper into the top to trap it within.

The pack's reaction was instant and dramatic as they gathered together into a tight group and began to leap and flow over each other in a mesmerising pattern of light and terrible sound. I landed beside the Serrate as the speed of the pack's interactions gained pace.

"What are they doing?" I asked, as it became hard to tell where one creature ended and another began.

"Nothing good," was Lytta's enigmatic reply as she hastened over to where Rasnich stood still, protected by the red haze of his wards.

"Let us in," Lytta said to the Low-Tsar, but he shook his head emphatically. "If you think I am dropping this ward while they are still around, you're crazy, Serrate."

"Do it now, or I will break this barrier down myself. Then you will see 'crazy' at first hand," she said sternly, and the two Succae stared each other down for a moment before the Low-Tsar looked away.

"Alright, alright," Rasnich said, and he relented, calling the spirits that were powering his ward back into a ritual Athame, which he had been holding on to as if his life depended on it. The long dagger was a piece of expert craftsmanship. Its wide silver blade was clearly enchanted with mystical sigils that had a bluish glow. As he recalled his spirits, the facets of multi-coloured gems embedded in the handle flared with light. Lytta and I turned to face the Tindalae, but they were gone, and in their place was a large ball of yellow light that pulsed with dark energy.

"That's a void," Rasnich said with a sort of hushed reverence, or maybe fear.

"A void? What is that?"

"It's a precursor to the conclusion of a summoning," Lytta said.

"The Tindalae must have sent for support," Rasnich said. "We should get out of this place before it arrives."

"I doubt we have time," Lytta responded. "Best we prepare to fight, and whilst we do, you have some questions to answer, Rasnich Low-Tsar."

"What do you mean?"

"I came here to get answers, and you will give them to me or you will die long before whatever is coming through that void gets the chance to kill you."

Rasnich looked vexed, but I was certain he had been relieved to see us intervene.

"We are only following your trail," I said, trying to be helpful.

Rasnich smiled. "Oh were you? And what trail is that?"

"The Shadowglass bottle you gave to your follower, Kjatz, was only made here. Vachs, the Lord Ancestral, immediately identified it. I presume that was deliberate?"

"You're that Angel ambassador, aren't you? Ash, or something?"

"It's Azshael, and yes, I have that privilege, to be the Seventh Flight's liaison to the Vod and his people."

"Then why are you here?"

"Never mind why he is here," Lytta said darkly. "You are accused of being a traitor and conspiring with rebel enemies of Vod Karsz. Do you deny it?"

"Traitor? Now wait a moment! I'm no enemy of Karsz!"

"Then why were you helping the High-Nin, Rukoi? It seems very clear he was plotting a pagan rebellion. Again."

"Was?"

"Yes. Death has a way of stopping plotters in their tracks."

"Rukoi is dead? You mean you killed him?"

"No, she didn't," I interjected, "although that's not to say she wouldn't have given the chance. He was dead when we found him."

"Dead! How? Who killed him."

"Not who. What," Lytta said. "We're not sure exactly who was behind it, but he had been attacked by *Yurei,* probably called from the Well. Maybe called by you?"

"Now listen here, Serrate. Rukoi and I were friends back when I was his equal, and I owed him a debt of honour, but I wasn't conspiring with him."

"That's not what Kjatz told me," I said, and Rasnich gave me a pained look. "Kjatz? He serves my will. He doesn't know anything."

"Well, that's definitely true now," I said without further explanation. "However, he confessed that you had plotted to steal the White Rood from Trinity Palace."

"I did no such thing, Ambassador. I had no idea what Rukoi was after. Just that he wanted me to find the best thief on the moon for a special task. If I had known it was to steal the regalia from an Archangel, I would have told Rukoi where to go, debt or no debt."

"Then how did Kjatz know you had the Rood in your possession?"

"He said that?"

"He did. He said it was being borrowed for a while but that you would return it when the task was complete."

"The only reason I am not cutting you to shreds, Low-Tsar, is the bottles here," Lytta said, indicating the sea of Shadowglass around us.

"I think you gave Kjatz a bottle as a signpost where I could find you. Now you'd better open up and spill your guts out – metaphorically speaking—or I will do it for real!"

The temperature in the auditorium dropped from cold to freezing and the yellow ball gradually drained of colour until it was just a barely visible patch of darkness. I could feel Necrene energy radiating from its core, pulling at my lifeforce.

"Looks like story time will have to wait," Lytta said. "Whatever is coming, its here."

I couldn't be sure if it emerged from the dark core or whether that darkness was just the shroud it wove around itself, but suddenly it was there in all its malevolent glory. A terrible stench filled the air as the thing shambled forward. It was the pack, remade into a horrendous mutated single entity. It looked like the daemon dogs we had seen attacking Rasnich's wards earlier, but its size had swollen massively so that it stood nigh on twenty feet tall with a wide body. A central canine head with bright yellow eyes filled with malign alien intelligence regarded us with keen anticipation. Its huge maw was filled with sharp white teeth and bright red gums. The jaws jutted out of its haunches whilst a dozen other canine faces fused into the thing's flanks, snapped, bayed and growled in eager anticipation of a feast. Its naked skin hung loose on its frame, and those leprous looking patches of some visible cancer leaked a black ichor that pitted the auditorium floor.

"It's cunning," Lytta said quietly. "I can no longer see individual spirits, just a massive life source. It has somehow fused both its physical and spiritual self together so that we cannot divide and control it."

"We need a new plan then," I said, but Lytta looked pensive and didn't reply.

Whilst we had been talking, Rasnich had reset his wards. The great beast padded in our direction with heavy, ponderous steps and paused mere inches away. It sniffed around the red haze and gave an ear-splitting roar. The multiple heads of the Tindalae, now fused with the beast's body, howled in a cacophonous chorus to chill the blood. It raised itself on its haunches, and launched forward in a ferocious snapping bite that could have cut me in two. The wards flared but held, and about a quarter of the bottles around us that still held the blue light of resident spirits went dark.

"We need to take action quickly," I said, and Lytta nodded grimly. "The wards won't hold for many more attacks." The beast circled away, and I saw Shadowglass being crushed under its weight, black ichor dripping from its pelt, melting the broken shards below. The beast howled and charged from across the chamber. I stood back as again the ward flared, bottles went dark, and the creature was repelled a second time. It fixed us with a baleful glare from a wide yellow eye and stalked away to prepare for another charge.

"How many more attacks can your spirit wards survive, Rasnich?" Lytta asked, and I could tell from the pallid look on the Low-Tsar's face that he was close to collapse, his blood having fed the spirits that were the power behind his Spiritcraft.

"One more pass. Maybe," he said, breathing heavily.

I watched the creature carefully, as it crunched across the sea of broken glass that now covered the auditorium floor. I noted it was avoiding places where the ichor had fallen. "I have an idea, but it's going to take all our strength to pull it off."

One more howl, and the creature loped towards us at speed.

"Draw from us," Lytta commanded, and Rasnich took hold of her hand and mine. The beast crashed into the ward, and I felt the Succae's pull as he sank his fangs into my flesh and drew life from me. It was like being stabbed with a jagged blade, but I managed to stop myself from pulling away. There was a discernible shockwave as the creature smashed into the wards for a third time, and Shadowglass bottles fractured and broke into pieces all around us. They shattered, but the ward held briefly as the beast turned away. Then it failed completely, and Rasnich fell to his knees. I looked at Lytta, and she nodded. We had just one chance to deal with this thing.

I took flight and headed for the monster's left flank as Lytta did the same on the ground. The Tindalae heads howled, but the great beast didn't stop taking plodding steps as it stalked to a charge distance. As it prepared to turn, I flew close to its left eye and increased my aura to blaze with blinding intensity. The creature recoiled and reared up on its haunches, and I shouted at Lytta to execute our plan. Together, we charged into the beast's flank. Blinded Tindalae heads snapped at me as I heaved with all my strength. At my side, Lytta joined me to do the same.

To begin with, nothing happened, and the beast's immense size seemed immovable. Then Lytta snarled, and I saw her skin grow tight against her bones as blood energy coursed through her. "Push again," she said through gritted teeth, and as I did so, the creature moved and toppled backwards. It crashed onto the bed of ichor and shattered Shadowglass shards. Snarls of anger became yelps of pain as I saw it trying to right itself. I had guessed that the toxic discharge that fell from its body was just as dangerous to it as it was to us. Great rents where acidic discharges had touched uninfected skin opened across the body, exposing white bone beneath. Black blood poured down its sides, and the Tindalae heads screamed in unison.

The great beast tried to get up, but the damage was done, and instead, it slipped and slid on its own blood before subsiding and lying still. The yellow eye fixed us with that hateful stare before the light went out, and it closed for the last time.

Chapter Nine

Lytta pulled Rasnich to his feet, but the Low-Tsar looked spent and unsteady.

"Thank you," he said with a thin smile, but Lytta was not in the mood for celebration.

"Now you will tell me what Rukoi was up to and your part in what has happened," she said forcefully.

"Alright, Serrate. I will tell you what I know."

Rasnich spoke at some length, and the pieces of the puzzle started to come together. He had been approached by Rukoi who, he said, was working for an Angel he had only met once. He was sure that this Angel was female and the description he gave reminded me very much of Kokael. She had approached Rukoi as a representative of a significant faction of the Flight unhappy with their Prince. She said they were seeking Succae allies who might help if a regime change were to take place. They were concerned that the Archangel would ask Karsz for support if an internecine conflict were to develop within the Flight. Rukoi, whose devotion to the Blood Goddess had been banned under the Dursc enlightenment, was apparently sympathetic and said that many Succae were unhappy with Karsz's continuing ban on pagan worship. That disenchantment had festered and grown over the centuries and driven worship of their old gods underground.

Rasnich said Rukoi had secured a pact with Kokael that should a new leader of the Seventh Flight arise, she would ensure the new regime would support a restoration of paganism and actively petition Karsz to listen to his people. For the High-Nin, Rukoi, it was about having the freedom and right to choose. Unsurprisingly, Lytta was unimpressed, and I thought, too, that Rukoi was an optimist at best.

Succae society had changed over time, and I doubted a return to the old ways would have more than fringe support. Unless you factored in the support of the Low-Nin, that was. For them, such a change would represent a new lease of life and the chance to change lives of drudgery and servitude into ones of meaning and achievement. It was the sort of great revolution I suspected many of them dreamed of.

Lytta went on to question Rasnich about his own role in these events, and his answers were simple and direct. He was not a believer in Rukoi's pagan vision; he was a Low-Tsar, and the High-Nin were his customers and his superiors. Rukoi had once been a friend, but there was still a dynamic between them of master and servant. Lytta was dismissive, saying that she thought the Low-Tsars were laws unto themselves, but I had the sense that Rasnich was telling us how things really worked when the Highers came looking for them.

Rukoi had asked him to find the best thief in the Low-Nin, and he had secured the services of a Succae named Rokh. He was never told what Rukoi wanted Rokh to steal, and he didn't want to know. Then things got complex. Using his skills, Rokh had secured the White Rood from the Trinity Palace three days prior to the day of unrest. Rukoi had told Rokh to go into hiding at an empty house in the Landing, and to stay there until he was sent for.

The next Rasnich knew, Rokh returned to the undercity with the Rood in fear of his life. He reported the unrest and said there had been an altercation between him and those who claimed to have been sent by the High-Nin. Rasnich's description left me in no doubt this was Malacaz and his rogues. Then, an Angel had appeared and demanded the Rood be handed over. One of the group murdered the Angel, and everyone had scattered. The Angel's killer had apparently tried killing Rokh in the ensuing chase, but he had managed to elude them in the labyrinthine alleys of the Lower Landing. He had stolen the Rood back from Malacaz later on the day of the protest.

"Where is Rokh now?" Lytta asked.

"And where is the White Rood?" I added.

"Here," Rasnich replied. "I told him to seek sanctuary and

followed him here when some madman came to the arena and threatened me."

"Did this madman have a name?" Lytta said.

"Yes. He said his name was Malacaz." I had a sinking feeling when Lytta looked at me. I had obviously been played.

As Rasnich led us through the temple complex and back out to the *Kolodesh* square, I thought long and hard about Kokael's actions and motivations. The Irin were known as being ultra-loyalists, and it seemed odd to me that their leader would entertain such a plot with a minor Succae rebel, unless it delivered on whatever ulterior motives she had. I didn't believe that Kokael would be moved by Anael's threats to her position—if they had ever been made at all. I thought it more likely she had been testing Vasariah's loyalty after his failure in the Benazzarr affair, and he had believed her sympathetic approach. It was classic Angelic deception, which Vasariah's soldierly mind was likely ill-equipped to handle. It made me wonder what she was up to and who the real targets of her gambit were. Maybe it was lingering desire on my part, but suffice to say, I didn't for one moment believe she was a traitor to the Prince.

Lytta stalked quietly ahead of me, following the Low-Tsar's lead as we made our way into the labyrinth of tight alleyways that led from the market square into the deeper city. We were heading into the western quarter, where cracked streets and buildings were mostly still intact. I had the feeling we were being watched, but Khrov was the kind of city where shadows had their own special personalities and made you continually look over your shoulder. We soon arrived at another wide plaza, where the statue of Vod Karsz towered into the sky. It was a surprisingly artistic depiction of the Succae warlord, and despite the naïveté of the artistic style, the sculptor had captured his stern demeanour and hulking presence perfectly.

Lytta looked around. "Where is he?"

Rasnich pointed up towards the Vod's head. "Up there. In the upper part of the statue." The Low-Tsar opened a hidden door located in the sculpture's heel. I could see stairs inside that presumably wound their way up through the body. Lytta didn't look back and headed inside with Rasnich close behind. I couldn't shake the feeling of being watched and decided to take a short cut to Rokh's hiding place somewhere in Karsz's sculpted head. I took flight and headed up, looking for a way in.

I eventually found an entrance point in the statue's right ear. It was a tight squeeze, but I was able to make my way inside without ruffling my wing feathers too much. Inside was a platform with a large wide copper cauldron, its purpose, I guessed, was multi-fold. First, it was a beacon designed to alert the other parts of the city when an enemy was sighted approaching from the vast, wide plains of Khast. Its second purpose, I thought, was pure theatre – to create the illusion that a Succae titan was alive. Wooden steps to my right led to an upper platform where a pair of eyes looked down at me.

"You must be Rokh," I said assumptively, and those eyes narrowed.

"What's it to you?" the man said gruffly, standing up and pointing an ornate and loaded heavy-looking crossbow directly at my chest.

"I think you have a burden that should be mine to carry," I said. "Rasnich and the Serrate, are on their way up currently." I paused to let Rokh listen to the sounds of the structure creaking as the pair made their way up the inside steps that wound their way up to the head chamber.

Rokh was the smallest Succae I had ever seen. His build was compact, but his body was lithe. He wore a black leather waistcoat and grey woollen leggings that pulled tight around rock solid legs whose muscular strength was clearly defined. He looked like a tightly wound spring, ready to uncoil at any moment. At the same time, he seemed personable, and I was relieved when he put the bow down beside him and bade me ascend the steps.

Rokh's hiding place was well concealed. Metal scaffolding that looked like it was part of the design of the support for the statue's head created struts that striated out from the platform above the beacon to reach a solid rectangular box fifty feet above me. Rokh acrobatically scaled the inner part of the statue's headspace, leaping from strut to strut to dangle briefly in space before hauling himself up and on to its top. I flew up to join him and saw that there was an access into the box itself, although I wasn't sure of its original purpose other for what it was now being used for – a space to retreat into and hide.

Concealed in cloth, I immediately sensed the White Rood once I had dropped inside. It was propped up on the back wall and Rokh pointed to it.

"There it is, Angel, although I need Rasnich's permission to release it into your hands." I was about to argue, but what was a few more minutes? Instead, I asked Rokh exactly how he had managed to steal the artefact from Trinity Palace and how and why he had ended up hiding out in Karsz's statue in the western district of Khrov.

Rokh sat cross-legged in the dark and cramped interior of his hidden lair and seemed happy to speak at length. I heard Rasnich and Lytta arrive about halfway through his narrative, but they didn't interrupt or try and stop him. So I listened and learned the truth of the Rood's theft, Cassiel's death and all that had happened since.

Chapter Ten

Rokh's infiltration of Trinity Palace had taken place three days prior to the day of unrest in the Landing. Rasnich had furnished him with maps and instructions on how to access the Palace's under vault and secret walkways. He said an Angel had provided these to the Low-Tsar, and although he hadn't met them directly, he thought their name was 'Iren'.

Hidden below the Day Hall, he had waited until things were quiet and entered beneath the Throne of the Archangel. Then he had scaled the interior wall, entered the tower, and scaled the heights to access the suspended vault that contained the Flight regalia. Rokh was quite matter-of-fact in his description of this athletic and acrobatic feat, but I knew he would have risked his life several times, and that was without the Honores catching him in the act. Clearly, Rasnich had chosen the right man for the job. I tried not to show it, but I was quite impressed.

Having acquired the Rood, Rokh had left the way he had come, dodging a couple of patrols before making his escape. I found it revealing that the regalia chamber was unlocked. which meant that someone had cleared the path for him. That had to be an Angel with normal access to the Palace. I remembered what Vasariah had said about the wards that protected the regalia vault and who had access to them. I was certain now that he and his Legio Honores were innocent, which left the High Steward, Anfial, Narinel the Wise, and his Cherubim. Of these, only Anfial seemed a likely candidate, given that Narinel and his staff only accessed the vault on ceremonial duties. I had known the High Steward for a long time, and it was difficult to imagine him being involved in a plot against the Prince. However, his participation at the request of a senior member of the

Flight was something I could believe, as he was known to be obsessively didactic about following orders to the letter. There had also been that odd incident on the steps of the Palace where he had cut short my talk with his junior steward, Evangelos. At the time, Anfial had said it was to protect him from the Irin's suspect list, but I was now wondering whether I had started delving too deep into Evangelos's recounting of unknowns fleeing the Palace grounds. An account that I now thought was probably fabricated.

"From there, Angel, I headed to the Lower Landing. I was told to hide out in the attic of a burned-out house near the northern wall and wait for further contact." I knew where he meant. It was a few streets away from the Red Roof Inn. The house had formerly been home to one of the Bonded, although I didn't know who. It had caught fire several months after Benazzar's attempted coup and had never been repaired or re-occupied.

"Then things started to go wrong," Rokh continued. "For the first two nights, it was all quiet. Then on the third night, I heard someone skulking about. They were making odd noises, and it took me a while to realise they were sniffing the air. Next thing I know, I'm surrounded by a right strange bunch of characters." Rokh went on to describe Malacaz and his pack of rogues.

"They knew I had the stave alright. They said they were there to take it off my hands. I said to them that I would need to see some proof, but they didn't like that one bit. I got a right ear-bending by their leader, who gave me some guff about doing something for the greater good. He blabbed on about how my kind would benefit from what they were going to do. Honestly, I thought this fella was mad, and I didn't like him. I said to them that the Rood was not mine to give. They would need to track down Low-Tsar Rasnich, and if he said yes, then, and only then, would I hand it over. Then things got tense. Malacaz ordered the sniffer – a big old wolf man—to take it off me. I could see he wasn't happy about it, but I reckon he would have pitched in were it not for what happened next."

"Which was?"

"An Angel suddenly flew in from above. She looked young, not at all like all the rest of you. She says, 'Give me the Rood or there will be trouble'. That caused a right bit of consternation among Malacaz and his gang. I thought she meant business. and I could see wolf man thought so too. All of a sudden, everyone made a dash for the stick but kid-Angel, she got there first and snapped it up. She was brandishing a fiery spear, and everyone backed off. I reckon if she had just headed straight off, only the black feathered bird-woman could have followed her, but she decided to hang about and give a lecture on right and wrong and how we should all be ashamed of ourselves. No doubt it was from the heart, but it was a little naïve, to be honest. I saw Malacaz give some sort of signal and then, out of nowhere, this masked man appeared. Fearsome-looking fellow, he was. He didn't say a word, just rammed a Shard Blade right into her back. It did its job, and a second later, she was dead on the floor. Malacaz grabbed the stick and was off, just like that. I could tell the others were shocked and the old wolfman wasn't at all happy, but he left shortly afterwards, and apologised for the trouble."

So Kaualakoo was Cassiel's killer after all. It made sense, as he was probably the most unhinged and dangerous of the lot. I felt that deep sadness steal across my soul again. Poor, young, and idealistic Cassiel. You had no idea of the danger you were in.

"What did you do next?"

"I ain't stupid, and this wasn't the first time something I had acquired had been taken away from me. I had marked the stick so that I could track it again, and that's what I did. At first light, there were a lot of folk crowding into the Landing, so I was able to blend in with the crowd and go hunting, both on the ground and over the rooftops. It didn't take me all that long to find Malacaz again. He was standing just outside the Lower Landing gates talking to a couple of tall, shrouded people."

"Can you describe these people? Were they Angels?"

"I don't think so. They were tall and slender, and I had the impression they were powerful. I'd say one was male and one was female, but I can't be certain."

"Then what happened?"

"The male took the stick in his hand and spoke words over it. I heard a clicking sound and felt a pulse of power. I heard him say something about Excelsis, and that whisper echoed off every wall around us."

"Yet you didn't feel any compulsion to act?"

"No. I am a little deaf in one ear though, so maybe I didn't fully hear what he was saying."

"I think you had a lucky escape, Rokh."

"Maybe, Angel. Ain't the first time my deafness has saved me."

"What next?"

"That was it. The fellow handed the stick back to Malacaz, and the two went on their way. The mad Mal looked right pleased with himself and went off in search of a celebratory drink."

"He took the staff with him?"

"Oh, yeah. Just made a little mistake when he got to the inn on Tether Street. It was closed, but he broke in. Whilst he was helping himself to some brandy, I helped myself to the stick and made a swift but silent getaway. He never knew what happened, but I am sure he knew it was me."

"No honour among thieves, I suppose?"

"Excuse me, Angel! I got plenty of honour but that don't keep an artisan like me in fine fettle. I decided to get out of the Landing as fast as I could, so I was gone."

"To the Tether?"

"Nah, far too obvious. To the Well Path, of course!"

"There's a Well Path in the Landing?" I said in surprise.

"Yes, there is," Lytta said from below. I peered over and saw Rasnich and the Serrate standing there looking remarkably calm and collected. Given the number of steps they had just climbed, I was a touch disappointed.

"We'll have to talk about that later, Serrate," I said darkly. "Where does that pathway go?"

"The undercity. Don't worry, Angel. None of the Highers know anything about it. It's a Low Path you see?" Cold comfort when your potential enemy has a conduit straight into your home. I admired Rokh's confidence, but if Lytta knew about it, then odds were high the Vod did too.

"You went back to Rasnich?"

"He did," the Low-Tsar said. "I took the Rood to Rukoi, but he didn't want it. Told ne to keep it safe until he sent for it. Honestly, Angel, I wasn't all that happy about that, but I had the feeling Rukoi wanted to keep its location hidden from various parties. My impression was that he was playing a game with them."

"A deadly game, as it turned out," Lytta said.

"He said it was a means to an end, although I didn't entirely understand what end that would be."

I thought I did. If Kokael had promised support for pressure on Karsz to restore pagan worship, I suspected Rukoi wanted to see something more than promises from his Angel ally, however silkily delivered they had been.

"Did you tell Rukoi about Malacaz and his gang of rogues becoming involved?"

Rasnich looked uncomfortable. "No, Angel, I did not. The Highers aren't interested in details, just results. He wouldn't have cared unless another High-Nin were involved."

High-Nin arrogance made sense, but that meant Zamalca and her brother, if that was what he was, were unexpected complications. Rukoi had been caught in a web, and I suspected that an Irin Angel had spun it for him. The question was whether that spinner had been aware that other spiders were closing in. I had a sinking feeling that they had known but had found the sacrifice of a Succae life at best, acceptable, and at worst, inconsequential. It upped the ante in my mind. Whatever Kokael and her watchers were looking at, it had to be a serious threat to both the Prince and the Flight itself.

"This Malacaz then came looking for you?" Lytta said as my mind pondered the Low-Tsar's testimony. "Yes, he did. Came swaggering into the arena saying he knew I had done something bad, and that it would be best for my welfare if I were to hand the Rood over to him. I told him to go boil his blood, but he just laughed at me. Said he would give me time to think. Said I didn't want to meet his other half, as vampire or not, I would be returned to the Well, and there I would be her prisoner. I didn't rightly know what he was talking about, but as soon as he left, I gathered Kjatz and the others and told them I was going away for a while. Kjatz got fixated on Rukoi's revolution and repeated much of what that Malacaz had said, so I told him it was connected, which wasn't that much of a lie."

"And you gave him the Shadowglass bottle so that we could find you?"

"I did. Since then, we've been hiding here, expecting that someone like the Serrate would come looking for us eventually. The fact it is you two," he said, nodding to Lytta and myself, "is quite a relief, and a timely intervention, as it turned out."

That was a salutatory reminder that we were all far from safety. It was clear, from the predicament in which we had found Rasnich, that Malacaz and his shadow sister had found him, too. They had to be close.

Chapter Eleven

I heard Zamalca before I saw her, the snap of metal links and the whine of axe blades slicing through the air from behind me. I just managed to pivot so my right wing wasn't shredded. Instead, the blade heads slammed into bone, and I felt a sudden sharp pain lance through me as it fractured. Rokh leapt to his feet as she was suddenly among us.

She had her deadly Angel catching *Sarigama* woven around her black-shrouded body, and as she moved in a silent dance, the axes on their chains whirled in deadly arcs. Rokh got caught by one in the right shoulder but turned acrobatically with the blow to vault from the upper platform down to where Rasnich stood, looking on, open-mouthed. Lytta was in motion, fangs bared, red blades naked and readied as she raced up the platform steps. I called Nimrod to my right hand in spear form, but Zamalca twisted her upper body in a sudden move to send the axes into the haft and it was sent flying from my grip to clatter on the threshold of the statue's right ear channel. She wove the weapon back around her and launched a two-footed kick which caught me square in the chest and sent me sprawling back the way I had come. I came to a sliding stop on my back at the edge of the exit to the outside. The Rood had slid out of my grasp with the breaking of my wing, and I saw it twenty feet away as Zamalca moved toward it. She was just within reaching distance when Lytta intercepted her in a crimson whirl of steel. Under pressure, Zamalca backflipped away as Lytta's blades flashed but failed to find their target by the narrowest of margins.

Zamalca spun in a circle, and her axes whirled around her, forcing the Serrate to duck and weave out of their path. I had started to get up when I was suddenly yanked backwards and found myself falling from Karsz's ear to land on his shoulder some forty feet below. As I slid to the edge, I managed to get a purchase on a ridge of decorative metal armour. Looking up, I saw Malacaz grinning at me insanely before he disappeared back inside Karsz's head. I secured purchase just as I saw sparks flying from the left side of the statue's head. I saw Zamalca leap, catch the top of Karsz's ear and then scale upwards to the top of his head. I briefly saw the glow of Lytta's blades, but not the Serrate herself. I had expected her to follow, but instead she disappeared back inside.

I wanted to take flight, but my broken bones were still knitting themselves back together, so I was stuck as an observer, and an unarmed one at that. Malacaz suddenly appeared back at the right earlobe and jumped down to join me on the statue's right shoulder. He landed perfectly and rolled forward to end up in a crouching stance. I could see he had the Rood in one hand, and, with a laugh, he ran towards me. I'll admit it was unexpected and took me by surprise. I heard a shout from above as Lytta launched Nimrod into the air, leaving me with a choice—to either stop Malacaz or re-arm myself. Nimrod and I had been partners for so long, it wasn't a hard choice to make, and I positioned myself to catch it as it sailed through the air.

Malacaz raced past me, Rood held high like it was a relay baton. Nimrod in hand, I turned just as the rogue leapt from the end of the statue's right shoulder. I had the target, but something stopped me from just killing Malacaz out of hand. I still had a feeling he was a pawn in someone else's game, and he could possibly have barged me off the shoulder as he was running past me. Maybe it was respect between rivals that was undeserved, but somehow my subconscious must have thought he had earned it.

Malacaz dropped around eighty feet into the open palm of the statue's outstretched left hand. He landed with incredible poise and grace, rolling forward with the impact to rise into a standing crouch. Then he leapt from there, disappeared off the edge, and I lost sight of him. I knew I needed to get after him and the Rood, but the pain of my broken wing was still sharp, and I knew full flight was out of the question. Seeking a swift solution, I looked down at the statue and saw sculpted folds in the detail of Karsz's tunic that could act as catch points between where I was and Karsz's hand below. Knowing time was of the essence, I took the chance and slid down the statue, using the metal folds to slow my descent. Everything went well until I missed my last catch hold and fell the last twenty feet to land chest-first on Karsz's palm.

Pain shuddered through my wing frame with the jolt of the landing. I peered over the edge to the last hundred or so feet to the ground and saw Malacaz landing on Karsz's left foot before somersaulting to the dusty square below. He turned to look up at me and gave me a jaunty wave before turning to run eastwards toward the centre of Khrov. I looked up to see Lytta and Zamalca locked in a deadly struggle. Lytta's swords sliced through the darkness, red arcs left by the light of her blades. Zamalca's black-clad form was a neat silhouette as the silver *Sarigama* whisked and whirled in defence and attack. It looked like the Serrate was losing ground as they fought across the top of the statue's head. but with Lytta you never knew. I didn't imagine there was much an ancient war spirit didn't know about fight tactics and strategy, but this was a cunning enemy and one I didn't want on my tail anytime soon.

I turned my attention back to Malacaz and was pleasantly surprised. He was in a scuffle with Rokh and Rasnich. It looked like they were trying to wrestle the Rood away from him. They had bought me time, but I didn't expect our rogue to be delayed for long. I looked down the legs of the statue, but there was less detail here, and I didn't think sliding was a safe option any longer. Karsz's left knee was slightly bent, and I guessed Mal had leapt to that point and then vaulted to the Vod's left foot below. I spread my wings and had to breathe deeply as pain lanced through me. It was like being stabbed, but the initial sharp flash subsided to settle into a painful ache that was just about tolerable. I watched as time slowed and Mal used the momentum to kick Rasnich away and throw Rokh over his shoulder. I launched myself from Karsz's hand and hoped for the best.

With only one wing, I initially dropped like a stone until I managed to initiate a spiral, dropping in ever-decreasing circles as I headed swiftly to the ground. On impact, I landed badly and felt new pain flare in my right leg which had taken the brunt of the controlled fall. I managed to stay upright and watched as Malacaz sped away from his Succae pursuers to disappear into one of the many alleyways that radiated off the square. As I regained some level of equilibrium, I dropped into a loping run and went in pursuit of my quarry.

Chapter Twelve

A huge tremor struck just as I caught up with Rasnich and Rokh at the entrance to the alleyway on the edge of Karsz Square. The pair stopped in their tracks as a crack split the narrow passage in two and shook the surrounding buildings. Choking dust blew up like a sudden squall, filling my lungs and stinging my eyes. The effects were not so debilitating for the Succae, but they had stopped anyway. Rasnich gave me a resigned look.

"That fellow is armed and insane. I think we should let you take it from here, Angel." I was about to say something smart-mouthed in response, but Rasnich was only telling the truth. It was my fault Malacaz had got here in the first place, and it was my responsibility to recover the White Rood.

"You said something about a Low Path, Rokh? Where is it?"

Rokh looked at Rasnich for permission to reveal a Low-Nin secret. The Low-Tsar nodded quickly.

"It's in the lower eastern hall of the Black Temple, but you'll need to be careful. The structure on that side is collapsed and it's quite a squeeze to get to the path entrance." I thanked Rokh for the warning and set off. As I did, I heard a distant scream and looked back at Karsz's statue to see a body falling from its head. I didn't have time to work out whether it was Lytta or Zamalca who had fallen, but I hoped the Serrate had prevailed. If it was Zamalca, I thought there was a strong chance I wouldn't get back to the Landing.

I made my way back towards the *Kolodesh* and Black Temple Square as fast as I could. I have always had a good sense of direction, so even though the lanes and alleyways were a twisting labyrinth, I managed to stay on track, and before long, I emerged back into the western side of the market square flanking the Black Temple. I had not seen hide nor hair of Malacaz en route, but I fashioned Nimrod into a sword just in case there was a need for close combat. I had a feeling that when cornered, Malacaz's smiling façade would turn into something more dangerous and unpredictable.

I climbed the steps and entered the quiet outer halls of the Black Temple to the Succae's old gods. A grand colonnade of black basalt columns marked the boundaries of the outer ward, and I stopped for a moment to let my senses adjust to the surroundings. It was as deathly quiet as Saur'Il's mausoleum, and just as bleak and dark. This outer space had once been a marketplace, and I could see the remains of stalls, pitches and tents left behind by those who had once traded here. Debris and discarded items were strewn across the floors, victims to what must have been a frenzied retreat into exile. Broken pots, overturned baskets, and other such items lay where they had been abandoned on the day the Seventh Flight had launched their final assault on Khrov and forced the Succae out of their capital city. At the time, I remembered, we had thought such a decisive victory would end the war, but that optimism was short lived as the vampire nation regrouped and came at us with renewed vigour and intensity in our own Garden.

The entrance doors to the temple's inner ward were open—great brass gates decorated with moulded faces that looked cruel and imperious. On closer inspection, it was clear these graven representations of the old gods had been defaced and defiled, presumably during Vod Dursc's renaissance when the pagan ways had come to an end. I had always known this history, but it was strange to see such clear evidence of an entire society's sudden change in belief writ so clear and large in front of me.

As soon as I made my way inside the Black Temple, I could feel the presence of the Necrene pathway nearby. It was a sudden pull at your senses, like the sharp cry of a raptor in the night hunting its prey, a jarring sound that set your teeth on edge. The Necrene Well devoured life itself and was still a mystery to my kind. I had experienced it first hand, and it had nearly killed me. No wonder my nerves were suddenly jangling.

I ventured deeper in, and with my sight now adjusted, I could see a vast inner chamber where the vandalised statues of the old gods lay in pieces. At one point, they had been tall and imposing pieces of masonry with the capacity to instil fear and awe. Now, they had a forlorn appearance, broken, sad and forgotten. I followed my sense of unease and was drawn east towards a pair of tall doors made of blackened wood that were partly collapsed, bowing under the weight of a caved-in roof that weighed heavily upon them. It was a wonder they hadn't given way, but so far, they remained intact, stoically resisting their inevitable destruction. I wondered if this was the tight squeeze Rokh had been referring to but quickly dismissed the notion. Even with an injured wing, I was able to sidle through the gap with little problem.

The floor in the hall beyond was broken and had subsided to the right. Great rents scarred the southern wall, where pressure from the partial collapse of this side of the temple structure had sent fissures running through it. I could see steps leading down at the hall's eastern end. On closer inspection, the stairs were blocked by large pieces of masonry that had fallen from above and rolled down the steps to block the way forward. There were small gaps between the stones but nothing that I could even begin to think about trying to squeeze through. As I thought through my options, another tremor shook the building and dust and debris fell from above. I looked up to see that the fissures in both the eastern and southern walls had grown, and both were in danger of imminent collapse. If I wasn't careful, this place could easily become my tomb.

I headed down the stairs and took a closer look at the obstruction. There were four pieces of stone nestled tightly together. I could only presume Malacaz had managed to pass through here just before the last one had fallen into its current resting place. I felt along its stone surface and noted that a hairline fracture ran along its left-hand side. I shaped Nimrod into a war pick and took a mighty swing at the fault line. Chips of stone flew, but the crack didn't widen any further. I reshaped my weapon into a war hammer and took another three swings. It looked like there was some small extension of the crack in the rock, but the overall piece remained stubbornly intact.

As I paused to examine my unsuccessful handiwork, I felt the vibration of another tremor shake the foundations. This one felt deeper and longer than the ones that had gone before, and I could hear the crashes of more debris falling in the hall above. Then there was a pause where everything went quiet. For a moment, I thought I might have been lucky, but that hope was short-lived. I heard a strange grating sound as the walls above and around me finally gave way. Great pieces of stone crashed down and shook the ground with a blast of dust and a cacophony of noise. I swung the hammer again, but the rock refused to break. A large piece of masonry slammed into the stairs above and rolled down toward me. It was massive and would have made me a permanent addition to the Black Temple, but instinct took over and my wing had healed enough to carry me aloft. I shot upward as the jagged lump of rock missed me by the narrowest of margins to roll down and smash into the blockage at the bottom of the stairs. Maybe it was due to its own momentum, or perhaps I had done just enough damage to the fault line, but when the dust cleared, the left-hand side had sheared off, leaving a hole wide enough for me to drop through and into the passage below.

The taste of Necrene energy was heavy in the air here, and I knew the entrance to the Low Path had to be nearby. I enhanced my aura, and Nimrod amplified my glow to illuminate the passage ahead that ran southwards in the direction of the temple entrance. After a few hundred feet, the passageway turned to the left, and I thought I could hear a voice speaking in whispers. It had a strange lilting tone, as though it was intoning a chant or a prayer of some kind. I turned my aura down, reshaped Nimrod back to spear form and advanced cautiously. Around the corner, another set of steps led down to a chamber that was lit with an eerie glow of blue light. It looked like it had been used as a storeroom, and boxes and barrels still lined the walls. The stone floor was plain and unmarked except for one wide stone slab that had been moved to one side, and it was from the resultant dark hole that the blue Necrene energy spilled into the chamber.

I heard the whispering voice again and tracked it to being somewhere on the far wall, concealed by barrels and boxes. The roof was no more than ten to twelve feet high, but that would be more than enough elevation to see who it was. I ascended and saw the tattered garb of Malacaz.

"I see you, rogue," I said. "Stand forward! Come out of the shadows!"

Malacaz stopped talking and looked up at me from where he lay sprawled among broken wood. His body lay in a contorted position, and I could see his jerkin was drenched in blood.

"I would do as you ask, Angel, but I seem to have a little problem with being vertical. Horizontal is fine though, as you can see."

I reinstated my aura and dropped back down to the floor. I moved obstacles aside to reveal the former demigod lying there, bloody and broken.

"What happened to you, Malacaz?"

"No honour among thieves, Angel."

"Kaualakoo?" Mal nodded and coughed. It was wet, raspy, and bubbles of blood appeared by his lips. I was surprised the assassin had left him alive.

"I thought he was working for you?"

Mal smiled that mad smile and let out a brief laugh.

"So did I, Angel, so did I. I thought it was over, that the rift was healed, but I was wrong." I wasn't sure what he was talking about. I wasn't aware that Malacaz and Kaualakoo had a prior history.

"I suppose it's in his nature, but your lot will find that out soon enough." Malacaz was bleeding out, although I wasn't sure if he could die. Either way, I wanted to understand what he was talking about before either a healing coma or a last breath came upon him.

"He has the White Rood?"

Mal's eyes were losing focus, and he muttered some silly rhyme before looking back at me.

"Where's Zamalca?" he asked. I honestly didn't know, so I just shrugged.

"Oh, my dark half has gone back to the Well, eh? I suppose I will see her there soon."

"Mal! Where is the Rood?"

"It will be in his hands now, Angel. Looks like he gets the last laugh."

"Who? Kaualakoo?"

"No, no. Charomos. Judge, jury, and my executioner."

Malacaz subsided into a still silence that looked like death to me. I say that because in my experience, demigods and their kind can be remarkably resilient, but this looked final. I guessed that Kaualakoo had stabbed him multiple times all over his body, and Mal was many things, but a fighter was not one of them. My mind raced with the implications of this whole affair being a plot of the Primogi. What was Charomos planning? And why? How did Kokael and her Irin fit into all this? I couldn't imagine Anael's most loyal order of watchers would suddenly turn on him in favour of an outsider god, no matter what had been promised. There was something I wasn't seeing. Whatever the truth, I had to try and intercept the murderous Kaualakoo before he handed the Rood over to Charomos for good.

I turned to the space below the floor, sensing the Low Path's power pulsing through me, and a visible corona of the Path's horizon below. Whilst it was much less intense than the Well itself, I could still feel the Necrene energy that powered the Path pulling at me, seeking a way to gain a hold and leech away my lifeforce. I felt repulsed by it and had serious doubts that I could survive long in its grip, but the facts were obvious. I was out of time and alternatives. I braced myself and crossed the Path's threshold.

Chapter Thirteen

I have known pain in many forms in my life. It has been my experience that physical pain is far easier to handle than mental pain, but neither should be sought after. Very shortly after passing onto the Low Path, I felt all my senses and my physical being becoming wracked with waves of nausea-inducing hurt. Around me, smothering darkness threatened to close in as blue flashes of light buzzed around me like a swarm of bees. They wanted to get inside me, and I covered my mouth, nose, and ears with my cloak as best I could.

Agonising seconds passed that felt like an eternity, and I could feel my body being stretched and warped under the pull of the Necrene forces around me. I imagined flesh tearing and bones breaking, as my mind dissolved into a dementia born of unbelievable torment. I clutched Nimrod close to my chest. It was a solid and tacit reminder of the real world and a departure from what my mind was telling me was happening to my physical body. I took one shuddering step after another as the lights around me began to lengthen into blue streaks that accelerated both toward and away from me at the same time. There was a strange sense of dislocation, and then it felt like I was in a bizarre horizontal freefall where I still had a grip on what was up and down, ahead and behind. I carried on walking, and tried to ignore the senses that were telling me I was in full flight. This sensation continued until, ahead of me, the flashing lights coalesced into a solid corona. At that point, stumbling steps became a run as I wanted to close the distance as soon as I could. Waves of pain rocked through me and grew in pace and intensity. I wasn't sure I could make it, but there was no turning back now. I would either reach the other side or the Necrene would feed on my life until there was nothing left. I pushed myself on, and in my growing desperation, found myself laughing like Malacaz had before he had gone still. I wasn't sure what was so funny then, and even less so now.

I reached the corona and passed through, probably on my knees although I can't be sure. There was a flash of light and the sound of wind rushing past me. The waves of pain ceased as suddenly as they had begun. I felt as though I had been underwater and just breached the surface. All around me, colours flashed, and my body vibrated with energy. As soon as I had got used to the sudden change, there was a popping noise as I exited the Path and found myself under a vaulted stone roof in a chamber lit by torches that flickered in their brackets.

I tried to stand, but whilst the mind was willing, the flesh wasn't. I felt utterly drained of strength and energy, and every part of my body ached. It was like I had been mercilessly pummelled for an extended period. I heard laughter, and was just able to turn my head to see who was talking. It was Charomos, and Kaualakoo was standing next to him. To one side, I could see Aethi and a hooded Angel I knew to be Kokael. I felt bitter disappointment as she walked forward and picked up Nimrod from where it had rolled from my hand. I imagined Duma Fallenstar was laughing somewhere as well.

"Best we keep this safe," Kokael said with a thin smile. "Don't want you getting any foolish ideas of heroics do we, Azshael?" I only had it in me to say two words in response. "Traitorous bitch." That engendered more laughter from Charomos and his tame assassin, who handed his new master the White Rood.

"Sleep now, Angels," he commanded, and as unconsciousness beckoned, I had the grim satisfaction of seeing the look on Kokael's face as she also collapsed to the floor. Nimrod fell from her hand and rolled towards me, but it was as the Primogi said as my eyes closed, "Too little, too late."

Chapter Fourteen

I awoke to the sound of distant cheers and much closer swearing. I opened one swollen eye and saw I was behind bars. Across from me, Kokael was trying to pick the lock to her cell, but didn't seem to be having much luck. We had both been stripped of armour, weapons, and most of our clothing. To see Kokael's body clad purely in sheer muslin was not the worst sight to wake up to, even if she *was* a traitor.

"About time you woke up, Azsh," she said as another thin sliver of wood broke in the lock. "Make yourself useful. I don't think we have much time."

My aching brain was trying to work things out, but it also wasn't having much luck.

"Why should I help you, Kokael? You're a traitor!"

She gave me an exasperated look. "If I am a traitor, then what am I doing here?" That was too difficult a question for me to answer at that moment, so I settled for something simpler.

"Where are we anyway?"

"We're in the prison beneath the Temple," she said, intent on finding another wooden sliver to use as a lockpick. "Charomos is addressing the Citadel Legions using the Rood and will soon have an army under his command. Shake it off, Azsh!"

My head hurt, but I am a sucker for being told what to do by half-naked females, so I got to my feet and looked around. As the brain fog cleared, I recognised where we were being held, just a few cells away from where Marok had been murdered by Kaualakoo. I was beginning to think we might have a hope of getting out of here, but I needed to understand Kokael's part in all this first.

"You want to enlighten me as to what's going on?"

Kokael sighed as her new pick broke in the lock. "You're a clever boy, Azsh. Why don't you tell me?"

"You set Charomos up?"

"Not exactly. We didn't know it was Charomos until very recently, although he was a prime candidate after Darophon witnessed your encounter with him in Registry Hall."

"Wait a second. Who's we? And what is 'it'?"

"After the incident with Benazzarr it was clear his cabal extended beyond the Succae and that various Bonded had materially aided and abetted the coup attempt. The problem was that Anael killed Benazzarr, and between you and your Serrate, the key plotters on the Succae side of things were also eliminated before they could be properly interrogated."

"So, you and Darophon set a plan in motion to root out the conspirators?"

"Not just Darophon and myself. The Vod and his Lords were also involved." I was momentarily speechless.

Kokael laughed at the look on my face. "What? You think you are the only member of the Flight who speaks to the Succae? You are sent when diplomacy is called for. I go when more intricate discussions are required."

"Is that how Rukoi got involved?"

"Rukoi had long been a thorn in the Vod's side. His pagan belief in his Blood Goddess never went away, and he wasn't the most discreet of plotters. Karsz thought he might be involved with someone on this side, so I reached out to him and set wheels in motion."

"What did you promise him?"

"Support. When the time came."

"What kind of support?"

"I said the Flight would back a liberalisation of worship, and that the Archangel would meet Karsz to suggest a restoration of the less dangerous gods in the Succae pantheon."

"Karsz would never have agreed to that!"

"No, but then he didn't need to. I just needed to convince Rukoi that we would back him, and as you know, I am very convincing." She winked at me and blew a kiss. I was not impressed. "Apparently not. Rukoi didn't trust you, did he?"

"There may have been a late crisis of faith, but nothing I couldn't have handled."

"He wanted more than words, I take it?"

"He wanted to meet Anael and hear it from the Archangel direct. I was in the process of setting that up when Rukoi got himself killed."

"Zamalca and her ghosts from the Well?"

"It would seem so. I was unaware of Zamalca's connection to Malacaz until it was too late. It would appear the Succae did know however, so perhaps you should blame them?" I remembered the duality that was Malacaz and Zamalca being depicted on the hides in the Hall of Keeping and the fact it had come as a surprise to Lytta. It looked like we had both been left to find our own answers.

"How did Charomos get involved?"

"Rukoi met with the Primogi on the eve of the troubles. He discussed the Bonded backing a change of the status quo in return for Succae support. Word of the Rood's alleged powers must have given him some ideas of his own."

"Charomos then got his rogue to recruit some help and steal the Rood from Rukoi?"

"Yes. That was unexpected. As was Vasariah's plot to steal the Rood."

"You didn't trust him?"

"Anael didn't trust him. He and his Legio Honores allowed Benazzarr right into the Trinity Palace. I had to agree with the Prince's evaluation that it was more than suspicious."

"You tested his loyalty as well?"

"It was Darophon's idea. He set up the very public dressing down which got Vasariah so angry and agitated. In truth, that exercise in humiliation was a setup to test his loyalty and see how he would react. In the aftermath, I played on his anger and suggested a show of force was necessary, using the White Rood to show the Archangel the limits of his power. He went for it, thinking the Irin were with him. I just didn't count on him employing one of the Juvenii to do it."

"That got Cassiel killed."

"If I had known about it, I would have stopped it. I am sorry about what happened to Cassiel, but that is on Vasariah and not me."

"So Rukoi got his loyal Low-Tsar to recruit a thief to capture the Rood as bait to hook the big fish. I presume you provided all the information and cleared the way?"

"To a certain extent, yes. It wasn't much of a challenge."

"But then Rokh loses the Rood to Malacaz, who takes it to Charomos on the morning of the revolt?"

"Yes. I'll admit things were out of control at that point. But then, no plan is perfect."

"Why didn't you move on Charomos then?"

"We didn't know it was him, and secondly, the Rood was missing. The Bonded were already militant. Arresting one of their leaders without evidence would have been a potentially incendiary act."

"That's when you decided to find the Rood, and that's how I got dragged into your sorry mess."

"Last I checked, you are Anael's servant and a member of the Seventh Flight. You were asked to do your duty!"

"Why didn't you tell me everything? I went into the Vod's presence blind!"

"We were not sure that Karsz was playing the same game we were. Only after the unrest you witnessed among the Low-Nin were we sure that something bigger was going on."

"What do you mean?"

"I mean, Charomos's plans don't stop with the Prince. He wants to rule everyone and everything!"

"And you gave him the tool to do it!"

"We can debate that point later. For now, we should stop talking, and you should help get us out of these cells so we can do something about it!" I was angry with Kokael, but she had a point. Nothing would be achieved unless we could get out of here.

I went to the bars of my cell and called out down the passage.

"Mama? Papa? You hear me?"

A welcome but distant voice broke the silence.

"Azsh? We hear you! Are you alright? You be looking dead when they carried you and the black-winged Angel past us!" It was Papa Famine.

"What are you doing?" Kokael said. "They're locked up, too!"

"How are the toothpicks coming along?"

"Badly."

"So let me try a different approach then!"

"Can't you use fire to melt these locks?"

"Kokael. This is an Angel prison. There wouldn't be much point to it if the bars could be melted by fire! Besides, why haven't you tried that already?"

"That's a soldier power, Azshael! I am not a soldier!"

I muttered something about excuses and called down the hall again.

"Papa? Can you get out of your cell?

"Mama says yes, of course we can," Papa replied with a derisive whine.

"Well, please do and then come and get us out."

"Alright, Azsh, alright. We be working on it." I heard the sound of arguing and then the sound of metal grinding and breaking. Moments later, Papa Famine and Mama Feast in all their Hyena-headed glory were standing in front of my cell.

"Look at you!" Mama said, her tone heavy with disappointment. "How them mighty have fallen, Papa," she said, turning to her diminutive mate.

I smiled but was slightly surprised when no smile was returned.

"I think Azsh would like to be released, Mama," Papa said with a sympathetic look in my direction.

"Oh, would he? Well, as an Ambassador, I am sure he knows favours don't come for free, no."

I sighed. The Hyenae were voracious gods in all sense of the word.

"Alright Mama. What do you want?"

Her yellow eyes sparkled. "First, we be wanting the deeds to the Inn. Sylvenell don't run that place no more. We do." I really wasn't sure of the technical status of the Red Roof Inn, which really belonged to the Flight now it had been declared an embassy, but all that could be sorted out later, so I just nodded. "Noted and I'll see what I can do."

"That be good enough for me," Papa said, but I could tell Mama wasn't finished.

"Second," she said, "we be wanting a personal favour from you!"

"What kind of favour?"

"We sure ain't decided yet! Sometime in the future we be calling that in."

I had a bad feeling I was setting myself up for trouble, but I agreed as there really wasn't much choice, and time was running short.

"Alright, Mama – you have my word, witnessed by a senior Watcher," I said, indicating Kokael, who I could tell found this whole thing highly amusing. Mama and Papa turned around, suddenly realising we were not alone.

"Oh, Missus Blackwings is here," Mama said, turning her attention to the Leader of the Irin.

"My name is Kokael the Watcher, and I don't do deals with Bonded souls," she said, with more authority than I thought appropriate, given the situation she was in.

Papa flattened his ears, a sure indication that this was the wrong answer.

"Oh, well that's alright," Mama said. "Dumb girls who want to stay locked up ain't no concern of mine, no."

I doubt anyone had spoken to Kokael like that for a long time, possibly ever. She looked astonished as Mama turned away and began to gnaw through the bars of my cell. It didn't take long, and Papa helped me remove them so I was able to step out into the passageway. I went across to Kokael's cell to see what I could do about breaking her out, but Mama blocked my path with a snarl. "She pays or she stays," she said, her vicious jaws wide open.

"She'll pay. I'll see to it Mama. I promise." Kokael gave me a sharp glare but managed to keep her mouth shut. Mama gave me a big smile and sashayed over to Kokael's cell to repeat her metal eating exercise. After Kokael was free, I told the Hyenae to hide until they were sent for.

"Now what?" I said as we advanced cautiously through the cell block toward the Iron Gates. The deeper cells were empty, and I wondered why the Hyenae had been left locked up. Then I came to the obvious conclusion that as we were connected, Charomos had kept them for additional leverage over me in case it was required. As it turned out, I was as susceptible to the Rood's powers as any other Angel, but it showed his capacity for cunning.

"We need to get the Rood from Charomos somehow," Kokael said as we came in sight of the stairs that led up to the Iron Gates.

"How are we going to do that?"

"I have a surprise up my sleeve, but his assassin will need taking care of. Last I saw, he stays very close to Charomos."

"Surprise?"

"Yes. The Rood has no effect on me."

"But I just saw…"

"Yes. I went along with it as Kaualakoo would have killed me in two heartbeats. We need to get Charomos away from his bodyguard. That's your job."

Oh, great.

Chapter Fifteen

Kokael and I made our way up out of the deep cells and into the upper gaol without encountering anyone. The sounds of cheering grew louder the closer we drew to the exit. In the upper cells, I found Ys and her 'mother' still behind bars. Naturally, Ysabeau was full of questions, but as we didn't have the means to release them, I assured them we would be back to get them out as soon as we could.

Ys's guardian changed shape back to her usual spider form, surprising Kokael, who took a step back as the former goddess sprayed the bars to the cell with black webs until she and her 'daughter' were completely obscured from sight. There was a sudden sound of metal shearing as the cell door was yanked free and hung in suspension before it could clatter on the floor and alert any nearby listeners.

"Mind if we see ourselves out, Azsh?" Ysabeau said, but Kokael warned her to stay put for a while. "Charomos probably has many Angels under his control now, and we don't know what orders they have been given. It would be safer for you to stay where you are."

"But we can help you!" Ys said, and she had a point. Certainly, they could present an unexpected surprise if things got difficult. "Alright. Stay here for now," I said. "We'll call for you if we need you." That seemed to satisfy Ys at least. Her mother's eight bulging eyes just stared at us impassively, but given she didn't move to follow us, it looked like she was letting her 'daughter' take the lead.

"I think we need to work on the prison's integrity," Kokael said as we headed to the gaol's exit and got our first sight of what was going on in Athenaeum square.

Angels were gathered below the steps of the Herald's Hall. So far, it looked like a couple of hundred of Lamechial's Legio Alba and maybe another century of the Acropolis garrison. It was a sizeable force, but, I thought, probably not enough to think of an assault on Trinity Palace.

"Looks like we have some time in hand before Charomos can execute his plan," I said, and Kokael nodded. She pointed to the ranks closest to where Charomos was standing in the shadow of the Hall's columns. Angels were taking flight and heading off in all directions, presumably to bring in outlying legions from the region to hear the siren call of the Flight's new would-be King.

The word siren made me wonder about his partner, Aethi. I couldn't see the former earth goddess, but we were still some distance away. I wondered where she was and what she thought of all this. I had to presume she was a supporter, but her conspicuous absence made the voice of instinct inside me wonder if she had a part yet to play in all this, whether for good or bad.

"We need to get round to the rear of the Herald's Hall," Kokael said. "I know a secret passage into the lower vaults we can use." We headed out into the streets surrounding the Athenaeum to find them mostly deserted. Along the way, a couple of Angels descended to advise us to head into the square and hear the words of Charomos's new gospel of peace and progress. Other than having to stop and listen to these brainwashed missionaries and nod enthusiastically, these encounters went without incident.

The entrance into the rear of the Herald's Hall was hidden in an arched passage that ran from the back of the building through to the back of the Hall's steps on Athenaeum Square. Round about halfway, Kokael stopped, and I stood guard as she felt around the walls and located the hidden door. She was about to push when it swung open with suspicious ease, and a hooded figure stood there looking at us.

"Get inside now," said a voice I immediately recognised.

"Serrate?" Kokael said, and Lytta threw back her hood to reveal herself.

"What are you doing here?"

"My Vod said you may need my help," Lytta said, and Kokael nodded.

"As long as it doesn't come with any additional needs or

concessions?"

"No strings attached," the Serrate replied, and once again, I could only marvel at how much I was unaware of. Like secret passages that everyone else knew about and I didn't. I supposed if it meant not having to fight others of my own kind, I was all for it.

Kokael led the way through the Hall's vaults, and Lytta brought up the rear. "Zamalca?"

"Gone," was her enigmatic reply. To my mind, 'gone' had multiple potential meanings but she didn't elaborate, and at that moment, there were more pressing concerns. Kokael guided us to a set of wide steps leading up into the back of the Chamber of the Word, where the Herald Council received and discussed the orders that came from Trinity Palace. The chamber had been busy during the war, but had declined in use in recent times. The Prince's proclamations were rare these days and required little in the way of debate. We exited onto the raised dais that held the thirteen seats of the Heralds. They were high-backed chairs intricately carved of white ash from trees that had been cultivated in the Golden City. The chamber was empty, and we dropped down into the auditorium before heading towards the exit to the main Hall. Kokael listened at the great doors, which were slightly ajar, and shook her head. The sound of the cheering crowd outside was close now, and unless she had amazing hearing, I doubt she could make out a thing.

Charomos was in full flow. He was busy vilifying the war with the Succae, and Anael's leadership. In his view, the Flight needed to establish itself as a force for good elsewhere and leave the Succae to heal and recover from our unwelcome intrusion. Of course, he would be the one to take us to this newfound destiny once he had full control of the Flight and Anael was deposed. I could feel my mind glazing over. He was obviously using the Rood, but unlike the previous command to slumber, which had been immediate, this was something more insidious. I could feel its pernicious hold like a serpent slithering through my brain. It sank its fangs into prejudice and belief, and its venom spread slowly but thoroughly, enhancing doubts and fears. I tried to resist, but I could feel indignant anger and bile at what had happened during the war and afterwards boiling up inside me. Thankfully, Kokael saw the change in my persona and slapped me hard across the face.

"Block your ears, Azshael!"

I came out of the initial daze and watched as Kokael tore strips from her dress and handed them to me. I stuffed them in my ears to protect myself from Charomos's siren speech. She indicated to me that I should scout ahead, and I was about to go when Lytta pulled me back.

"Let me help," she said, indicating that I was still unarmed. She had a point. If there were any dominated Angels on patrol, it was likely they would do more than ask me to go listen to the Primogi. Not that I was happy with the Serrate taking more innocent Angel's lives, but there was more at stake here than we had previously realised. I whispered to her that she was only to kill as a last resort, and she nodded curtly before slipping sinuously through the gap between the doors and off to the right side of the outer Hall. I headed left and moved as quietly as I could around the Hall's outer ward. Here, statues of Heralds from bygone ages stood an eternal watch, immortalised in marble. They looked like trustworthy patricians whose wisdom and great deeds had guided the Seventh Flight to its undeniably eminent place in the annals of history. A history they had written, of course, and which was largely unreliable as a result.

I encountered no guards or patrols, and I was about to return to Kokael when I saw a flickering light ahead. I turned back and went in search of the source, only to find the fox woman Flynx, last of Marok's shape changer rogues sitting a few steps down on the stairs leading to the repositories beneath the auditorium. I removed my ear blocks and asked her what she was doing there. Cradling a small oil lamp used to light memorials, she looked up at me, and in that lilting double speech of hers said, "the Green Lady weeps. The Lady weeps in green." She pointed down the stairs and changed shape to lead me down, her white-tipped fox tails beacons in the dark.

The repository, a wide oval space, was really a glorified storage area cum library of laws and proclamations. Here, the Heralds and their helpers, mostly Narinel's staff from the Scriptorium, could review Princely rulings and Council decisions from across the ages. These important words of precedent held in thousands of books, scrolls, and sheaves assured a consistency in the Flight's ethical and moral compass. Personally, I found it amusing that someone needed to check what a Prince had once said to know what to do the next time a similar situation arose. To me, that just said that no-one really knew what we truly believed so we had to make it up as we went along, but perhaps that is the definition of cynicism.

In addition to many ancient but well-maintained tomes and ordered shelves packed with scrolls and bound documents, there were large tables and reading lecterns dotted around the floor. The central area of this wide space was dominated by seven great stone caskets where the Flight's founding Heralds were entombed. Six eternal fires placed in large copper cauldrons created an outer ring, and the flames within sent shadows running, leaping, and dancing around the curved roof and walls. In the darkness on the edge of the light I was unseen, and I approached to its edge to see who was doing the talking. It was Aethi, Bonded goddess of the fields and woods, Charomos's partner and a Primogi in her own right. She was talking to a shrouded body laid out on the stone slab that sat in the centre of the chamber, the Herald's caskets arrayed in a semi-circle creating a kind of silent honour guard.

She was gently caressing its face and smoothing its long flowing locks. Even from a distance, I could tell it was the body of Marok the Wolf. I was caught in momentary indecision, but my instinct about Aethi's commitment to Charomos's plan was, I thought, being validated in what I was seeing now.

"I'm sorry Aethi," I said, emerging into the light and breaking the silence. Aethi looked up and smiled at me. It was the dreamy smile of someone lost in their own thoughts and memories.

"Ambassador Azshael. How lovely to see you. Have you come to pay your respects to my fallen one?"

"I have done so already, Primogi. I was there when he was killed."

Aethi looked at me in shock, as if I had just slapped her in the face.

"I am told he was murdered by your White Legion. Just like

Virdae the Feathered, another victim to your Archangel's incessant paranoid need for control!" It was clear where she was getting her news from.

"Indeed, he was murdered, Aethi, but not by any Angel."

"Who then? Who did this?"

"I suspect you already know but I will name the killer if you wish."

Aethi looked at me, and tears sparkled in her clear green eyes. "Say it then," she said quietly, and so I named Kaualakoo.

"But why?"

"He was acting on orders, I believe."

"Orders from whom?"

"Do I really need to tell you?" Aethi looked back at Marok's dead visage, and tears ran down her cheeks as her body quietly shook with grief.

"I visited him and his pack so many times," she said. "I was their goddess of the strange seasons on their world. They called me in winter when my warmth could save them from the snow. They called me for the rites of their short spring and summer, where I made food bountiful and pups played in the warmth of a nurturing sun. Then back again to mark the start of winter and the great migration. For aeons I watched, and they prayed to me. Marok was the last of my High Priests before you and your kind descended on them in the name of your Excelsis. If only you knew what harm you had done."

"What is done is done, Aethi. I can't change it any more than you can restore the old wolf to life."

"Then who is to say Charomos is wrong, Azshael? Maybe it is time for change!"

"You see what Charomos's change involves laid out before you. His ambition is purely for himself. He doesn't care who gets hurt along the way. One of my own kind, a young innocent from a sect of ours that rejects Excelsis, paid with her life, not to mention others like Virdae, who I believe venerated you as well?"

Aethi nodded, and I knew that she had been used by Charomos to gather supporters who would follow his rogue, Malacaz. "Marok knew what he was doing was wrong. He stayed loyal, not to Charomos, but to you. Except he was lied to and misled, just as you have been."

Aethi looked miserable and said nothing, but the remorse was clear on her face.

"We must stop this madness, Aethi. Hundreds, maybe thousands, will die if we don't, and all for Charomos's vanity. You have to help us." Aethi wiped away her tears and replaced the shroud over Marok's face.

"Very well," she said calmly. "Tell me how I can help you."

We headed back to where Kokael and Lytta were still hiding in the shadows. I briefed the others on my plan, and together we took stock of the situation. Charomos was several hundred feet away from us on the steps of the Hall, and I could see Kaualakoo standing behind him, along with several large Angels from Lamechial's Legion. He continued to speak, although it was merely repetition of the same words again and again. I presumed this was to ensure new arrivals fell quickly under his spell. The shadows of the outer hall gave us some protection, but it was probably a good fifty feet or so from where that protection ended to where Charomos stood, bathed in daylight on the steps.

"Can we do this?" Kokael asked. In truth, I really wasn't confident of success, even with Aethi and Flynx's aid. We would need to be quick, and have a hefty amount of luck on our side. I was worried about the growing number of Angels falling under Charomos's spell. Any edge Kokael and I had in the power of flight was effectively neutralised, and none of us knew how swiftly, if at all, the Rood's powers of suggestion could be reversed. The record of the end of the War of the Tribes gave little comfort on that score. As far as I could tell, Kemuel's enforced peace had lasted for centuries.

Aethi materialised out of the shadows, and we retreated into the Herald's Hall to finalise our plan. Once I had finished talking, it was clear no-one, except for Flynx—a mad rogue—and a stoic Serrate thought we would succeed. It was going to be a challenge, but it was us or no-one.

Chapter Sixteen

The plan went wrong from the very beginning. I hoped to draw Charomos away from his guards so that we could rush him and hopefully wrestle the Rood away from him. Kokael would fly off to the Trinity with it, probably pursued by some of the Legio, but she was confident her speed could outpace them. She could also potentially use the Rood to talk them down if things went badly. There were a lot of unknowns, but it was my hope that if Charomos lost the Rood, then sense or confusion would descend on the gathered mass. Either way worked for me.

On cue, Aethi emerged from the shadows and called to Charomos. Initially, I thought things were going even better than planned as he stopped talking and turned to look back up the steps at his Primogi partner. Aethi beckoned to him to join her, but Charomos stood stock still. He rocked back and forth on his heels, and I could tell he was scanning the shadows of the Hall to see if she was alone. Kokael, Flynx, Lytta, and I were hidden behind one of the columns of the outer ward, and as his eyes tracked towards us, I shrank back behind it. I had no idea exactly what Charomos's powers were.

"He's been Bonded, Kokael, right?" I said, and Kokael nodded tersely but remained tight-lipped. That gave me all sorts of bad feelings. If Charomos had escaped the full Bonding process, this could be a very bad plan indeed.

"The bodyguard is moving," Lytta said, and I risked a quick peek at what was going on. Sure enough, Kaualakoo was sauntering toward Aethi and spinning Nimrod in his hands as he did so. I could feel the weapon reaching out to me. We had been bonded too long, and I was in range to call it to me this time. It was difficult not to act immediately, but to do so would concede any element of surprise. Given that our plan was already desperate, we needed every bit of edge we could get. Kaualakoo climbed the steps and reached out for Aethi's arm, presumably to manhandle and drag her to Charomos if necessary. Quietly and calmly Lytta said, "We must go now." I guessed she was right. It wasn't perfect, but it would have to do. I wished everyone luck, and we made our move.

Lytta sprang from the dark into the light and, in a single high arcing jump, collided heavily with Kaualakoo, severing his right hand with a slicing sword strike before putting a hefty spinning kick into his chest to send him sprawling back down the steps. The Serrate had severed the hand in which he had been holding my spear, and I called Nimrod to my hands as I charged toward Charomos and his guards. The assassin made a semi-recovery of sorts, hurling small razor-sharp throwing knives at the Serrate. Lytta's red blades wove a defence equal to the attack, and those knives that presented a threat to her or Aethi were deflected wide of the mark.

Kokael flew past me at full speed and landed by Charomos, who, disappointingly, looked neither surprised nor concerned at the turn of events. She tried to grab the Rood from him, but she wasn't fast or strong enough as Charomos wrestled with her for control. Around him, guardian Angels were closing in, and I heard him tell them to kill her. I wanted to get to him and help her, but Angels around her were rising, and the air was suddenly full of fiery lances. I saw Kokael collapse forward as a wide spear blade punched through the right-hand side of her chest. It was clearly a heart shot and it should have disabled her completely, but her hand stayed firmly clamped on the Rood. Our eyes met, and I saw a mixture of desperation and resolve. The Angel who had stabbed her was setting up for the second strike that would end the Irin leader's life, so I adjusted and propelled myself at him at the same time as Flynx bounded forward and leapt at the Angel's face. He saw her coming and took a step back, and I was relieved that if nothing else we had saved Kokael, although for how long, I didn't know.

Kaualakoo was on his feet, and I saw him stab a curved dagger at Kokael's hands. Her wounds were grievous, and her white dress was drenched in blood, but somehow, she kept going. Lytta had retreated to guard Aethi, but now she also charged forward and, in the growing melee, carved a path to the assassin whose remaining hand was being savaged by Flynx. Lamechial's legionnaires fell back under a ferocious onslaught from the Serrate and me. Nimrod sang in my hands as I punched through feather, flesh, and bone, forcing Angels to retreat. I saw Lytta's red blades slice through one Angel's head as she kicked another clear.

Above us, I saw the light dimming as the beat of Angel wings filled the sky. They were coming to Charomos's call, seeking safe landing points to enter the fray. Kaualakoo shook Flynx off and stabbed Lytta in the face, but she hardly flinched, and the pale wound did not bleed. It was the assassin's final and fatal move. In a vicious double slash, Lytta's blade opened him up from neck to sternum, first on the left side of his body and then on the right. I doubt he knew what happened until his body slid apart in three pieces.

My two attackers had become four as new arrivals tried to circle around me. I was still standing over Kokael, who was slipping and sliding in her own blood as she tried to stand whilst holding on to the Rood. Flynx had also clamped her jaws around one end of the Rood and was trying to pull it loose. For his part, Charomos remained calm but resolute in his firm grip upon the staff of command he had put so much stake into acquiring.

"My fault," Kokael said, although I was not sure she was really speaking to me. "Must stop him," she added, no doubt a rallying cry to herself as she finally found her feet. I parried heavy blow after heavy blow, Nimrod now fashioned into the shape of a hoplite shield, blocking spear thrusts that would have spelled the end for both Kokael and me if they found their targets. It was a chaotic, blood-soaked battle crush as more Angels joined the fight, and we were pushed away from Charomos and back up the steps. My sinews screamed and I could feel my strength beginning to ebb. I tried to pull Kokael with me, but she was locked in her struggle with Charomos and Flynx. He pivoted suddenly, and there was a flash of gold. My heart sank as I saw him bury his justiciar knife into Kokael's chest. I shouted, "No!" as she turned to look at me for one last time.

Then her hand slipped from the Rood and she collapsed, trampled underfoot by advancing Angel soldiers.

More and more Angels were landing on the steps above and behind us. Our plan had failed, and I feared the end was drawing close.

Chapter Seventeen

What is a miracle? Something I don't generally believe in. Well, that's not true. It's more that I don't believe they ever happen to me. Yet on this day, at this moment, I would argue I was witness to one, and it came from an unexpected source.

As we were being pushed back, I could see Aethi standing at the top of the steps. She was aghast at the carnage she was witnessing, and when Charomos stabbed Kokael, I could tell it was as if she had been stabbed herself. She stood tall and spread her arms, and the air was suddenly filled with the scent of spring. All around us, flowers bloomed, and new life grew from every crack between every stone. This new life's acceleration was remarkable, and with every bloom, seed and pollen burst forth in little yellow clouds. The air was saturated with a heady perfume that came upon us with the promise of peaceful slumber in a leafy bower, wrapped in the arms of a loved one. All around us, Angels collapsed, and weapons fell from hands as they all surrendered to deep sleep.

Aethi walked toward Charomos, who had stopped talking and was standing still on the Hall's steps, no more than a foot away from where we had first seen him. Flynx still held on to the Rood, but he ignored her, her lean fox body dangling in space. He smiled at Aethi, but as her back was to me, I couldn't tell whether she smiled back. As Aethi drew near to him, Charomos held out his hand, inviting her to be his Queen in a new dawning. For her part, Aethi raised her hand, her palm apparently empty and open. As he reached for her, she clenched her fist and turned her palm downwards. Black seeds fell from it and bounced on the steps around them, before falling between the cracks in the stone. A second or so later, black bushes bristling with thorns arose and shot towards the sky. They surrounded Charomos, and his eyes went wide as sharp black thorns pierced his flesh at every angle. He made no sound as the plants impaled him, and he shuddered as they pushed through his flesh. A second or so later, he released his hold on the Rood, and Flynx dropped to the ground with it still held in her mouth.

When he went still, Flynx trotted up to Aethi and released the White Rood into her hands. She walked back up the steps among my sleeping brothers and handed it to me. "For Marok, my wolf," she said.

Epilogue

Kokael's memorial took place at Trinity Palace amid much solemn pageantry. Pellandriel stood to my left, whilst Lytta and a Succae honour guard stood to my right. The Irin led the service but did so in anonymity, the grey cowls of their sect hiding their faces. Prince Anael watched from his throne with the Heralds, led by Darophon, arrayed around him. It was a day of pomp and circumstance that would last in the Flight's collective memory. Whether Kokael herself would have welcomed it, I don't know, but there was no doubt her attempt to set right a course that had gone desperately adrift was worth remembering.

In the final event, however, it was the former goddess, Aethi, we had to thank. She became the leader of the Primogi, something that was welcomed by Darophon and his Heralds, mainly because she did not want the job and had to be persuaded into taking it. A Bonded soul with no interest in power or position was probably what we needed now, although I did hear mutterings of 'too much protesting' from some quarters. Such is the nature of the Flight; we find it hard to trust or believe that someone would not want power or position. It's just the way we are built.

Cam returned to the Red Roof Inn a few weeks after the ceremony and didn't want to talk about what had happened. Pell told me he had left the Juvenii colony soon after I had left for Khrov and that he hadn't been seen around their islands, so Excelsis only knows where he went. Our uneasy friendship endured. Vasariah recovered from his wounds and resigned his command of the Honores. He returned to become a protector of the Juvenii enclave with the Archangel's blessing.

Kemuel's White Rood was consigned to a secret vault under the control of Narinel the Wise. It has never been seen or heard of since, which is undoubtedly for the best. The truth of Kemuel's peace among the warring Angel Tribes was never explored, although Sariel did write a treatise on it for academic reference. Be prepared to fail if you try and find it in the Black Vault, though. It's not where it should be, no doubt conveniently misfiled.

Lytta went back down the Tether with her people. The rumours of rebellion quickly faded, and a relative level of equilibrium was restored as the threat of the *Yurei* seemed to recede, albeit not for me. The dream I had seen at Zolorel's house became a constant recurring nightmare, and I couldn't shake a sense of impending doom. I made it my business to explore the anomalies on the Pilot charts of Cerule's space, but what I found is a tale for another time.

"The only truth that matters is the one that most people want to believe." It sounds innocent until you realise that a truth twisted can have devastating, sometimes fatal impacts on the lives of others. Perception is reality and prejudice is a weapon. We underestimate liars at our peril in such circumstances. I believe the old maxim should be updated as follows: "The only truth that matters is the one that most people want to believe *but it's the lies that become that truth that can destroy the world."*

THE END

Printed in Poland
by Amazon Fulfillment
Poland Sp. z o.o., Wrocław
13 September 2023

2aa3d39f-99d2-4674-9179-97f2a74bd710R01